HOUR
OF
THE
BEES

HOUR

OF

THE

BEES

LINDSAY EAGAR

CANDLEWICK PRESS

Copyright © 2016 by Lindsay Eagar
Bee illustration copyright © 2016 by Kristina Closs

The publisher gratefully acknowledges
the contributions of Teresa Mlawer.

First paperback edition 2017

Library of Congress Catalog Card Number 2015954524
ISBN 978-0-7636-7922-4 (hardcover)
ISBN 978-0-7636-9120-2 (paperback)

17 18 19 20 21 22 BVG 10 9 8 7 6 5 4 3 2 1

Printed in Berryville, VA, U.S.A.

This book was typeset in Berkeley Old Style.

Candlewick Press
99 Dover Street
Somerville, Massachusetts 02144

visit us at www.candlewick.com

This first one is for me.

Something flies too close to my ear. For a moment, its buzz is the only noise in my world.

"Hey," I say, out of reflex, and swish my ponytail like it's a weapon.

"What?" Dad turns off the radio. The quiet brings attention to how bumpy the highway is.

The bug zooms out the truck window, its jeweled body glittering black and gold in the sunlight. A bee. "Nothing," I say, contemplating the grim view. It's been mile after mile of "nothing" for more than an hour. Up ahead, a line of mesas comes into view, flat as tabletops and crumbling along the edges, rock-cakes going stale, eternally baking. I snap a picture with my phone, but on the screen the mesas blur into red smears beneath an empty sky.

"Are you sure we didn't miss a turn? Maybe we're in Mexico."

Dad snorts. "Trust me. I'd rather go to Mexico." He switches his twangy rock music back on and checks his rearview mirror. My mom and one-year-old brother, Lu, follow in the minivan, the only other vehicle on the road.

My legs ache from being cramped in the truck for almost three hours. "How much longer?" I groan.

"Excited, are we?" Dad says.

No. Definitely not excited. Instead of a summer filled with pool parties and barbecues, I'll be spending my days on a dusty sheep ranch with a grandfather whom I've never met. At least Mom and Dad are dreading it, too. I'll have some company in my misery.

We turn off the highway and rattle down a long dirt road for about ten minutes. As we curve around the base of a mesa, Dad lets out a sigh. "There it is. Home sweet home."

Across the rose-colored land, a run-down rambler

sits in a browned pasture, its roof sagging, the porch beams warped with age. The entire property is tucked between the buttes—out of sight, out of mind. Forgotten by civilization. Grandpa Serge's two-hundred-acre sheep ranch, the place where Dad grew up.

My dad may have grown up here, but he also left the first chance he got. I can see why.

Dad pulls into the gravel driveway, right next to the house, and kills the engine. "Now, Carol, don't be nervous."

"I'm not," I lie, and take a wobbly breath.

I squint until my eyes focus through the bright white desert sun. The ranch is literally in the middle of nowhere. No hint of the highway or of the rest of New Mexico; the ranch is its own little city, the sheep its woolly citizens.

Dad told me this was still a working sheep ranch, but other ranches just outside of Albuquerque have hundreds of sheep. Here I count only a dozen sheep, moping in the massive pasture—if you can even call it a pasture. The grass was once green, I'm pretty sure, but is now the color of swamp water, and crunchy. Hasn't Grandpa ever heard of a sprinkler?

I swallow my disappointment. I've been trying to think of the ranch as a summer getaway, almost a vacation, only a few hours from my room, my school, my friends. But it might as well be on Mars.

Home sweet home, indeed.

Dad holds out a wrinkled and worn pamphlet titled "The Seville's Guide to Dementia for Caregivers." How many times has he made me read this? How many times have we already had this conversation?

"Let's go over it one last time," he says. "Our number-one goal this summer is . . ."

". . . not to upset Grandpa," I recite.

"No confusing sentences, no complicated questions, no loud noises, no word puzzles," Dad lists.

No talking about Grandma Rosa, I add silently. But that's always been Dad's rule.

"If he gives you any problems, come find me." Dad shifts in his seat.

The Seville—the assisted-living facility we're moving my grandpa into—filled our heads with horror stories about how dementia can transform even the sweetest grandparents into kickers and biters. "What happens to grandparents who aren't so sweet?" Dad had wondered.

Mom comes to my window, Lu slung on her hip. "Are we ready to go in?"

"Well, we didn't drive all this way for the scenery," Dad says.

I laugh for Dad, for his tiny joke. He fumbles slamming his truck door shut, then drops his keys in the dirt. I've never seen him like this—like a nervous kid.

I step onto the scorching desert dust, so hot my sandals are useless. The air feels like it'll drown me. I grab my Gatorade from the truck and take a swig.

Mom grasps Dad's hand until their knuckles turn white, and they walk up the driveway together, looking like they're about to knock on a rabid stranger's door, when it's only Grandpa Serge.

But he is a stranger, I remember. To me.

"Last time I saw you, you were climbing out of the backseat of the sheriff's car."

The gruff greeting sends butterflies into my stomach. In the shadows of the porch, the outline of my grandfather hunches in a wicker chair. The legendary Serge.

"That was years ago. You've seen me plenty of times since then." Dad's turning red.

"Well. Here you are." Grandpa Serge doesn't sound especially happy about this. He stands, and when he comes into the light, I hold back a gasp. I've only seen pictures of Serge, and Dad warned me he might seem different in person, especially now that the dementia has gotten hold. But I'm not prepared for just how different.

A skinny green oxygen hose links behind his ears and feeds into his nostrils. His skin, in the photos, was always ripe brown, earned from hours sizzling in the desert, working the ranch—but now it's pale, and hangs from his bones like it's melting. And his eyes . . . His eyes in the photos are true blue, clear as the midday sky.

But the eyes of the Serge before me are watery blue, like faded jeans. They move beyond me and focus on some invisible person on the ridge. Those eyes are what I think old looks like. The Serge I know from those few photographs Dad showed me at home—that Serge is nothing like this version, a rusty old man parked on the porch like a leaky, broken-down car.

This is why we're here, I remind myself. *Because Grandpa is sick.*

"Rosa." Serge points right at me, and the butterflies in my stomach flap so hard, I worry they'll leave bruises.

"No, I'm Carol," I say quickly. "Not R—" But I can't say it, the forbidden name.

"This is Carol," Dad cuts in. "Your granddaughter. And here's Lu, your new grandson."

"Yes, I know," Serge snaps. "Carolina. And Luis."

Mom taps the back of my shoulder. "Say hello," she prompts.

"Hi, Grandpa, it's nice to meet you." The words come out exactly like I rehearsed them, thankfully, because my mind is focused on Serge's skin, how it folds and wrinkles, mottled with splotchy sunspots. Lumps pop out on his face and neck, like tiny marbles under the skin. Those were there in the photos, I remember, but subtler because his face was fuller, his skin tighter. What are they, anyway? Measles that never healed?

"*Hola, chiquita,*" he says. "*El gusto es mío.*" The pleasure is mine, he says in Spanish, his eyes glowing. And then, in English, "You look just like her."

"*P-Papá* . . ." Dad stutters, as if there's more to say. He's been gone for twelve years—there is everything to say. Before he can fill in the blanks, something hobbles down the porch steps, a creature with frizzled black fur and a wet nose.

"Inés?" Dad whispers. "No way!" He kneels to scratch behind the ears of this mangy dog, grinning at Mom and me. "Inés was my dog growing up."

I pat the old dog's rump as she walks past me on stiff, arthritic legs. I've always wanted a puppy—Mom's never let me have one—but this is not exactly the dog I pictured. Her bloodshot eyes droop at half-mast, and her fur is peppered white and gray around her snout.

Mom balks. "How is she still alive?"

"Some dogs live longer than you think," Dad says.

"Not for thirty years, Raúl." The dog brushes against Mom, and she backs away, suspicious, like it's a zombie. The dog flops into the dry grass and lets Dad rub her belly.

"You're right," Dad whispers to Mom. "This can't be Inés. Must be one of her puppies."

"More like her puppies' puppies," Mom mutters.

"What's the dog's name, *Papá*?" Dad asks.

"Don't tell me you don't remember Inés," Serge says.

"Of course. But this isn't Inés," Dad says.

"Who else would it be? Inés is the best sheepdog in the state." My grandpa shakes his head. "What else have you forgotten about your home?"

"You're right. Sorry." Dad looks at each of us, silently communicating that we should let the old man believe this is the thirty-year-old Inés.

A great silence follows, tossed over all of us like a quilt. I want to talk, but this is a historic moment, and a scary one. Dad hasn't been home in years—since before I was born. That's why I've never met my grandfather. The moment is a pulsing, living quiet, about to smother us, but I keep my mouth shut.

"Serge." Mom saves the day. "Remember me? Raúl's wife, Patricia? It's so good to see you."

A grunt from the porch.

"We're going to bring our things inside, okay?" she adds gently.

Serge says nothing, just walks to the other end of the porch and starts scrubbing a wool blanket in an old-fashioned metal tub. Weird.

"Is it the dementia," Mom whispers to Dad, "or is he always so . . ." She searches for the word.

"Prickly?" Dad finishes. "No, that's just my dad."

Grandpa Cactus, I think.

"Carol." Mom pulls me aside. "Could you stay out here with Lu? Dad and I want to go in first; we don't know what state the house is in."

"Sure," I say, fanning myself with the Seville pamphlet.

"And keep an eye on Grandpa, too, please." Mom sets Lu in the dried brown yard and disappears through the front door, gripping hands with Dad again, like the dark house is haunted.

"And Grandpa, too," I whisper.

The name "Grandpa" tastes weird. It doesn't fit. "Grandpa" is for someone who always keeps his cookie jar full, someone who gives bear hugs, someone who keeps a straight face while spinning a yarn at the dinner table.

I climb up the creaky porch stairs and bend over the railing to get a visual of Lu. He's scooted his way over to the gravel driveway and is tossing pebbles at the dog. She's being so patient with him, considering he's disrupting her afternoon siesta.

I tighten my swinging black ponytail. I can already wring sweat from my hair, and we only just got here. I'm no stranger to the desert, but at home, in Albuquerque, I could hide from the heat in the pockets of shade, in frozen yogurt shops, on the cool, fresh-cut grass between houses.

Here, there's nowhere to hide.

I peer around me. The ranch house is the tallest thing for miles, until the land rumples up into a ridge, a kind of mesa that never was—a wall of rock that makes the ranch seem like it's in a bowl. No trees, though there's a scabby black tree stump on the edge of the pasture, so there *was* a tree at some point. Whose bright idea was it to chop it down and get rid of the only shade for miles and miles? No sounds, except the *swish-swish* of Serge washing that blanket. Quiet and flat.

The desert seems alive and breathing, a huge, sandy monster that sucks moisture from bones and blows the dry, dry air up, where it rolls and churns and boils.

Another bee buzzes around my shoulder and lands on my earlobe.

"Go away!" I wiggle my body and swat at the bee. The dog lifts her head and sniffs in my direction. Finally the bee carries itself away, until its lace-thin wings are camouflaged against the beginnings of sunset.

"Are you dancing for rain, *chiquita?*" Serge is behind me, still washing that blanket.

"No, I don't know any rain dances." The dog rests her head back in the grass, and she dog-sighs. Lu throws another pebble at her and laughs.

"We need a rain dance," Serge says. "My bones are so dry, they itch."

"It's almost the rainy season, isn't it?" I say. We relearn about New Mexico's desert water cycles every year in science. It's mercilessly dry until July, then it rains in buckets through autumn—sometimes so much that the rivers flood. Monsoon season, we call it.

"No rainy season in this desert," Serge says. "No rain for a hundred years." He folds himself in half, spine curled, trying to pull the blanket out of the tub. But the striped maroon wool, heavy with water, is too much for him to lift with his shaking hands, which are frozen into claws. Useless hands. Old hands.

The Seville pamphlet warned that this can happen. Body parts shut down without notice.

"Here, let me help." I unhook the blanket from his fingers and re-rinse it. To my relief, he lets me.

"Where are your boots, *chiquita?*" Serge says.

"It's too hot for boots." A bead of sweat rolls off my forehead, proving my point.

"Fiddle-faddle." Serge clacks his own boots on the porch floorboards. They're as antique and leathery as he is, real cowboy boots, embroidered with vines and fleurs-de-lis. They look like they were once black, under layers of dirt and sheep grime. "Everyone needs a pair of snake-stomping boots here."

I dip the blanket in and out of the tub, relishing the chilly water. "Why?"

"Snakes are braver in the drought," Serge says. "They didn't use to be so bold." He pantomimes crushing a snake beneath his heel. From the grass below, the dog softly growls.

"No rain for a hundred years," Serge continues. "No rain makes the ground crackle, makes it harden. Makes it sharp. Like walking on a shattered stained-glass window."

I glance down. Through my sandal straps, my feet are already coated in cinnamon-red dust.

"And no rain for a hundred years means no bees."

"Bees?" I echo.

"Sí. No rain means no flowers. No flowers means no bees."

"I saw a bee earlier," I say. "Two of them, actually."

"Here?" He frowns. "No, no bees in a drought."

The heat and my grandpa's circling words and sentences are making me dizzy. I dig my fingernails into the links of the wool, but the last flakes of soap refuse to wash away. "This wool is impossible!" I toss the blanket back into the water.

Below the porch, Lu laughs and babbles, "Impah! Impah!"

"Impossible, yes." Serge plucks that word from the air like a fish from a river. "Bees, impossible. But it's only impossible if you stop to think about it."

He tries to stand, and his legs tremble like cold noodles. I rush to be his crutch but he barks, "I can do it."

Your loved one with dementia may seem cross with you or snap at you when you've done nothing wrong, the words from the Seville pamphlet recite in my mind. He yanks himself away and plops back down in his wicker chair. "If you see any more bees, *chiquita*, tell me. The bees will bring back the rain."

"Don't you mean the rain will bring back the bees?" I ask, hoping my correction won't upset him.

But he shakes his head emphatically. "No. The bees will bring back the rain. But first we need the bees."

This is one of the things that happens when you have dementia, the pamphlet warned—it's called "word salad." Serge will arrange words in a way that doesn't make sense, like saying the *bees* will bring back the rain. I should stop pressing him, but I'm trying to understand.

"So it never rains here?" I say.

"No rain for a hundred years," he responds.

"Then where does your water come from?" Please, please, tell me there's still running water at the ranch. If this becomes a camping situation—brushing teeth with bottled water, sponge baths, no ice for drinks in this thick heat . . .

"The ranch has wells," Serge says, "but we don't waste water. Every drop counts. No rain for a hundred years."

No wasting water. That explains the pasture. From the porch, I can see the creosote bush and yarrow that have crept through the grass, belly high to a horse at this point. Soon this will be all the sheep have to eat: scrubby, thorny, wild desert plants.

Well, since we're not supposed to waste water . . . "The blanket needs to soak a little longer," I say, and it sinks to the bottom of the tub. "Maybe overnight."

"Yes, drought dries everything to bones," Serge says, seeming not to hear me.

Dad says our brains are like a strand of Christmas lights, and Serge's lights are shutting off, one by one. Dementia means Serge confuses names and faces. He forgets what day it is, what year it is, his memories a deck of cards that keeps shuffling and reshuffling. He loses things, he'll put the milk back in the cupboard instead of the fridge, or he'll forget to eat altogether.

When Serge fell last winter and almost broke a leg, a paramedic called Dad and said it was time. Time to move Serge off the ranch and into an assisted-living facility, before he really hurts himself.

I guzzle my Gatorade. One drop falls from the bottle and sizzles, evaporating as it hits the dirt. A few sheep wander into the yard from the pasture, bleating at me with bulging black eyes.

No rain for a hundred years . . . It sounds like something from a book, an evil curse from a grudge-holding fairy who wasn't invited to a party. Except curses in fairy tales always come to an end, and here the sky is cloudless for miles. Forever. If this is drought, it's miserable. Every inhale scratches my lungs.

Get used to it, I tell myself. *There's two long months of summer ahead.*

"Carolina," Serge says.

"Carol," I say.

"Carolina," he says again, stretching out the *i* into a long *eee* sound. It's exactly the kind of drama I remove from my name on purpose.

"I go by Carol," I tell him.

"Raúl doesn't call you Caro-leeen-a?"

"Not unless I'm in trouble."

"Raúl." He tut-tuts, like of all the stunts Dad's pulled, this is unforgivable.

"Caro-leeen-a," he says, "is a beautiful, strong, Spanish name. You should use it. Every day. For everything."

As if Serge has any idea what it's like to be a twelve-year-old girl. I roll my eyes. "I'll go by Carolina the minute all my friends go by *their* Spanish names."

My friends Gabby and Sofie are really Gabriela and Sofía, but we don't call them that, not since Manuela

Rodriguez, *the* Manuela Rodriguez, started going by Manny. And when Manny started straightening her hair with a flat iron, plucking her eyebrows, and sharpening her cheekbones with blush, the rest of us had to keep up.

This is how it is in sixth grade. Sink or swim, eat or be eaten. Keep up or be forgotten.

My gut lurches when I think of junior high, starting in just two months. It's only going to get worse.

"Rosa's sister was Carolina, you know." Serge is so worked up, his oxygen tube squeaks with extra air. "Carolina was not ashamed of her heritage."

"I never met Grandma's sister," I point out. *I never even met Grandma Rosa,* I want to add. I take a breath, but the air is so hot, it doesn't even cool itself down inside my body. I feel like I've swallowed the sun.

"Carolina is your namesake." Any smile in Serge's eyes is gone. "Why do you spit on your roots, *chiquita*?"

His question rattles through me, but I don't have a good answer.

2

I peek over the porch railing to check on Lu. The rocks
he was playing with are abandoned, half buried in dirt.
The dog is asleep.

Where'd he go?

"Lu?" I jump down the porch steps. "Lu, where
are you?"

"Luis," Serge corrects. *Why do you spit on your roots?*
I think.

"Lu," I say pointedly. "We call him Lu."

"Luis," Serge begins, "is a strong Spanish name . . ."

Conversational déjà vu. I run to the chicken coop,
void of any chickens. Lu would think it's funny to kick

these old poo-smeared feathers into the air. But he's not here.

My heart skips. If Lu wanders off the ranch, he's buzzard food.

I run back to the house, sandals slapping the gravel driveway.

"Did you see where Lu went?" I call to Serge.

"Luis," he corrects again, and so I ignore him.

"Lu!" *Don't freak out,* I tell myself. I force my breaths to be metered and easy, and concentrate on filling my lungs to the brim. I scan the ranch for a sign, any sign, of my brother. There's nothing.

"This would never happen back home," I mumble. There are no cliffs at home, no dangerous ranch equipment, no troughs of water for him to drown in. No jackrabbits to give him rabies, no fire ants, no coyotes. No buzzards.

Tears sting my eyes. I didn't even want to come here!

"No bees in the drought," Serge says. He's just background noise now. "The bees, the bees . . ." This chant drips out of his mouth like water from a leaky faucet.

I dart past Serge, nearly tripping over his oxygen

tank, and cry "Mom!" through the front door until she and Dad come out.

"What is it? What happened?" Mom's gaze lands on Serge, still safely parked in his wicker chair, and she sighs with relief. The dementia keeps my parents on edge: Serge will be like another toddler to babysit this summer.

"I can't find Lu." My spit tastes bitter in my mouth. "I promise, I was watching him. I just took my eyes off him for one second—"

Dad leaps from the porch steps like a mountain lion. "Lu!" His voice echoes off the ridge.

"Quiet," Serge calls. "You'll scare the bees."

"We'll find him." Mom pats my back.

"He's not in the coop, or the driveway, or the pasture," I say. Mom checks those places anyway and searches each room in the house. When she walks through the pasture a third time, her panic level has risen from shaky to emergency.

"Did you check the barn?" she asks.

"What barn?"

Mom points to a weathered structure, leaning on the edge of the pasture—patchwork roof, crooked windows.

Maybe it was a barn—about a million years ago. I jog to it and push the squeaky door open with my foot.

Goose bumps rise along my arms. It isn't cold in the barn, of course, not when it's a million blazing degrees outside, but my skin must know something I don't.

"Lu?" I whisper. This barn makes me want to be quiet, like it's a church. The boards are gray and splitting down the middle, and it smells as if a puddle of hundred-year-old rain has pooled in a corner, growing stale for a century. There are pyramids of dusty ranch equipment—garden tools, wheelbarrows, barrels for storing feed.

But no Lu.

When I turn to go, I spot something. Highlighted for a millisecond, in the stream of a sunray, is another bee. I blink, and the bee is gone.

Serge said there were no bees in a drought. Was that the dementia talking, or is he right? Are these miracle bees?

"Carol!" Mom's shout pulls me out of my daze.

I back out of the barn slowly, almost reverently, then run to the house. "Did you find him?"

"The little stink's under the porch." Mom shrugs:

crisis over. My heart stops twittering, and my hands calm their quaking.

I want to be mad at my baby brother for scaring me, but when I bend over and peek at him, he squeals and laughs. I shake my head and smile at Mom. An angle of sunset caresses her face. Her hair escapes from its braid in soft wisps, and her eyes glitter like black diamonds as she smiles back at me.

Mom was married once before, when she was younger. They got divorced, then she met Dad, and it's no wonder he snatched her up. Even with the beginnings of wrinkles on her forehead, she could be in a magazine.

My phone vibrates in my pocket. It's a message from Gabby.

I made my friends promise to text me every five minutes, since they get to stay in Albuquerque and hang out while I'm stuck here for the summer. It's been five hours since I last heard from them—I was starting to think they'd forgotten about me.

We're going to Manny's end-of-the-year volleyball party! Gabby's message says. *How's the ranch? Awful?*

Before I can text her back, a hair-raising sound comes from under the porch.

A sound like maracas.

My eyes meet Mom's. I've never heard this sound before, but growing up in New Mexico, I've listened to enough stories from hikers and farmers to place it.

"Rattler?" I whisper. Mom crouches, peering into the darkness. The dog growls from the grass.

Dad comes up behind us. "What, Patricia?" he asks quietly, catching our tension like a fever.

"R-rattlesnake," I tell him. I can barely get the word out, I'm shaking so much. It was only half an hour ago, wasn't it, that we were safely driving on the highway? Half an hour ago that summer hadn't started yet?

Dad cheeks fade, seashell pale. "Get out of the way."

He tries to shove in next to Mom, but she hushes him. "I've almost . . . got him." She stretches her arms beneath the steps. "Come on, Lu, nice and easy."

"I told you, *chiquita*," Serge says. "Drought makes the snakes braver. *Locas*."

The rattler hisses again, and I hold my breath. *No, no, no, please don't jab Lu*, I think, in case the snake reads human minds. *He's only a baby, please don't bite him.*

In a smooth, gliding movement, Mom yanks Lu out, like pulling a turkey from a piping-hot oven. A spiral of dust twirls around my brother, who's giggling and clapping, unaware of the trouble he's causing.

Mom passes Lu to me while she shakily stands, and I plant a hurried kiss on his dark hair.

Dad runs into the house and reappears with a shovel and a dingy pillowcase. "Move," he commands. Mom and I shuffle backward.

Serge leans over the porch railing, drool dangling from his mouth like fishing line. "Where's your snake-stomping boots, Raúl?"

"Not now, *Papá*," Dad growls. He kneels in the dirt and pokes the shovel under the porch. The snake rattles its tail, an eerie percussion solo.

"Dad knows what he's doing, right?" I ask, but Mom doesn't answer. Words keep falling out of my nervous mouth. "He grew up here, so he knows what he's doing, right?"

No answer.

When Dad pulls the snake out by its tail, the ugly thing doesn't bite, but kindly lets Dad coil it into the pillowcase. He dusts off his pants and puts the bagged snake in the back of the truck.

"Are you going to kill it?" I say.

Dad gets into his pickup. "It's illegal to kill rattlers," he says. "I'll take it up to the ridge."

"What if it slithers back?" I say, but he's already driving off.

"No bees in a drought," Serge says. He reaches into the tub and grabs the wet blanket, successfully this time. Mom joins him on the porch and helps him wring the wool out and drape it over the railing. "If you see a bee," he says to her, "tell me. The bees will bring the rain."

Word salad again. I watch for Mom's reaction. Maybe Serge is sicker than we thought. Maybe the Christmas lights in his brain have all popped.

But Mom flashes him one of her warm, sparkling smiles—a smile that could put the sun out—and Serge melts. Even I feel the last of my snaky jitters go away; Mom's smiles are legendary. "If we see any bees, we'll let you know. Right, Carol?" She winks, then whispers to me, "How long has he been talking about bees?"

One of Mom's jobs this summer is to keep a mental catalog of Serge's dementia symptoms, especially what she calls "slips," when he slips out of the present moment and out of reality. Bee talk, filed away.

"The whole time," I say. "He's got a real thing about them. Mom?"

I stare at Serge, who's pouring fresh suds in the tub so he can rewash the blanket he just hung up to dry.

"Mom, has he always been this . . ." A thousand words flit through my mind. *Weird? Crazy?*

Strangely magnetic?

Mom puts her arm around me. "His brain's deteriorating, honey. I know it's hard to watch. But remember, this is still your grandpa under all the sickness."

But I don't even know my grandpa, I want to say. *How am I supposed to know where the dementia ends and Serge begins?*

Mom takes Lu from me, leaving a toddler-shaped stamp of red dirt on the left side of my tank top. She's about to head into the house when a pair of headlights spring above the curve of the main road. Someone's turned off the highway, heading for the ranch.

I watch the car's every twist around the mesa until it pulls into the driveway. It's a powder-blue, bullet-shaped two-door convertible.

"Who's that?" Mom asks, and I shrug. No one I know drives a fancy car like this. But when the driver opens the door, I know exactly who it is. The first thing I see is her leg, golden tan with a high platform wedge on her foot. Not exactly ideal shoes for a summer at a sheep ranch, but if anyone can make it work, my big sister, Alta, can.

"Hey," she says, stepping out of the car with movie-star grace.

Dad's returned from dumping the snake on the ridge. When he sees Alta, he makes the tiniest groan and shifts his feet, bracing himself for the onset of enemy fire. Alta has that effect.

Her wedges stomp down the crunchy, dry grass, flattening the blades. Her cobalt-blue purse is the color of the shadows beneath the ridge and looks as expensive as the new car. The dog leaps up, tail wagging, and greets Alta with more enthusiasm than I thought the old canine could muster.

I didn't get a tail wag.

"Nice wheels," Dad offers. Alta grins at him. She has the same heart-melting smile as Mom—only Alta's has fangs.

I didn't inherit the smile. I got Dad's stitched-on, serious mouth instead, and my eyes are nothing like

Mom's shimmering black jewels; mine are more like dull black olives.

Mom crosses her arms. "You're late."

"Well, sorry. We were birthday shopping." My sister turned seventeen last Sunday, but she's dragged out the celebration for another five days, as only Alta can do.

Mom gestures to the car. "You and Gael? Shopping for this?"

Alta beams.

Gael is Alta's dad, Mom's ex-husband. Alta stays with him every other weekend, except this summer; Gael is going to Europe on business, and Alta wasn't invited to tag along.

"How's Grandpa?" Alta asks Dad, and I snicker at how blatantly she changes the subject. It's a typical Alta move, acting like she volunteered to come here to help, out of the kindness of her heart. Really, Alta doesn't care about Serge. Every time we bring him up, she's quick to remind us that Serge isn't even technically her grandfather.

I hate when she measures our family's relationships like that, reducing it to who shares whose blood. But she loves keeping those details in her back pocket, so she can whip them out in the heat of an argument: "But *my* dad lets me have my laptop in my room at night! I don't even belong here!"

She wants to be the black sheep of the family so badly, we all let her.

Mom's not finished. "Gael bought you this?"

Alta tosses her hair, like the gorgeous specimen of a car behind her is No Big Deal. "I paid for part of it."

I'm trying to decipher which version of Alta is here to visit. Some days she's in a butterflies-and-rainbows mood. She paints my toenails, and lets me sit next to her at dinner, and talks to me in full sentences. She goes shopping with Mom and lets Dad help her with calculus.

But if it's Moody Alta who's arrived at the ranch, then she won't stop brushing her hair, and she'll look at me with cold eyes, like I'm a cockroach to her. She'll swear at Dad and make Mom cry in five syllables or less, growled through her teeth.

It's like having two older sisters instead of one.

"That's just how teenagers act," Mom explains when Alta lashes out. "You'll do the same thing someday." But

I hate it when she excuses Alta's behavior with something as silly as her age. Twelve isn't easy, either.

I decide to test the waters: "How's Marco?" I ask. Marco is Alta's on-again, off-again boyfriend, so this is a risky question to ask.

But Alta smiles. "Good. I need to call him, actually. Do we even get reception here?"

I release a shaky breath. It's Happy Alta, for now. "It's pretty spotty. And there's no Wi-Fi."

"That's okay. I've got a hotspot. Hey, baby brother." Alta grabs Lu and tosses him into the air, sprinkling dust in my hair.

"Come help get dinner started," Mom directs. "And we're not done talking about that car."

Alta rolls her eyes and carries Lu up the porch steps. I catch a whiff of her department-store body spritz. Three hours driving in that teensy car, and her shirt isn't even rumpled.

"You mean *my* car," she can't help saying to Mom.

"We'll see," Mom says, her voice raspy with fatigue. She goes in the house, followed by Alta and Lu and the creaky dog.

"Dinnertime, *Papá*." Dad tries to help Serge up, but Serge slaps Dad's hands away.

"Don't touch me! You've got snake stink on your fingers."

"Aren't you hungry?" Dad says. He's being so patient with Serge, even though I can tell he's exhausted. Less than an hour at the ranch, and he and Mom are already tapped out.

"Stinks like death." Serge folds his arms, his ancient eyes glassy, staring at the horizon. "I'm staying here. Waiting for the bees."

"Okay, okay. Fine. Whatever." Dad stomps into the house a tad harder than necessary.

Mmmm, dinner. Lunch was hours ago. I go up the porch steps but stop at the screen door.

There's a sound, a droning. Another rattler? My stomach clenches.

But it's a bee.

"No bees in a drought," I whisper. It circles my head twice, then buzzes toward the pasture.

When I unfreeze and turn back to the door, Serge is next to me, steady on his feet. He puts his hand on my elbow.

"A bee, Rosa!" he says.

"Not Rosa," I say quickly. "I'm Carol. Remember?"

"I never thought the bees would be back." His eyes burn a hole in me.

Our number-one goal this summer: don't do anything to upset Grandpa Serge. But would it be more upsetting for him to know that I saw it, too, or to think he'd just imagined it?

"No," I whisper. "No, it must have been a trick of the light." Up close, Serge's eyes are less yellowed, more like rings of light blue and gold. Rings, like the inside of a tree trunk.

My phone vibrates in my pocket. Gabby's message from earlier, still unanswered, demands attention: *How's the ranch? Awful?*

Yes, awful, I write back. *Too hot.*

I look at Serge. He's staring at the barn, its roof silhouetted in the last gulp of sunset light.

This is going to be a weird summer, I finish, and send the text.

Then I go inside, and leave Serge alone on the porch.

3

I curl up on a futon next to Dad, who isn't so much sitting as he is melting, the cushions molding around his limp-noodle body. Through slitted eyes, he watches the tiny discolored TV, which is tuned to a grainy cowboys-and-Indians Western, badly dubbed in Spanish.

Serge is perched in the corner recliner, his own eyelids drooping. The dog snoozes at his feet. Somewhere in the house, Alta lurks.

Mom and Dad were prepared for the house to be filthy, since people with dementia sometimes hoard junk, or refuse to vacuum, or simply forget to clean. But

Serge's house is surprisingly tidy. It's old-fashioned, with tacky 1970s southwestern decor hanging on the wood-paneled walls: a flat lizard made of rainbow beads; a dusty straw sombrero, the kind tourists go for; a huge handwoven Navajo rug, with geometric shapes and stripes like sunrise—blues, indigos, yellows, reds . . .

There's no clutter. Not even a fun attic full of forgotten treasures that I could have spent the summer rummaging through. The ranch's boringness runs deep.

Beep, beep. Beeeeep.

Dad's phone is ringing. He unclips it from his belt loop and answers in a creaky voice, "Benny . . . Did the electrician get there? Then call him, not me. Yep. Okay."

He hangs up, then digs his thumbs into his temples. His phone rings again, almost immediately.

"*Silencio,*" Serge mutters, squeezing his withered hands into fists. A growl steeps in the dog's throat.

"Just a quick work call, *Papá.* Sorry," Dad says. Annoyance is written all over his face. He's a contractor, and tried to leave behind projects that could run like clockwork with his crew members. Day one at the ranch and already his crew needs him.

Alta walks into the room, quiet as a shadow, and

sits on the futon, leaving a foot of space between us. Apparently I have cooties.

Her thumb flies across her phone screen as she scrolls through every social media account she has, her nail perfectly polished neon orange.

"Girls?" Mom calls from the other end of the house. "Come help with dinner. Alta, put your phone away."

My sister rolls her eyes but doesn't move. I get up and find Mom in the kitchen.

She's a blur, whipping from counter to stovetop to fridge, and back again to counter. She points to a head of lettuce. "Rinse that for me, *por favor*?"

"Por favor?" I raise my eyebrows. "What are you making?"

"Caldo tlalpeño," Mom says. Lu's in his high chair, devouring a board book.

"Translation?"

She gives me a look. "Chicken soup."

I rinse the lettuce.

"Don't let the water run," she says. "Water's scarce here."

"Because of the drought?"

She nods. "One of the worst ones in the country.

That's why the grass is so brown, and the sheep are so thin. There's just not enough water to keep everything alive."

"Serge said it hasn't rained in a hundred years," I say, letting one last burst of delicious cool water pool in my hands before shutting off the tap.

Mom shrugs. "I believe it. We need to be careful with our water use. Five minutes, tops, for showers. And only flush if it's number two."

"Alta's going to love that," I say. I concentrate on drying my hands for a moment, then ask, "Mom? Serge said there's no bees in a drought. Is that right, or is that his dementia?"

"*No lo sé,*" Mom says. I don't know, she means.

"What's with all the Spanish?"

"I can't speak Spanish?" she says. "We're Mexican, after all."

"Mexican American," I correct under my breath, "and we never act like the Mexican part."

Alta does, though—at least a little bit. She and her friends drop snippets of Spanish into their sentences, and no one gets teased. They've figured out how to make the Mexican part of Mexican American cool. Of course, it helps that she doesn't have a long, dramatic, embarrassing Spanish name: she's just Alta.

My friends and I would rather show up to school in just socks and underwear than have our "roots" brought up. I don't want to be Mexican. Or American. Or Mexican American, or Caro-leeen-a.

Just being Carol is hard enough.

"Why can't we eat something normal?" I say. "Like Hamburger Helper? Stuff we eat at home?"

Mom snorts. "Oh, come on. I'm making something that isn't from a box for once."

"Exactly," I say.

"Hey." Mom's voice has a barbed-wire edge. "Think about why we're here."

Surround your loved ones with things that make them happy, the pamphlet from the Seville suggests, *things that remind them of home and of the person they used to be.* That's why Mom's speaking Spanish and cooking a traditional Mexican dinner.

For Serge.

Caro-leeen-a. Serge's question chimes through my head. *Why do you spit on your roots?*

Mom slices a red chili into pine needle–thin slivers

and rubs a lime against a grater, making it snow green citrus flakes. Next she claws the cloves out of a bulb of garlic and tosses the ingredients into a pot with one hand while flattening a made-from-scratch tortilla with the other.

I didn't know she could cook this way. Like she's conducting a symphony.

After a minute she asks, "Where is your sister?"

I don't answer. We both know where she is.

"Tell her to come here. Now."

In the living room Alta's still on the futon, pretending to be fascinated by the actor in the cheap, historically inaccurate Indian costume riding a fake horse on TV.

While she's distracted, I stare.

It's obvious that Alta and I are only half sisters. She has Mom's round, gleaming mineral eyes and toasted brown skin, Gael's bold cheekbones, and a dainty mole on her right cheek. I have Dad's squinty eyes and a stranger's blunt nose, which always seems okay in the mirror, but photographs like a pig's snout. My lips are thinner than Mom's and disappear if my smile gets out of control.

Alta's black hair is cut bluntly at her shoulders; when she moves, it sways like an expensive silk scarf, draped across her clavicle. She doesn't wear much makeup; just a swipe of mascara and some goo that makes her lips shine baby-blush pink.

Me, I'm a natural tumbleweed, with frizzy dry hair that has to be fried into submission with a flat iron. Mom won't let me wear real makeup, not until high school, only clear mascara and lip gloss. But I don't even come close to resembling Alta when I put it on.

"You're supposed to come help," I tell Alta.

"I will at the next commercial." She tries hiding her phone in her lap, but it glows against her red shorts.

"Alta!" Mom shrieks from the other room. "Put down your phone! Get in here and help!"

"I am!" Alta glares at me like this is my fault and stomps to the kitchen.

The silence only lasts a second. Dad's phone rings again. *Beep, beep. Beeeeep.*

"Argh, Rrraúl!" Serge rolls my dad's name around in his mouth, then spits it out like a habanero seed.

If I stay here, in the eye of their storm, I'm going to get a headache. I leave them to their Spanish-infused argument, the TV flickering static-shadows on their faces.

In the kitchen, it's not much better. Mom and Alta bicker, two angry hens clucking and snapping, pots banging against the stovetop. Lu's adding to their percussion by slapping his hands on his high-chair tray.

I need quiet. I'm thirsty for it.

I walk to the other side of the house and peek through the open doors of the bedrooms.

Mom, Dad, and Lu will be sleeping in the pale-yellow guest room. The bed and dresser look like they were carved in another century, giving the room an old-fashioned feel.

The next room down is where Alta and I are staying: Dad's old bedroom. It's a plaid nightmare of a room, still decorated from when he was a teenager. Posters of some mullet-sporting rock star in a denim vest are pinned to the wall above the bed. The room is cluttered with knickknacks: a hula-dancer doll with hips that bobble, one of those hats from Russia with the fur-lined earflaps, a miniature Eiffel Tower. . . . If there's a theme to all this junk, I'd say it's *Anywhere but here*.

Only one twin-size bed for Alta and me, which

means I'll be sleeping on the hardwood floor, unless I can convince Alta to let me share the bed. Doubtful; hierarchy says big sisters get the bed.

Even on the opposite side of the house, the echoes reach me—a pollution of noise and contention:

"Put the phone away and finish chopping the tomatoes!"

"The TV volume doesn't go any higher, *Papá*!"

"Then stop breathing! You breathe too loud! Helicopter breathing!"

I go to the only other room in the house.

The door creaks open until I'm staring at my own shadow on a bedroom floor. I squint in the gloom, taking in the details of what I decide must be Serge's room.

The bed is neatly made, a patchwork quilt tucked over two plump pillows, and the nightstands on either side of the bed hold identical gold lamps. Squares of cardboard are shoved into the window frames, blocking daylight.

I cough. The room is stuffy, and even in the darkness I see a layer of grime coating everything. No one's been in this room for a long, long time.

But I hear a whirring, coming from the closet. No, not a whirring.

A buzzing. Like a bee. Like a *thousand* bees.

I put my ear up to the closet door. Yes, an entire military fleet of bees.

But . . . why? Bees in a closet? Is hoarding animals a symptom of dementia? I don't remember anything about it in the Seville pamphlet.

I jiggle the handle, but the closet door won't budge.

It's eerie, the thought of bugs scuttling along jacket sleeves, in and out of pockets, inside shoes. I leave the door handle alone. I should leave the ranch's secrets alone, too.

"Caro-leeen-a."

I jump. Serge stands next to me, only half of him in a stream of the hallway's fluorescent light. His wrinkles trap shadows in their valleys, making frown lines around his mouth, like scribbles from a marker.

"What are you doing in here, Caro-leeen-a?" There isn't even a whisper of anger in his words. Everything about him is relaxed, cool as a stone smoothed by a river—nothing like the Serge I met on the porch, who was spilling out of his own leathery skin.

"I'm sorry," I say. "I was looking for . . . looking for . . ."

He doesn't even blink, his eyes clear blue coins. "You were looking," he says.

"There you are." Dad charges past me and links his arm in Serge's. "I thought you wandered off."

Serge rips himself away from his son's reach. "I can wander. It's my house."

"No," Dad says. "You can't wander. Not too far. Things are different now."

"*Silencio,* Raúl," Serge says, his jowls quivering. "Make that phone stop ringing."

I look at Dad. His phone is clipped onto his belt, quiet.

"Dinner's ready," Dad says, and Serge stalks to the kitchen, wheeling his oxygen tank behind him.

Dad waits until Serge is out of earshot, then says, "Grandpa doesn't go in the bedroom. No one does."

I think about this. "Then where does he sleep?"

"On the porch, I would imagine. He always slept outside when *Mamá* was gone." He coughs once. "I don't think he's opened that door in twelve years."

"I promise I wasn't snooping," I say.

"I know." Dad pats my back. "But let's remember the goal this summer."

I make myself smile. "Don't do anything to upset Serge."

His return smile is just as wooden as mine.

In the kitchen, Serge lets Mom guide him to the table. He plops into his chair like a dropped ham.

Alta heaps her bowl full of Mom's chicken soup and licks the drip that spills on her wrist. "Mmm, this smells divine."

I hold my breath. Alta's attempts at sucking up aren't working; she's in trouble, and we all know it.

Mom doesn't waste any time. "You know, we have to talk about that car." She slams a tortilla onto her plate.

I serve myself a teensy bowl of *caldo tlalpeño* and wait for the fireworks.

Alta flares her nostrils. "Fine. Let's hear it."

My first bite of soup, and I'm thrown into a sprawling garden, bursting with every chili in existence. It's the most flavorful thing I've ever tasted, like I swallowed a piece of heaven, so rich I'm in a stupor.

"This is so good," I tell Mom, but she's not listening to me.

"I don't think a seventeen-year-old needs her own brand-new, fully loaded—"

"Tons of seventeen-year-olds have their own cars," Alta interrupts. "You're just pissed because Dad was the one to help me pick my first car out, not you."

"Whoa, it's spicy," I say, trying to cover for Alta's use of the word "pissed."

"No, I'm not," Mom says. "Not at you. Your dad completely went behind my back and ignored our agreement."

"What agreement?" Alta says.

"Really spicy," I repeat, louder. It's a slow-burning heat, fanning from the back of my tongue to my lips. Mom passes me water without a glance. It's lukewarm— no ice in a drought.

"The agreement was," Mom says, "that if you wanted your own car, you'd earn the money yourself. Your daddy won't pay for your toys forever. He's not made of money, even if he thinks he is."

My dad grunts: a laugh in disguise. Mom rarely

talks about her ex-husband, but when she does, she aims below the belt.

Gael lives in Placitas, in a rich bachelor-pad town house with a pool. Alta has a private entrance to her own bedroom and a queen-size canopy bed. Gael is a businessman, some kind of analyst, whatever that means—I never get details. Mom just says Gael's job sounds too good to be legal but apparently is.

Alta stops pretending to eat and pushes her bowl away like a boxer clearing the ring for the final throwdown. "I paid for my car. Well, most of it. Dad only covered the rest because I got a four-point-oh."

"What's a four-point-oh?" I ask.

"Straight A's," Dad says, serving up his third helping of soup. Alta's grades are always perfect—part of her Alta-ness—so this isn't a surprise.

I pull Lu's empty bowl off his head and help him scoop a bean onto his spoon; Mom's too worked up to pay attention to anything but winning this argument.

"So your dad buys you a car for getting the grades you're supposed to get anyway? Does he give you money to breathe? To maintain your tan? Is that how you paid for your half of the car?" Mom's sarcasm is so deadly, I wince.

Alta narrows her eyes. "Dad pays me to clean his place. I scrub, pick up, dust, mop . . ."

"He pays you to do chores?" Mom hasn't taken a single bite of her soup.

"I've been saving for over a year," Alta says.

"I think she should keep the car," I offer, but I get no response, not even a mind-your-own-business death glare from Alta.

"You just hate hearing that Gael is a good dad," Alta says, and Mom can't recover from the stinging truth in that statement. "I'm keeping the car. It's my birthday present. He got me insurance, he'll help me schedule tune-ups, everything. So stop worrying. You don't want me to be the only one at Mesa High without a car."

Mom picks up her spoon, finally. "You wouldn't be the first high school kid to survive with no car."

I let out a breath. Mom's retreating. She knows she can't win against Gael, not with the new car, and the town-house pool, and all the future ways that Gael will throw his money around. The fun parent wins, always.

That's what Alta said after her birthday last year. Mom offered Alta a sleepover party with pizza and ice cream, but Gael wanted to throw a pool party with a taco truck and a live band. A boy-girl party. "The fun parent wins," Alta had said, and she was right.

"Can I be excused?" Alta asks, flashing a white victory smile. Her phone's vibrating under the table.

"May I. And no. Not until we're all finished." I know this strategy. Mom's payback for losing the car argument will be to micromanage Alta, whenever possible, for the next two months. "And you're grounded from driving that car until Gael is home. I need to have a talk with him."

"But he won't be back in the country until August!" Alta barks.

"Then go ahead and put your keys somewhere safe," Mom says.

Summer's going to feel much longer than two months.

Alta slumps down, and her phone stops ringing. But her sourness melts away; the car is hers. She's smug as can be.

To be honest, I'm kind of happy, too. Over the

years I've learned that Alta's victories will one day mean my victories. Like when she was eight and fought to get her ears pierced. When I turned eight, Mom took me to get mine pierced without a fight. Seventeen-year-old Carol will definitely want to use her saved-up lifeguarding paychecks to buy a cute car.

But still, Mom looks like she needs a hug. She surveys the table, dribbles of her delicious dinner clinging to bowls and spoons that will have to be washed. Behind her, the window's open, the flat desert stretching to the ridge, and Mom, profiled against the twilight, seems small. The desert could swallow her up. I catch the weariness in her eyes before she blinks it away.

4

We're quiet, except for the sounds of clinking utensils.

"Eat your soup," Dad tells Serge. "It's good."

Serge folds his arms. "No." The sight of my grand-father, pouting like a toddler—I don't know whether to giggle or cry.

"Come on. You've got to eat. You'll be hungry," Dad insists.

After a moment, Serge takes his spoon and scoops it into the bowl. His hand trembles—the only movement in the room—and we watch him spill each spoonful he tries to lift.

"*Papá*," Dad says, and I cringe at the awkwardness of this moment, of the child feeding the parent. "Let me—" Dad reaches for the spoon, but Serge shoves the bowl with all his might. The soup splashes down the table in a tidal wave, soaking Mom's lap.

"Uh-oh!" Lu crows—one of his favorite phrases—and repeats it over and over, banging his spoon on the high chair as percussion.

"Hey!" Dad shouts at Serge and slams his napkin down on the table. "Watch what you're doing!"

"It's my house! My house!"

"It's okay." Mom wets a dishcloth and mops up the spilled soup. "Accidents happen."

No one calls her on the lie that hangs there. That was no accident. It's right in the Seville pamphlet, the warning of aggressive and possibly violent behaviors, *as your loved one attempts to navigate through their new and frightening reality.*

Dad takes a calming breath, then changes the subject. "*Papá,* we drove past the Seville on our way down. They're getting the grounds ready for summer." *Discuss upcoming changes with a positive outlook.*

"Seville?" Serge twists his wrinkles into a confused face.

"Remember?" Dad says. "The Seville? The new home I—we—found for you?"

Serge reacts to the news with as much enthusiasm as Alta would give a sheep. "I'm staying here."

Dad shreds his napkin into bits. "We decided this was the right choice."

"No. You decided," Serge says, and he's right. Earlier this year, when Dad first learned that his dad was sick, Serge wouldn't agree to move away from the ranch. Doctors told him he needed to be somewhere safer, somewhere closer to a hospital, but they couldn't convince him. "He won't even discuss it," Dad had told my mom while tugging his hair in frustration. "He just keeps shouting, 'This is where my roots are!'"

"So what does that mean?" Mom had wondered.

Dad had sighed. "It means I have to hire a lawyer." And he did. He hired a lawyer to make Serge move—*for his own good,* Dad kept on saying.

"I'm not going to some raisin ranch," Serge says now. "You can't make me."

"Papá." Dad groans, and I see a flash of what he must have been like as a teenager, with a flawlessly executed

roll of the eyes. "It's not a raisin ranch, it's . . . it's a private residence. Practically a hotel."

"Too expensive," Serge says.

"It's not, remember? We looked at the numbers? It's completely doable," Dad says. "There's round-the-clock medical staff, jetted tubs, a four-star chef. It's the best place in New Mexico." Dad's guilt is bright as a sunburn. Serge would never care about Jacuzzi tubs or gourmet food; Dad picked the swanky Seville to feel better about putting his dad away against his will.

"Then move in yourself." The oxygen shoots through Serge's tube and squeaks with rage.

"The ranch is too far for hospice to drive. You need hands-on care. The dementia is just going to get worse."

"I'm not leaving the ranch, Raúl," Serge says. "Not when the bees are coming."

"Beeee, beeee," Lu chants.

My heart pulses. Bees.

Dad rubs his temples. "What are you talking about? Bees, *Papá*?"

"*Sí, sí,* the bees! They're coming; they're bringing the rain."

"There are no bees here anymore. It's too dry for them, you know that."

"No, the bees are coming! Caro-leeen-a saw one!" Serge points a chalky-yellow fingernail at me.

"I—" I start, then realize everyone's staring. Our number-one goal this summer: don't do anything to upset Serge.

"Um," I barely whisper, "it was just a fly."

My lie is painful to deliver: Serge's hope melts out of him, his mouth goes slack, and his eyes become blurry, icy-blue watercolor versions of themselves. "No bees?"

"No," I say. "No bees." I wish I could dive headfirst into my bowl.

"The Seville's the best care center in the state," Dad says. "It'll be a vacation after the ranch. You can relax for once in your life."

"We'll be able to see you more often," Mom adds, ignoring the fiery look Dad gives her.

Serge's hand reaches out, a clammy, pasty claw. "Water, please."

I pass him a glass, which he drains. "Bones are so dry," he says. "Drought dries everything to dust."

Dad clears his throat. "So this week, we've got to meet with the real estate agent."

"Real estate agent?" Serge repeats.

"We decided," Dad says carefully, "that it's time to pass the ranch on. This way, everything at the Seville will be paid for."

"You were born on this land," Serge says. "Raised on this land. Your mother—"

"I know." Dad's voice cooks hotter and hotter. "But it hasn't been properly maintained. When we sell it, somebody else can clean it up, get it up to speed with the twenty-first century. It will have a future—another family to look after it. Won't that be great?"

"This land belongs to my family, Raúl. To your family. *Tus raíces significan nada para ti.*" Your roots mean nothing to you, Serge says. "You'll pass it on over my dead body!"

"That's what I'm trying to avoid!"

Dad storms out of the kitchen. Seconds later the TV volume cranks up.

Serge pushes away from the table slowly, trembling as he stands. Mom opens and closes her mouth, trying to find the right thing to say, but it doesn't come in time, and Serge goes outside, carting his oxygen tank behind him, and parks himself on the porch.

Alta starts texting.

"Okay, guacamole monster. Time for a bath." Mom plucks Lu from his high chair. "Will you girls get the dishes cleaned up? That means *you*." She narrows her eyes at my sister.

Alta makes a big show of putting her phone away and carrying her own dishes to the sink. "I *am*," she says.

"What about . . . ?" I say, pointing at Serge on the porch. "Should someone go talk to him?"

Mom glances at him, crumpled in his wicker chair, staring across the land at nothing. "Give him time," she finally says.

Bzzz, bzzz. I jerk my head around. "Bee," I whisper. But it's Alta's cell phone, vibrating on the countertop.

"Alta. Clean up first. Then phone."

"Fine." My sister, queen of the monosyllable. But as soon as Mom's out of sight, she abandons the sink and grabs her phone.

"Hey, Mom said you have to help." My heart thumps as I say this; I'm risking being yelled at, or pinched, or worse.

Alta's eyes flash danger. "I won't tell her if you won't." She slips out of the kitchen, her only contribution clearing her own dishes. It's more than she usually does, anyway.

It's not fair. Alta always manages to talk or walk her way out of work. If I tattle to Mom, Alta will spin an excuse, elaborate as lace, and get away with it. She always gets away with it.

"*Chiquita?*" Serge calls through the open kitchen window. "Did Inés get fed?"

I peer at the dog's food and water. Both full. "Yes."

"She's a good dog," he says.

I wash dishes like a factory worker, letting the cold suds drip down my arms. I breathe, forgetting the unfairness of the evening with every exhale; the ranch is no place to rewrite the rules of my world.

"*Chiquita?* Did Inés get fed?" Serge pops his head in the window this time.

I stare. "You just asked me that."

"No, I'm asking it now."

"Yes, she's got food," I say.

"And water?"

Sigh. "And water."

"She's a good dog."

Loved ones with dementia may repeat the same phrases or questions, or repeat the same tasks, such as washing their hands, getting dressed, or showering. Do your best to be patient.

"I'm trying, I'm trying," I reply to the pamphlet in my back pocket. I finish washing the last plate and declare the kitchen clean.

In the living room, Dad faces the general direction of the TV, but he looks through it, his eyes puffy, an unopened can of beer in his hand. Both he and Alta won their arguments tonight, but unlike my sister, Dad isn't the gloating type.

I zone out for another hour, shifting my lukewarm attention between the TV and my phone. When my text conversations with my friends drop off one by one, I watch the movie. It's in Spanish, but it's still nice to be lost in someone else's world, someone else's problems.

Mom comes in. "Bedtime."

"It's only nine," I say.

"Okay. Let's play a game where I'm the mom and

you're the kid." Mom squeezes the bridge of her nose. "Trust me, you need sleep. Tomorrow's going to be a long day."

"You mean a long summer." But she's right, I need sleep. My muscles ache—I'm shattered.

"What exactly are we doing tomorrow?" I ask.

"Same things we'll be doing every day," Mom says. "We pack. And clean. And try to fix things that are falling apart." She drags one hand along the hallway wall. "This ranch is so full of junk, it'll be a miracle if we fit half of it into one moving van. A lifetime of junk. Of memories."

"Mom?" I say, as quietly as I can without whispering. A thousand questions line up single file in my throat. *Will Dad be okay? Is it going to kill him to be here with Serge for two months, or is he just being dramatic? Why are there bees here? They're not supposed to be. And why does it seem like they're following me? Why do I feel like the ranch is brewing something extra weird? Am I going crazy, like Serge, or is it just the heat?*

I want to tell her how Serge's eyes glow, how they are cat's eyes, wide as a newborn's, ringed like an ancient tree trunk. I want to tell her how lucky I feel that Lu's alive, and talk to her about Alta, how I wish I could transform into a giant, just so I can pick Alta up and say, "You're not the biggest, not really." I want to tell Mom that living with Alta is like having a rattler in the house.

But what I ask is "Mom? What happened between Serge and Dad?"

Mom comes out of slow motion and studies my face. "You'll have to ask Dad. That's his memory to share." She kisses my forehead. "Get some rest. See you in the morning." Then she goes into her bedroom, and I'm in the hallway with no answers.

The door to Dad's old bedroom is closed, so I knock.

"What?" Alta calls, instead of "Come in" or even "Who is it?"

"It's me," I say. She doesn't respond.

"Mom says I have to go to bed." Still no answer.

"Can I come in?" Nothing.

I go in.

She's scrunched in the corner of the bed, painting her toenails purple, copying the flower pattern from some fashion magazine. She's alternating between this, texting, and watching a teen vampire show on her phone.

"I thought the ranch didn't have Wi-Fi," I say.

She points to a thin black box plugged into the wall. "My dad let me take his hotspot," she answers in a bored voice.

"Oh, right." I wonder if my dad even knows what a hotspot is. "How should we—I mean, do you want to share the bed?" I say this cautiously. My communication has to be void of emotion, purely neutral, because if Alta's in a mood to bully me, she'll deny me anything I seem to want.

"Not really," she says, and locks eyes: a dare to challenge her.

In the closet I find a sleeping bag and a Superman pillow. I unroll the makeshift bed, then lie on the floor, flat as the desert.

Above me is the tangled cord of an old Nintendo video-game console, dusty on a shelf. "Can you believe Dad grew up here?" I say.

"So?" Alta's glued to her phone.

"I just can't picture him here."

"This place is awful," Alta says. "No wonder Raúl waited until Serge was on his deathbed before dragging us out here."

I sit up. "You think Serge is on his deathbed?"

She shrugs. "Serge makes me hope I die before I'm forty. Just so I don't ever have to be that old."

"It's not his fault," I say. "Everyone has to get old."

"He's like the Crypt Keeper."

My blood warms. "Alta. He's not *that* old."

"His skin's falling off his bones and his teeth can't even chew," she says.

I glare at my sister, but earlier on the porch, when I saw Serge for the first time, the same things paraded through my mind: old, decaying, one foot in the grave. The living dead.

"What about his eyes?" I say.

Alta's unimpressed. "Old-man eyes."

"Yeah, but . . ." *But there's something alive behind them. Like he has X-ray vision to your thoughts.*

Bzzz. It isn't Alta's phone this time. *Bzzz.*

"Ew, get it." Alta points at the window, where a winged insect hurls itself against the glass, trying to escape. It's too big to be a mosquito. A fly, maybe? Some kind of evil winged ant?

I grab my sandal and crawl on the bed, ready to swat it into a stupor. It's not an ant or a fly—it's a bee;

of course it's a bee. Perfectly striped in black and golden yellow, buzzing along the windowpane. My throat goes dry. A bee, again.

"Kill it," Alta commands.

"Hold on, I'm trying to let it out." But before I can budge the window open, Alta crunches the bee with her rolled-up magazine.

"Alta!" I cry. "I was letting it out."

"Flies will crawl in your mouth while you sleep," she says.

"Gross, don't say that." The window finally opens, the dead-bee grit blowing out into the night. "And it wasn't a fly," I say, but Alta's head is on her pillow, eyes closed, headphones in. Conversation, done.

I lie wide-eyed in the dark, my mind a pot of hot water about to boil over.

Alta snores, a delicate, feminine sound, like a chipmunk breathing on autumn leaves. The rest of the house is quiet.

My dreams are full of bees.

5

There's a thunderstorm outside.

I wake in a cold sweat. For the record, cold sweat is way worse than hot sweat.

I crawl to the window, heart thumping against my ribs. Thunder means rain. Rain, after a hundred years of drought, I can't believe it! Serge was right—the bees brought the rain!

But it's not a thunderstorm, just Dad's truck engine growling outside. I rub my eyes and reel at how ridiculous I am—did I really think it was rain? And that somehow the *bees* had brought it?

Going back to sleep seems as impossible as seeing a bee in a drought. I stand up and catch a glimpse of Alta, relaxed in dreamland, her face like a statue of an angel. When she's sleeping, she looks almost nice.

My phone says it's close to midnight. I wrap a blanket around my shoulders and walk to the porch. Serge snoozes here, in the openness of night, sitting upright in his wicker chair, a quilt tucked over his knees. Asleep, he seems frailer than ever. His skin is papery-thin, and his eyeballs move under the spiderwebs of veins on his purple eyelids.

"Carol?" Dad tinkers beneath the truck's open hood. "Did I wake you? Sorry."

The dirt is chilly under my bare feet. How can the desert be so scorching hot during the day, then freeze at night? "What are you even doing?" I ask Dad.

He climbs into the truck. "The pasture gate didn't get shut. One of the sheep got out."

I must have a glow of neediness, because Dad smiles a tired smile and waves for me to join him. "Come on, I could use another set of eyes. Mine are down to their last wattage."

"Ever heard of sleep?" I get in the truck next to him.

He laughs. "No rest for the wicked."

I finger-comb my rat's-nest hair as we drive through the pasture. "So Serge really does sleep on the porch."

"Whenever *Mamá* is gone, he sleeps outside."

"But she's been gone for twelve years," I say, tightening the blanket around me. Twelve years of sleeping in a stiff wicker chair with the moonlight, and the jackrabbits, and the desert bats. . . .

"It doesn't feel like twelve years," Dad says. "When we pulled up to the house today, I half expected *Mamá* to come bounding down the porch steps, like she always did." He smiles. "The ranch was different when she was here. Brighter. Bluer skies, and more air. She loved to travel, and whenever she was gone, and it was just *Papá* and me . . ." He goes quiet.

"I can't believe he won't go in his own bedroom," I say.

"Grief does funny things to people." Dad's jaw keeps clenching and unclenching.

"And dementia," I suggest. Behind us, the ranch house is illuminated by the moon, the wood warped, the windows dingy. "Dad?" I say. "Does he have to go to the Seville?"

"Where else would he go?"

My reply is tiny. "With us?"

"Live with us?" Dad nearly pops a lung with his laugh. "In our house? No. No. No." He shivers, his whole body shaking. "Believe me, I hate that we have to move him. But it's better that he goes to a home. For all of us."

This is an off-limits topic, but it's after midnight; it feels like the rules can be bent until they snap. "Dad? What happened to Grandma Rosa?"

"What do you mean?" Dad says.

"All I really know about her is that she died on my birthday," I say. I was born at noon, and she died right before dinner.

"I'll never forget that day," he says. "Full of hellos and good-byes. Happiest and saddest day of my life."

"I don't even know how she died," I say.

He coughs. "Cancer."

"Cancer," I repeat. What an ugly, scary word.

"She fought it. Fought hard. It kept leaving and coming back, leaving and coming back. In the end . . . Well, it took *Mamá* a long time to finally go. She sure was stubborn."

"What else was she like?"

For a moment, I panic that I've gone too far. We're in uncharted territory, talking about Grandma Rosa. Dad tightens his grip on the steering wheel. "She had lots of fire. Never let anything go unsaid. She was adventurous—definitely adventurous."

"Fiery and adventurous," I repeat. What was she doing married to Serge?

"*Papá* couldn't ever get her to stay put. No one could." Dad's voice hardens. "She hated the ranch as much as I did."

He parks the truck on the edge of the ridge, where the pasture ends and the desert begins. "All this openness," he says, "and still, I always felt trapped here. There's only one thing I love about the desert." He switches off the headlights and points outside. "The sky, *niña*. Just look at the sky."

I get out of the truck and gasp.

Golden-white stars freckle the black sky. A wisp of midnight cloud uncurls itself into hazy purple smoke, then disappears. The moon is round and bright and the color of harvested corn. All of this stretches above the miles and miles of sparse desert—a heavenly ceiling.

"Say what you want about the ranch," Dad says, "but you sure don't get skies like this in the city."

"This belongs in a movie," I whisper.

Dad squeezes my shoulder. "I'm glad you're still young enough to gawk at the stars with your old man."

"I'm not that young." I lean against his truck, lost in the sea of stars. "Dad? What are those bumps on Serge's face?"

"Believe it or not," he says, "they're bee stings, from years ago. They never fully healed."

"Wow." I wasn't expecting that. "No wonder he's obsessed with bees."

"Like I said, grief can do funny things." He pats my back.

"Dad?" One more question. "What happened between you and Serge?"

He looks down at me, and I watch something harden behind his eyes, like a puddle drying into crackled dirt. "You don't need to know that," he says, and grabs a rifle from the truck bed.

It's dark, so he doesn't see my scowl.

He hands me a flashlight. "Don't go on top of the ridge," he warns. "Stay in sight of the truck. Just shine that around the edge of the pasture, and if you see the sheep, holler."

Dad vanishes, and I'm left with the stars, the moon, and a flashlight.

Something howls. A coyote, I think. That's probably why Dad took his rifle.

I don't have a rifle.

I walk into the night, picturing ghosts of dead bees and long-gone grandmothers swirling around me. Invisible eyes follow me from every crack in the ridge.

The ridge is a buildup of multicolored sand, stuck together in a giant wall about a mile from the back porch. When moonlight hits the ridge, it glitters like a Christmas ornament. The bottom is inky purple, from a million years ago when the universe banged itself together. Star dust. Above the purple, the sand turns rusty red, the color of caveman blood. Then a stripe of orange, and a bright yellow stripe at the top. It's a prehistoric Popsicle. The Painted Desert, they call New Mexico. Like some god reached down from the clouds and dragged his palette along the mesas.

Beyond the ridge, the land dips into a basin. The grass becomes rose-colored, ragged, and the scrub recedes like a balding hairline. There's just desert on and on until you hit Mexico. It's easy to get lost in the vastness of the night and the land, even in your head.

At home, the city has a vastness to it, too—a vastness of cars, of people, of pavement, of never-ending lights. Little patches of perfectly manicured grass—fake Mother Nature—are inserted into the metropolis.

But I've never seen anything as beautiful as the ridge.

The ridge isn't safe to play on, as pretty as it is. On the drive up, Dad gave me the rundown of its many dangers. Coyotes prowl there, and scorpions, and fire ants make their hills on the ridge's peaks. There are rattlers, always, hidden among the stones, so camouflaged you don't see them until it's too late.

I need snake-stomping boots.

An owl hoots. I spot it, a silhouette against the dime-round moon; it soars past me and lands on a lone cactus, ruffled-feather breast, unblinking eyes.

I scan the flashlight around me. No sheep.

Something tickles my neck. A trio of bees hovers around my head like it's their hive.

"Go away!" I cry, running in a wide circle to lose them, my blanket fanning out behind me like a cape. "Quit following me!"

But when I stop, the bees swarm back around me, too close.

"Rain's been gone for a hundred years," I whisper. "You don't belong here anymore."

Bzzz, they drone. *Bzzz,* around and around me, until I'm dizzy.

"You stop teasing my grandpa," I say, and flick my hands until the bees go.

Then it's me, and the sky, alone in the great, loud silence of desert.

Living in Albuquerque means I'm used to sharing close quarters. There's always been at least thirty kids in my class. At home there's limited closet space and not enough room in the yard to set up a trampoline. Some nights, I open my bedroom window just to breathe new air.

But there's such a thing as too open. Too wide. Here in the dark, I'm nothing. I'm less than a smudge on the pages of the world's history, tiny on the number line of forever. The lost sheep, Alta, Serge's dementia, even junior high—everything seems laughably small. What's one missing sheep to eternity?

Chilly night air creeps into my blanket. I think I'll wait for Dad in the truck, with the heat on.

In the truck, maybe I'll feel less small.

I turn around, and a scream bursts out of me before I process what I'm seeing: the missing sheep, lying mangled in an unnatural position—legs bent back, spine arched, wool tangled. The head is missing, and a cloud of flies pick at the corpse. Ribs, real ribs, jut from the body. They look fake. I never knew real bones were so clean, so yellow-white.

Where's the head? I'm too nauseated to search with the light. Blood makes me sick, makes my stomach churn and my head spin.

"Carol!" Dad runs to me, rifle in hands. I point, trying not to breathe in any of the flies. When I finally take a desperate gulp of air, I inhale the stink of rotting flesh and dry heave.

"Coyotes," Dad diagnoses.

"They, uh, didn't take much." I speak with my hand over my nose to filter the death stench.

"Drought makes the sheep spindly." Dad waves his

flashlight around the perimeter, and we spot it at the same time: the head of the chewed-up sheep, dragged about two feet from its body. The sheep's lifeless eyes are round black mirrors, reflecting the flashlight's gleam.

I'm still shaky with nausea, but Dad doesn't seem bothered.

"How are you not grossed out by this?" I ask, my hand still firmly covering my nose.

"Coyotes used to get into the chicken coop all the time," Dad says, waxing nostalgic. "We used to wake up to feathers and blood all over the pasture."

"I get the picture," I say, trying not to imagine this carnage of poultry.

Dad gets a shovel and a tarp from the truck bed and scoops up the remains, wrapping them up like left-over dinner. "So the meat doesn't attract buzzards," he explains, "and so the coyotes don't take it as an open invitation to help themselves." The sheep corpse goes into the bed of the pickup.

I hear a buzz.

No, not a buzz. A different sound.

A rattle.

"Carol," Dad says, his quietness a warning. "Stay still."

My whole self seizes up. "Snake?"

Dad angles his light on the ridge. "Oh, wow," he says. I follow the light, and now I really feel sick.

A knot of rattlesnakes has made a nest in a crevice on the ridge. I count a dozen heads, but can't tell which snaky head belongs to which body. The tangle of snakes makes a collective hiss, a few tails rattling.

Dad whistles. "That looks like a nightmare come true."

"What do we do?" I ask.

He shrugs. "It's their desert, too. Nothing we can do except watch where we step."

I scramble into the truck, my bare feet tingling with phantom snakebites. Dad gets in and starts the engine. "Don't tell Mom about the snakes, or she won't sleep the rest of the summer." He yawns, leans over, and kisses my forehead. "Let's get some shut-eye."

"Okay, good. I'm beat." That's a lie. I couldn't be more awake.

"Too beat to drive the truck back?" Dad offers.

I grin. He doesn't have to say another word—I know the drill. We switch spots, and I scoot the seat up as far as it will go, though I still have to stretch out my toes to press the gas pedal. But once it's in gear, my handling of the truck along the bumpy desert drive is as smooth as Dad's.

After Alta almost failed drivers' ed last year (and boy, it took all my strength not to gloat), Dad decided it wouldn't hurt to give me a jump on things, and taught me how to drive on empty roads outside the city.

I really love to drive. The concentration required to handle the truck means everything else—dead sheep, rattlesnake nests, senile old grandfathers—blurs. Driving makes me feel in control when everything else in my life feels out of control.

Death lurks around every corner of this ranch. It's under the porch, slithering around Lu. It's dragging sheep out of their pasture to eat them alive. It's sleeping in scaly piles on the ridge. It's dusted all over the abandoned bedroom, where you can practically see the indent from where Grandma Rosa laid her head on the pillow.

Most of all, death hangs on Serge like a wet towel, tangled in his salty-white hair, dripping down his shoulders. . . .

Next to me, Dad yawns and rubs his eyes, but there's no way I'll be able to go back to sleep tonight; it'd be a parade of bad dreams—of snakes and dead sheep and those darn bees, always, the bees.

"Do you want to talk about it?" Dad says as I pull into the driveway.

"About the bees?" I blurt.

"Uh, no," he says, looking at me strangely. "I meant about the dead sheep."

Great, bees are buzzing aimlessly in my mind, just like Serge. "Sheep, I meant sheep. No, I'm okay. Circle of life and all that."

Dad yawns and can barely reopen his eyes.

"It's past midnight," I say.

"Okay, okay."

I snicker. First Dad acting like the parent with Serge, now me acting like the parent with Dad—this ranch makes everything all topsy-turvy.

6

"Will you kill the headlights?" Dad says as we get closer to the ranch house. "We don't want to wake anyone up."

I switch the truck's lights off and pull into the gravel driveway as slowly and quietly as I can.

We climb out of the truck and walk up the porch stairs. I lean over the railing to get one more peek at that sky, at that cosmic mess and glow. A speck of light whizzes across the horizon. "A shooting star," I whisper, but Dad's already slumped into the house. I pass the star's wish on to him; seems like he could use it even more than me.

"Rosa?" Serge scares a gasp out of me. I forgot he was out here.

"No, it's me," I say. "It's Carol."

"Yes, I know it's you, Caro-leeen-a," he says. "You just look so much like her. You shine like she used to shine."

"Me?" I say.

"You belong with the stars, like she did."

I shake my head and walk over to him. "I don't think so. Dad says she was full of fire."

Serge's cat eyes gleam in the darkness. "But so are you, Caro-leeen-a. A hidden fire. A volcano."

"That sounds more like Alta. Not me." The truth of this statement burns, right above my stomach. Alta's the fiery one. Not me.

"No," Serge insists. "Sounds like you, Caro-leeen-a."

His ancient hands carve into a piece of sandy-white wood with a knife. They work fast for old hands. He barely has to look down at them; he's probably done this a thousand times, a thousand nights.

"What's it going to be?" I lean closer to look.

"Who knows," he says. "My mind wants to sleep, but my hands want to work."

I sigh. "I can't sleep, either."

Some unidentifiable critter makes a noise in the

pasture, and I jump. "This place gives me the heebie-jeebies."

Serge nods. "Bees. Snakes. A whole sky full of magical things." He coughs, a raspy hyena bark. "Caro-leeen-a, I need water."

I fill a glass in the kitchen and take it out to him. He guzzles it and asks for another, and his cough finally stops. "Drought dries everything, inside and out," he says. "Did you know there used to be a lake here? Right there." He points beyond the ridge.

"It dried up in the drought, too?"

"No," he says. "One hundred years ago, the bees flew away with our lake, and there's been no water since. Not even rain."

More word salad. Even when he seems just fine, the dementia simmers underneath, waiting to burst out. The patchy starlight gives every one of his bee-sting scars its own shadow, so his face mirrors the desert landscape: bursts of scrub and rocks, miles of flat.

"How could bees take a lake?" I say, a heavy dose of skepticism in my voice. I'll fight dementia with logic.

Serge leans close to me, like it's a secret. "One drop of water at a time." He smells of campfire, of old wood burning. "If one bee can carry a single drop of water, a thousand bees can steal a puddle. To take our lake, our green-glass lake, the bees came by the millions. They took the lake, and it's been drought ever since."

Part of me knows I should wake Dad, let him know Serge is lost in time and space, but I'm frozen to the porch floor, with an image in my head: an army of sickle-winged bees, each with a drop of clear green water held in its spiky black legs.

"We never thought the bees would come back . . . but you've seen them, haven't you, Caro-leeen-a? They're coming home at last."

"This is just a story, right?" I whisper.

"It is my best story," he says. "You're twelve this year, *chiquita*." I'm surprised he knows this—surprised he remembers. But he's probably kept count of every day since Grandma Rosa died. "Twelve is the border between childhood and old. Are you too old for my stories, Caro-leeen-a?"

Caro-leeen-a. He pronounces my name like it's the secret ingredient in one of Mom's Mexican dinners. "No." I cross my legs and settle near his snake-stomping boots. "I'm not too old."

Serge smiles, his watery-blue eyes crinkling. "The story begins, like all good stories, with 'Once upon a time . . .'"

O*nce upon a time, there was a tree, bigger around than three men could hug. Its leaves were emerald green, the bark black. The tree's branches dipped and curved like a lazy river, and its roots kissed the shore of a green-glass lake.*

White blossoms burst from the branches. Summer, winter, and the days in between, the tree was always in bloom. The flowers breathed out their sweet scent, spicing the dry desert air with their honey-vanilla fragrance. Bees made colonies in the branches, and like good tenants, they kept the blossoms tidy, kept them pollinated, kept them healthy.

The bees kept the whole tree alive.

On a day hot enough to boil eagle eggs in their shells, a boy and a girl climbed to the tree's highest branch. From here, they could see all the way to the ridge, which was striped in the fuzzy violets and peaches of sunset.

"Your turn," the boy said.

"No." The girl dangled from one twiggy arm, lop-sided above the lake.

Inés, the rascally black puppy, barked and chased a butterfly.

"Rosa," the boy said, only he stretched the name out into long, dramatic syllables: Rrrose-uhhh. "Tell me."

"Why?" she said.

"I won't laugh," the boy promised. He shifted on the branch, legs shaking. Heights terrified him. The lake terrified him. The girl, also, terrified him, but in an entirely different way. He was rounder than the other boys in the village, and moon-faced, wearing an embarrassingly too-tight pair of linen trousers. "I told you what my wish would be. Now you."

Rosa closed her eyes. The boy watched her soar miles away from earth, just with her imagination, her rose-petal lips pursed in thought. "My wish would be to leave the village," she finally said. She let go of the branch and fell thirty feet—splash—into the cold water.

For a minute, the only sound was the buzz of the bees.

When Rosa's head bobbed out of the water, the boy's jaw was still dropped. "But no one ever leaves!" he called.

"I know." Rosa's crow-black hair spread behind her in the water like a fan.

"No one has ever left before," the boy said.

"Sergio, I know." She waded onto shore. "That's why it's just a silly wish."

Every step she took, bees followed her in a halo around her head. They trailed behind wherever she went. No one else in the village had the bees follow when they walked; only Rosa. No one knew why, but no one really asked why—the village had plenty of mysteries. Bigger mysteries.

Father Alejandro, the priest of the village's mission, told his parishioners that these mysteries would never be explained by man, because some mysteries were gifts from God. The tree was a gift. The land was a gift. The bees, too, were a gift.

If you asked Sergio, he would say that Rosa herself was a gift, and they were all blessed to know her. Father Alejandro insisted that she was the same as everyone else: born of an old village family, raised to tend the communal crops and attend church on Sundays. But Sergio knew different. Rosa was teeming with life. She was so full of life, it overflowed, like the village wells after a rain, and that's why the bees always danced around her like honey-making angels. Where there was Rosa, there was life.

And where there was Rosa, there was also Sergio.

Rosa ran her fingers along the tree trunk, patting the lucky knothole. "Father Alejandro says with God, all things are possible. Mysteries. Miracles."

"Rosa!" Sergio cried. "You're bleeding!"

She kept walking, circling the tree.

Sergio dropped from his branch faster than an autumn leaf. "I said you're bleeding!" He grabbed her shoulders and made her stop.

"Am I?" Rosa looked down at all her limbs. There it was, jagged down her shin, a stream of blood. Every time she put weight on that leg, blood oozed from the deep cut. "I must have scraped it on the rocks," she said.

"Shh." Sergio knelt next to her leg, waiting, watching.

Then it happened—the cut sewed itself whole, the

flaps of broken skin pulling together as if with invisible thread. He touched the healed flesh in wonder, as he always did. Father Alejandro once told him that in the world outside the village, pain and sickness weren't healed like this. Cuts had to be stitched together with actual thread; injuries hurt; pain scorched like a fire in the flesh. Some wounds killed.

Sergio couldn't even imagine . . . Outside the village, would a cut like this keep bleeding forever? Would such a wound have killed Rosa?

He splashed lake water over her leg to clean it, and when the blood washed away, the skin was smooth, not a trace of the wound left. Then he sat against the tree trunk, panting until his pulse leveled.

"It was a little scratch," Rosa said, flicking away a bee that buzzed too close to her ear. "It was nothing."

"It was not nothing." He wiped sweat from his forehead. "I could see your bone."

"So?" Rosa's eyes burned. "I could have bashed the bone to shards and it still would have healed. It doesn't make any difference."

"It does to me," he muttered. A smoky wind blew past the children, rustling the leaves.

The village was preparing for their annual fiesta. Every year, when summer turned up its heat, they slaughtered a lamb, and the people would mix the blood with green onions, lard, thyme, and dried red chili, and make a feast out of it. It was Sergio's least favorite day of the year.

"You're the only one in the village who's scared of blood, you know that?" Rosa suddenly said.

"Am not," he said.

"Are too," she said. "Why?"

Sergio blew a gust of air out his mouth. "I'm not scared. It just makes me a little sick, is all."

She filled a nearby pot with lake water and let Sergio take the first drink. "Blood's a part of life," she said. "Blood and bones. It's normal."

Sergio sat up as though he had just grown a spine. "No. It's not. You scraped through to the bone. The bone, Rosa—that's not normal. And what about this morning? A thorn went straight through your palm." He reached out, almost daring to touch the place between Rosa's thumb and wrist where earlier a cactus thorn had driven through an inch of her flesh. He put his hand back into his lap before he could make contact, but his point stood: where a fresh, painful wound should have been bandaged and still healing, Rosa's skin was smooth, clean as an apricot.

"You worry too much." She climbed back into the tree, bees following her up the trunk. "I could slip right now." She dropped upside down, swinging by her ankles. "I could land headfirst on a rock. Crack my head open like a gourd. Blood, bits of brain everywhere—"

"Stop, stop." Sergio paled.

"It. Doesn't. Matter," she said. "The tree heals us, every time." She sighed. "It's boring. It's too safe here. Nothing new ever happens."

"But that's why no one ever leaves," Sergio said quietly. It was impossible to understand Rosa sometimes. He liked that they were safe, that really bad things didn't happen in the village. Rosa was so restless—Inés the puppy was better at sitting still than she was.

"I want to go." She looked at the lake, her face soft, and stood, balancing on the branch, toes gripping the knobbled bark. "I want to see things. I want to know what's out there."

He climbed up next to her, pulled out his whittling knife, and carved a piece of dried rose locust wood. His fingers worked on their own; they didn't need his eyes. He was busy watching Rosa's every movement, her arms rising, hands pointed like a prayer, eyelids falling shut.

"I want to see the corners of the earth. I want to see oceans. Mountains, forests, even other deserts. Snow." This last word she whispered.

"No one leaves," Sergio whispered back. "Not ever. Not even you."

"I'll find a way."

Sergio wondered if she would unfold hidden wings and take to the sky right now, but she sat back down next to him, toes tucked beneath her. As though she were glued to the tree. Stuck.

"Don't you ever think about those things?" she asked. "The things the Father told us, about the world?"

Sergio carved away a strip of wood and thought. Father Alejandro—the wiry, birdlike father of the mission—was born somewhere else. A kingdom of olive tree orchards, castles surrounded by sprawling gardens, and bullfighting. He came on a ship with a crew, hired to tear the desert apart until they found gold. They searched in rain-soaked jungles, atop the peaks of breathless mountains, along white beaches . . .

Instead of gold, when he led his expedition north into the dry rainbow desert, he found the lake. And the oasis.

He found the tree.

That was in 1480, Father Alejandro told them. Two hundred years ago – though the village had no use for years. He founded the village and built the mission with the crew, who also felt the tree was worth far more than gold. They made houses of stone and red desert clay, with yarrow thatched roofs.

The village grew. That group of sailors married local women, then raised children and grandchildren, and kept sheep and goats. Their children and grandchildren built huts of their own on the lakeshore. No one ever left. No one ever died. Those sailors grew old, yes, enough to be called the elders of the village, but their aging was slow. They were cheating time.

"I saw shorelines made of pebbles," Father

Alejandro would say, remembering his former life, "and flowers the size of my head. We sailed on gray oceans for so many days and nights that we lost the memory of ground beneath our feet. Sometimes the wind died, and we didn't move for weeks. I saw cities glittering silver and gold, people made of feathers." Rosa was always the one begging the Father for these details.

Even now Rosa's cheeks glowed at the mention of Father Alejandro's travels, but Sergio knew she missed the whole point of the Father's stories—that the world was the empty clam shell and the tree, the pearl. Nothing outside the village would ever compare with what they had.

"Is this the tree of life?" a grown-up had once asked.

"The tree of life bore fruit," Father Alejandro had counseled. "Our tree grows only blossoms."

"Then it is a magic tree!" Rosa had said.

Father Alejandro's face had darkened. "Magic is the devil's tool," he'd growled. "Our tree is simply a gift. A gift from God."

"What about everything else we have here?"

Sergio tried to say to Rosa now. *"What about the lake? And the stars? This tree gives the perfect shade, and the flowers make the village smell so nice, and the bees . . ."* The bees bring life, just like Rosa does, *he thought.*

Rosa scoffed. *"I've had enough of this lake, these stars, this tree."* She glared at the nearest blossom. *"We've seen everything there is to see here."* She sipped the lake water from the pot, and the two of them quieted as the sun fell.

Inés, finally worn out, curled up next to the tree trunk and snoozed.

The village, if one had a hawk's view, would be a vivid green dot in the middle of the thirsty desert: *un oasis.* The pale-green lake filled a basin between mesas, and where its water ended, lush, cool grass grew. If the village were an eye, staring up at the sun, the tree was its black pupil, dead center.

Rosa was right. The same people in the village did the same things every day. The only excitement was when a new baby came, born of the same old village families. But even that excitement wore off eventually; because of the tree, babies took longer to grow up than desert tortoises. A dozen years of watching the same baby coo erased the novelty of infancy.

Time in the village moved slower, decades coming and going, almost in a dream.

If time even existed in the village at all.

And of course, when the babies finally did grow up, they stayed.

Everyone stayed.

Travelers were rare, since the village was far off the beaten path. Few souls crossed the desolate heat of the southwestern desert, and anyone who did find the village passed through quickly, as though somehow sensing the strangeness of this place—though they never suspected the truth about the oddly mesmerizing black tree. In their memories, the village was a helpful but forgettable stop on their journeys to bigger, better places.

"Father Alejandro says the tree is—" Sergio said.

"A gift, I know," Rosa said. "Then we should use that gift to see the world. What else is life for?"

Sergio shrugged. "What about love? And marriage?"

Her teasing grin glowed through the foliage. "Me, married? To who?"

"No one. I don't know." He stared at his whittling knife.

Rosa stood. "Marriage is just another kind of sameness," she said. Suddenly she sprang into a swan dive and disappeared in the water, a white ring of foam rippling into stillness.

"Rosa!" Rosa's younger sister, Carolina, rang the mission bell. "Mamá says to come help make the chile caribe!"

Rosa let out a sigh that could be heard from the ridge. "I hate grinding the chilies. Makes my eyes burn." She trudged to the shoreline. "It's a child's chore, anyway."

"But you are a child," Sergio said.

Rosa scoffed. "I'm a century old! Father Alejandro says that in the world outside the village, children become adults when they're twelve. Twelve!"

"Yes, but he also says people die when they're fifty. Sometimes even younger. And that's if they don't split their heads like melons," he added, feeling queasy at the thought.

"Then maybe it's time we grew up."

Inés wagged her tail as Rosa passed, whining for attention. "When are you going to make a sheepdog out of this puppy, eh?" She patted the dog's head.

"Wait!" Sergio called. "Rosa, what if I"—he turned red—"or someone could make you a life worth staying here for? Would you get married then?"

Rosa plucked one of the blossoms from the branch above her and handed it up to him. "Only if you can figure out how to turn this lake into an ocean."

She walked back to the mission, a cloud of bees orbiting her head.

Sergio inhaled the blossom's honey-vanilla fragrance. Rosa was his oldest friend. Just as the village was contained inside the perfectly green, perfectly safe circle of the oasis, Sergio lived his life contained inside a smaller, safer circle. But Rosa always pushed him past his limits, and he always ended up thanking her for it.

He stayed in the tree until the village was dark and the fiesta was over, the lamb's blood drained and ingested, and the stars were out. He stood, the same way Rosa had, clinging to the branch the way she did.

He wondered if he looked as she did, like an eagle perched on a crag, strong in the uncertainty of midnight's shadows.

When his own family called him home, he leapt into the lake, arms flailing. As he plunged under the chilly water, he pictured Rosa, splayed bleeding on the rocks, vultures circling overhead.

And as usual, he was terrified.

7

"Rise and shine, girls! Breakfast!"

Mom's call comes five minutes after I fall asleep. At least that's how it feels. The disorientation of waking up in a strange new place hits me like a volleyball in gym class. Instead of my crisp white bedroom walls, I open my eyes to a poster of some ancient band called U2. Crackles in the blue ceiling reach out to the corners, like spindly tree branches.

Where am I?

"Girls?" Mom pokes her head into the room, and I remember. The ranch. Dad's old bedroom. Serge. Bees.

Bees. I dreamed of bees. They're following me, even when I sleep.

I sit up, so Mom sees I'm awake.

"Morning, hon," she says, a smear of flour across her forehead. "Breakfast is ready. Come eat, Alta."

The lump known as Alta grunts.

"You have ten minutes to get up and dressed, or your phone stays in my pocket all day." Mom's warning to my sister may seem harsh, but my family knows not to underestimate Alta's sleeping-in abilities. A zombie apocalypse could start and Alta would snooze right through it. She'd be so zonked, the zombies would mistake her for one of their own.

How is the desert already preheated and ready for baking at eight o'clock in the morning? The warmth seeps through the walls, dry and oppressive. I'm already sticky with sweat. I kick off the sleeping bag like it's suffocating me.

I remember last night: Dad's truck woke me, and there were stars, and snakes, and a bloody sheep's head . . .

There was Serge's story, about the tree and the lake and the children, Rosa and Sergio.

Funny that he used his and Grandma's names in the story. Funny, and also sad; he misses Grandma Rosa so much that she creeps into his fictional world.

My phone vibrates with a message from Gabby. *Raging Waters day! It sucks that you aren't here. :P :(*

A picture tries to download but stalls. Reception at the ranch flickers more than Serge's memory. I know what the picture will show, anyway: Gabby and Sofie squinting in their striped tankinis, sunscreened head to toe, both of them hovering near Manny in the first row of the group shot.

Raging Waters day is for kids who graduate sixth grade. A bus picks them up in the morning, and they swim and talk and play at the water park until closing time.

I wonder if my friends left my space empty, the spot I usually occupy in photos, right between them, since I'm the shortest.

I peck out my reply to Gabby with extra force in my fingers. *I know :(Eat a mango-tango snow cone for me.*

Is it going to be like this all summer? My friends send me updates on all the fun things I'm missing, and I start every morning in a jealous haze? And then, a worse thought: *How long until they forget to send me updates at all? Until they forget me?*

You'll get caught up, I reassure myself. *Two months at the ranch. Then junior high will be here, and you and Sofie and Gabby will pick up right where you left off.*

I almost convince myself.

Almost.

I get dressed and leave Alta to face the harsh reality of morning alone. The divine smell of breakfast leads me to the kitchen. Mom's cooking again, apron tied around her middle, whipping up another gourmet Mexican meal from scratch: spinach omelets, *pan dulce*, and fresh spiced chorizo.

Mom waits until I've got a mouthful of cheesy eggs before she says, "I need you to help Serge in the barn today."

Suddenly my food tastes of bribery. "Aw, Mom," I say.

"Serge says the sheep need to be dosed and sheared." Mom flips another perfectly symmetrical omelet onto a plate, a delicious bribe for some other unsuspecting soul.

"But I don't know how to do any of that sheep stuff," I say.

"Serge will take care of the sheep." Mom lowers her voice. "I just need you to . . . supervise." She cracks more eggs into the pan. "Alta! Get up now!"

"I *am* up!" comes the holler from the other side of the house, even though Alta's most likely still horizontal under the covers.

Mom turns back to me. "Dad and I have our own to-do lists today. And you and Serge seem to have a special thing—"

"No, we don't," I say automatically.

"Sure you do," Mom says. "You're the only one he's talked to besides Dad."

I scowl, not wanting to admit that she's right.

From the moment I met him yesterday, something about Serge has drawn me in—maybe the glow of his eyes when he looks at me, or the way his forehead is always furrowed, or the way he stares at his ranch, like he's lost in love with this land.

When my parents told me we'd be spending the summer here, I expected to have stiff, forced conversations with this grandfather I'd never met. I expected he'd ask me about school, about my friends, about what I wanted to be when I grew up. I didn't think he'd have anything interesting to say.

I didn't think he'd spin a magical story about a tree and a lake and a boy and a girl. . . .

"Okay," I say. "I'll supervise. But I'm not touching any sheep."

"Thanks." Mom lifts Lu into my arms. "Will you take Lu with you?"

Humph. My friends are hanging out at the water slides, and I'm stuck babysitting Lu and Serge.

After breakfast Serge and I walk down the rickety porch steps, Lu in tow.

Dad's on a ladder angled to the roof, holding a paintbrush. "Morning," he calls. "How's it look?" He gestures to the wood trim around the house.

To me, there's no difference between where he's painted and where he hasn't—it's all the same moldy beige.

"Looks good," I say.

Dad hops down in front of us. "Where you heading?"

"Sheep need shearing," Serge says.

"Mom's making me," I add, in case he thinks the real Carol was body-snatched by a new, alien Carol who's a sheep enthusiast.

Dad frowns at his father. "In the drought?"

Serge folds his arms. "The ranch doesn't shut down because of a drought."

"But they're so bony," Dad says, his eyes weary. "Don't they need their wool?"

"Are you a sheep farmer now?" Serge stretches, taller than I've ever seen him, his anger stretching tall, too.

Dad digs the toe of his boot into the grass like a little kid. "I'm just trying to help."

"I've been running a band of sheep longer than you've been alive," Serge says, "and don't forget, *niño*: You left. I stayed." He kicks up a tornado of red dust as he stomps to the barn. His oxygen tank leaves tracks in the dirt.

Dad bursts the bubble of silence. "Carol. Grandpa is . . ." Whatever he's about to explain, it melts away in the heat. "Let me know if he does anything out of the ordinary."

I sling Lu onto my hip. "I've never sheared sheep

before. How will I know if he's doing something out of the ordinary?"

Dad's eyes flash black, the only cold in all the desert. "Just come get me if he does anything weird."

Weird. I turn the word over in my mind. Does Serge's story about the lake and the tree count as weird?

Dad's already back up on the ladder, muttering to himself. He paints in violent slaps, marking the wood with splotches shaped like little witch brooms. Of the two of them, Dad's the one acting weird.

I follow my grandpa to the barn.

Yesterday, when I was looking for Lu, the barn felt like a sacred space, a cathedral in disguise. It must have been the illusion of sunset, because today, in the bright morning light, the barn is just a barn. Lu squirms, turning to jelly in my arms. I drop him, and he waddles to a worn-out saddle and bounces on it.

"You must forgive your dad," Serge says, propping the square doors open. "He forgets how long it's been since he was home."

I don't say anything. We all know how much Dad hates this place. Mom about keeled over in shock when

Dad brought up staying at the ranch to help Serge move. "He's still my father," Dad had said. "He needs help. There's no one else but us."

"I know, but can't we find a hotel?" Mom had said.

Dad had snorted. "There aren't any hotels, Patricia. It's the middle of the desert. The middle of nowhere. If we could camp outside and not be roasted alive, I'd buy tents tomorrow. Nope, we'll have to stay in the house . . . with him."

Mom had said, as an answer, "School starts August twelfth." That's when I knew my summer of sitting in Sofie's front-yard hammock, walking to the gas station with Gabby for slushies, and splashing in the pool with my friends for hours flew out the window on an eagle's feathered wings.

I chew on a hangnail. "It has been a long time for Dad" is all I say. I mean it as a defense both for Serge's gruffness and for Dad's meddling in sheep affairs.

"You don't have to tell an old man about time," Serge says. "I'm as old as time itself."

His top half disappears as he rummages deep in a metal bin. "But let me tell you something I've learned, *chiquita*. Measuring time isn't as simple as adding or subtracting minutes from a clock." He hauls out his sheep-shearing things. "You must find your own measuring stick."

"What do you mean?" I ask.

Serge gestures to the pasture. "Some count sheep to fall asleep. I count sheep to count time." He hands me a bottle of tonic and a gray rubber spoon.

"I'm not touching sheep," I say.

"I'll hold them," he says. "You shovel in the tonic. One spoonful per sheep. Get it all the way past the tongue, or they'll spit it back out."

I want to protest such a disgusting chore, but the shadows on the wall catch my eye. Four hands: two are mine, two Serge's. His hands tremble, even in silhouette. Mine are young and steady.

I can lend them out for a while. I'll help Serge measure time.

Serge fetches a sheep from the pasture while I uncap the bottle. Ugh! The stench of the tonic is so foul, my nose tickles. Serge tilts the poor sheep back, in a sort of choke hold: my first victim.

I've never stared an animal square in the face. The sheep's eyes bulge out from its skull in two different directions. It struggles, but Serge tightens his grip, so the sheep sinks back, relaxing, like a giant ugly infant succumbing to a lullaby.

Now that I see a sheep up close, I understand why Dad didn't think Serge should shear them. Its wool is scraggly, bug-ridden, and dirt-caked, a blanket of tangled split ends. Sheep are supposed to be puffy white cotton balls, clouds with legs. This sheep's skeleton juts past its scrawny wool, like its bones are hangers for future wool-knit sweaters.

This is what drought is. Skinny sheep; desperate biting flies; desert sand so dusty it hovers in the air, because the sky has more moisture than the land. The feeling of joints and muscles tightening, because heat makes bodies wring themselves out, mummifying us alive.

This is the drought of my dad's childhood, of Serge's every day.

A dying land.

Lu's bored with the saddle and is now banging two little garden shovels together to entertain himself. Serge and I dose sheep after sheep. Serge cradles their heads with such tenderness; he and the sheep have been doing this dance for years. I do my thing: hold nose, pour tar, insert spoon.

"Oh, the sheep I've shorn in this barn . . ." Serge scans the rotting wood rafters above us. "Do you know how Raúl measures time? In money. And bills. Things that time turns into dust and blows away in one breath." He waggles his finger. "You must find a measuring stick that means something, *chiquita.*"

A sheep escapes Serge's grasp and trots out to the pasture. Serge looks at me, a smile hiding in the corner of his mouth. A triangle of light hits his eyes. They're blue as cornflowers, every line in his irises pulsing. Rings in a tree trunk.

We work, Lu plays. Our conversations drift through every possible sheep topic: sheep diseases, the best lamb cuts for Easter dinner, the way these sheep used to have dark bones and long hair, but they've changed over the years . . .

If it was anyone else, I'd be bored to tears, but when Serge talks, it feels like the only sound. My ears are magnets for his words.

Lu munches on Goldfish crackers, and they look ridiculous and modern, too orange, out of place in this barn full of secrets.

By the time I spoon tonic into the last sheep's mouth, I'm ready to drop. But Serge never stops moving, never tires, just trades the spoon in my hands for a pair of rust-splotched shears.

"Uh," I say before he pats my shoulder.

"I'm not going to make you touch a sheep," he answers. "But shearing wool is a handy skill to learn, even for a city girl."

That's debatable, I think.

"This will at least make a good story to tell your classmates," he says, fetching a sheep from the pasture.

Stories.

"You never told me the rest of the story last night," I say. "Does R—I mean, does the girl ever leave the lake?" I don't want to say the name "Rosa" aloud; after all, our number-one goal this summer is not to upset Serge.

Serge reaches around to the sheep's belly and begins clipping. "Let me ask you something first, Caro-leeen-a. What would you have done? Would you leave the lake?"

I shrug. "I wouldn't want to stay in the middle of the

desert for eternity." *An entire summer is bad enough,* I think, but don't say.

"You would throw away the gift of the tree?"

My palms itch. This smells like a test, one I'm bound to fail. "I don't know," I fumble. "It's a big world out there."

Serge turns the clippers sharply at the sheep's hind legs. "You're right, *chiquita.* It is a big world, full of things that steal your breath and fill your belly with fire." He pauses, holding out a shaky finger for emphasis. "But where you go when you leave isn't as important as where you go when you come home."

"So the girl did leave the lake," I say, trying to steer him back to the story—that's what I want to hear about. "She does leave, but she comes back? Is that what you mean?"

"Caro-leeen-a." Serge's whisper is rough, like a rattler's dancing tail.

"Carol," I correct him.

"Your name is Caro-leeen-a," he says, louder. "Forget about the story for a moment. Close your eyes. Think of a tree."

Grudgingly I shut my eyes and picture a gnarled,

black-barked tree, with leaves so green they shine gold, branches reaching like fingers into a cloudless sky.

"The roots of a tree stretch deeper than you think," Serge says. "No matter how far away you are when you bloom, you are always tied to your roots."

I open my eyes. He stares at me, his forehead knitted with wrinkles.

"Your roots are part of you, Caro-leeen-a. You must never spit on them."

The freshly shaved sheep in his arms bleats, and Serge pats its rump. "This wool!" He stretches out what he's shorn so far, and it's pathetically sheer, a few strands of sheep hair held together by air. "And Raúl said the sheep were too bony."

The barn is mostly shadows, but Serge would have to be blind to miss the sheep's bones sticking out from its skin so far that you can practically see the white of them. This isn't good, usable wool—it's garbage.

"Look, Rosa," Serge says, and goose bumps prickle my arms.

"I'm Carol," I say, frowning. What happened? He was fine just a second ago, wasn't he?

"Have you ever seen such wool?" he says. "We'll get

fat coins for this wool, once you spin it into your magic scarves."

"Carol. I'm Carol, your granddaughter," I try again.

"It must be all this rain," he continues, clipping the measly wool around the sheep's neck. "A whole week of good rain. Rain always keeps the sheep happy, keeps them growing this happy wool."

I check every wrinkle on Serge's face for hints that this is a joke. But his eyes glitter sharp blue, no laughter in them. "It hasn't rained in a hundred years, remember? The drought?"

But my words seem lost on him, adrift in the shipwreck of his mind. I should call for Dad—Serge is stuck in a memory.

"All this rain." Serge holds his hand flat, as if rain is spilling onto it now.

But none of this makes any sense. Serge doesn't have any memories of rain. The ranch has had one hundred years of drought, only drought.

He spots Lu in the corner, making a spooky castle out of red dirt. "Raúl! ¡Ven aquí, ahora! You want to feel this wool! So soft, eh?"

"But that's Lu, remember?" I say, and again, the

words seem to go in one of his bat-winged ears and out the other.

"If we get any more rain," he says, "our little lake is going to be an ocean. But that's what you wanted all along, isn't it, Rosa—"

Brrrk!

He's cut off by the horrific noise of the clippers nicking the sheep's leg. The sheep panics at the pain and flails, hooves scraping the barn floor. Blood trickles down its leg, spoiling the wool Serge just sheared.

Go get Dad! my brain shouts. *Go get Dad!*

But it feels like the architecture has been knocked out of my legs. My stomach churns, rolling like a stormy sea, but I can't look away from the sheep, the cut, the waterfall of blood.

Serge breathes heavy. All the color's drained from his face.

"Are you okay?" I ask shakily.

His eyes are watching other worlds, and he mumbles, "I'm not scared. It just makes me a little sick, is all." It's a line from his story.

"I don't like blood either," I say.

Serge nods, then pulls a wadded-up tissue from his

jeans pocket and presses it against the cut. It isn't that deep after all; the sheep's just a dramatic bleeder. With the blood mopped up, Serge lets the poor sheep scamper out to the pasture, then leans into a wall, panting.

"We shouldn't be shearing such bony sheep," he says. "Drought's nearly dried them out to dust."

Like a light switch, his brain blinks back to normal. He loses that hazy, million-miles-away glaze. He packs the shearing tools and nasty tonic in the bin, leaving the pile of bloodied wool. "Thank you for your help, *chiquita*. These old hands are not as steady as they once were."

My pulse calms when he calls me *chiquita*, not Rosa.

8

I scoop up my brother and we walk to the pasture,
squinting, the sunshine blinding us after the darkness
of the barn.

Lu burrows his face in the crook of my neck, a fuss
about to spill out of him. It's naptime.

Serge stretches his arms out. "Oh, *chiquita*. The land
is dying. It's been dying for a hundred years. But even
the land still has its own ways of measuring time. Is it
sunrise? Look for rosy pink in the sky. Sunset? The sky
is burnt orange when the sun goes to bed. Is the eagle
hunting? Watch him fly: if his wings flap, he's in a hurry
to find a tasty snake for supper. But if he's soaring,
then he's just enjoying the view beneath him."

My brother is heavy in my arms, asleep, or nearly there. But I stay at Serge's side, trying to see the huge, empty desert through his eyes.

"The land measures time with the ridge. It gets taller every morning, like a child growing. Or the land measures time with the stars, twirling in the heavens. Tick, tick, tick, with every twirl."

He swallows. "It used to measure time with bees. Flowers slept in winter, yawned open in springtime. But the bees took our lake and left. No more blossoms. No more bees. No more time."

Bees again. Just when I thought he was back to acting normal.

The naked white sunlight beats down on us, the heat like invisible hands on my back, making me dizzy.

He nudges me, like one of my friends would do in the cafeteria. "Your turn, Caro-leeen-a. What can you see measuring time?"

My heart thumps. Another test. I shrug, but he shakes his head. "No, no. Tell me. What do you see?"

All right, fine. I shift Lu to free my hand, block the sun from my eyes, and scan the land.

The first thing I notice isn't part of the desert. It's a

shiny red truck parked in the gravel driveway, a monster-size machine big enough to haul away a house.

A well-ironed man steps out in polished leather cowboy boots that gleam as much as the truck does.

"Who's that?" I say.

But my grandpa barrels past me, snorting steam from his nose like a bull. "This is private property!" he shouts at the man. "You can't park that here!"

"Hey, wait up!" I call, trying to run without jiggling Lu.

"Are you Raúl?" The man extends a hand. "We spoke on the phone."

"Liar," Serge spits.

"Mr. González, hi. Good to see you." Dad trip-traps down the porch stairs and takes the handshake meant for Serge. "I'm Raúl. Thanks for driving out."

"This is private property," Serge repeats. "If you let him park here, then they'll all park here."

"What are you talking about?" Dad says.

But Serge has fallen into a full-on meltdown, shouting in garbled, jigsaw-puzzle Spanish that none of us can follow.

Your loved ones may lose their temper at seemingly little

lost battles, or they may throw tantrums and yell when they
don't get their way.

"Don't be rude," Dad says. "Mr. González is your real estate agent."

"Quite a nice property you have here. Quite the potential. I'm anxious to see what we can do with it." Mr. González flashes a smile that could glow in the dark.

Serge stares at his son as if Dad had strangled a sheep. "Wait until your mother gets home. Wait until she hears what you're up to!"

My gut lurches. Serge is slipping again, down the rabbit hole of patchy memories.

Dad rubs his red-rimmed eyes. "*Papá,* Mr. González is going to find the very best people to take care of the ranch. We're passing it on, remember?"

"Why do you spit on your roots, Raúl?" Serge says, and walks across the pasture, where he sits on the scabby old tree stump. From this distance he seems perfectly still, like someone painted him into the landscape.

"I'm sorry," Dad says to Mr. González. "My mom passed away twelve years ago. Like I said, he's tail-spinning into late-stage dementia."

Mr. González shakes his head. "Don't worry about it. My aunt had Alzheimer's. She could throw a mean punch before her time was up. We'll make this whole process as easy as possible for your dad."

The two men stroll off, clicking photos with their phones and chattering, sentences overlapping each other. My dad doesn't even look at me.

Serge stays where he is.

I take Lu into the house and put him in his port-a-crib, a lump of frustration bubbling in my throat.

Back in the kitchen, Mom's removing ancient layers of grime from the cabinets.

"So we're really getting rid of the ranch," I say, voice sharp enough to cut metal.

She notices my stink-eye and stops scrubbing. "Not getting rid of," she says. "It's just time to pass it on. Like Dad said. There's your lunch."

I nibble at the quesadilla Mom fixed for me. "How long has this ranch been in the family?" I ask after a moment.

"I'm not sure," she says.

"Does Dad know?"

"I can't imagine he's ever cared about the history of the ranch," she says with a chuckle.

"Well, he should," I say. "It's his history, his family. It's his roots."

Mom raises her eyebrows. "And now you care about your roots?"

I'm surprised, too—this sounds nothing like me. Caring about my roots? Worrying about what will happen to this ranch, this land? But try as I might to push this frustration away, my eyes sting with tears.

I hide my face with a glance out the window. Dad and Mr. González are still pacing the pasture. Are they debating how much this ranch is worth? Probably not much to the rest of the world—not much in dollars— but it's Serge's home. The place where sheep tell time.

"Will you go get Grandpa for lunch?" Mom asks.

"I'll bring it out to him," I offer.

Mom puts his quesadilla, rice, and banana onto a tray, and I carry it through the pasture. Inés hobbles along with me, and I match my steps to her arthritic old-lady pace.

A soft, hot wind blows the scrub around Serge's

snake-stomping boots. The dog nestles beside him, putting her head on his lap.

"Hi," I try. "Brought your lunch."

When he doesn't acknowledge me or the food, I set the tray next to him. "I measure time, too. With changes."

I clear my throat.

"Changes, like a stranger who shows up at the ranch in a red truck that looks too clean to have ever done a day's real work. Changes, like when Alta cuts her hair short, with no warning, and now looks like she's twenty instead of seventeen. Changes, like when Lu started crawling and it wasn't safe to leave anything lying around the house anymore."

The wind bends a weed into my sandal, tickling my foot. "Changes, like a new school in the fall. Junior high, where I have to learn new hallways, new lunch lines, new rules about what to wear and when to laugh."

No reaction from Serge, but I continue.

"When all the changes start piling on top of each other, stacking up, then I know time is flying."

My grandpa's eyes gawk at the desert. No clue if he

heard me, or if he even knows where he is. All I hear is his oxygen tube as he breathes, in and out.

"Will you tell me the end of the story?" I say. "The story about the tree?"

He says nothing.

"Look." I sigh, and sit cross-legged in the dirt. "Maybe if the girl—if Rosa, in the story—if she leaves the lake and is okay . . . maybe it means that when you leave the ranch, you'll be okay, too."

This is what I've been thinking all day, but it wouldn't fit into sentences. I stroke Inés's downy neck, and the lump of frustration in my throat dissolves.

Serge cracks free from the ice that held him, and his blue eyes find me, like I'm the only thing visible in a blurry world. "Once upon a time," he starts.

"No, not the beginning," I say. "I want to hear the ending."

"Stories don't end," he says. "They just turn into new beginnings."

I think for a moment. Beginnings, endings, beginnings . . . Like a circle.

Rings in a tree trunk.

"Once upon a time," he says, "there was a tree."

"You already told me about the tree," I cut in again, impatient.

"We always start with the tree," Serge says. "Now, listen, *chiquita*. Once upon a time . . ."

And I button my lips, scoot closer to the scabby tree stump, and let my grandpa tell me a story.

O*nce upon a time, there was a tree, with green leaves fat enough to block out the pale beams of a midsummer moon. It was early evening, the warm stripes of sunset fading, and the tree stood extra tall, like a boy stretching his spine to impress a señorita passing on the street. Copper lanterns dangled from the branches, and the flames bounced their light off the blossoms, making them glow like white stars.*

The bees buzzed and hummed in unison on this night. If they had had human faces, they would have shown faint smiles and dreamy, half-closed eyes as they siphoned pollen from the flowers.

The villagers hummed the same droning tune as they performed their own dull tasks: rinsing the vinegar from the pinto beans, tending horses in stables, gathering enough water to give the children their weekly baths. Busy as bees, yes, but on this night, happily busy.

Tonight, there would be a wedding.

Once upon a time, the groom-to-be tied and retied the strings that laced the neck of his cotton shirt. A simple shepherd's shirt, but of the two Sergio owned, it was his finest. Tie, untie, retie . . .

To give his shaking hands something else to do while he waited, he dug up weeds from the village's row of garbanzo plants.

"Inés!" He whistled at the black dot on the horizon, which became more and more dog-shaped as it ran toward him. "Good girl," Sergio said, rubbing the dog's ears. He looked at the tree, lanterns mirrored in the green-glass surface of the lake below . . .

On the other side of the tree, the bride allowed her sister to fuss with the garland of snowberry blooms in her hair. Rosa held as still as the tree trunk—not like her at all, to be holding so still—and watched Sergio.

He'd grown since that day they made wishes. His baby chub had melted, his limbs lengthened. His arms were strong enough to haul hay bundles, take barrels of water to the troughs, carry the sheep above his head. That boy from a century ago was now chiseled as tree bark, and every girl in the village tracked him like bees tracked flora.

Sergio had eyes only for Rosa. Always.

And Sergio was the only thing in the village that didn't bore Rosa.

The only one who could make marriage an adventure.

"Oh, Rosa." Carolina spoke in a voice thin as lace, and held her sister's cheeks gently. "You look like a bride."

"Then it must be time," Rosa answered. She gripped her sister's arm, and for a second Carolina thought she saw the impossible: a flicker of fear in Rosa's eyes.

"Will this cure me?" Rosa whispered. "Will this make me want to stay?" She thought about this daily, that there was something wrong with her.

Carolina held her sister still. "He loves you the way you are, Rosa."

But Rosa still worried. No one else in the village

burned and ached to leave like she did. No one else had a wanderlust like a fever.

Once upon a time, villagers prepared the bonfire for their annual summer fiesta. Their eyes and hands still burned from grinding the chilies for the lamb's blood, but the tears that flowed were merry ones as Rosa stepped down the aisle, clutching yarrow in her hands, bees flying in and out of her flower garland. Her rose-petal lips calmly gifted a smile to each person watching her, and Sergio, waiting with the Father beside the lucky knothole, felt like his next inhale was different, the most important breath of his life so far. Breathing as a husband.

Once upon a time, Sergio and Rosa wed beneath the tree, and the village celebrated. Celebrated the new union with crullers and cakes, celebrated summer with the slaughter of a lamb, celebrated life and love with a sleepless night dancing on the lake's shore.

The newlyweds sneaked up to their favorite branch and exchanged wedding gifts. For Sergio, Rosa had made a deliciously cozy wool blanket—burgundy, soft as clouds. He threw it around his shoulders at once, delighting in its scent: honey-vanilla, like Rosa.

For Rosa, Sergio had nothing in his hands. "Your wish," he simply said. "I want to make your wish come true."

Rosa gasped. "Leave the village?"

"A honeymoon," Sergio said, "to see the world."

"But no one ever leaves." She repeated his own words back to him, and he shook his head.

"We leave. After the harvest."

Rosa kissed him until the yellow morning light came. Then she happily set up home as his wife, cooked for him three times a day, tossed handfuls of dried corn to the chickens every morning, and chased the occasional rebellious sheep that ran from the shearing line.

Autumn brought the harvest, and when the crops had all been plucked and gathered and divided among the villagers, Rosa asked Sergio, "When do we leave?"

"Soon," he said. "We must first shear the sheep. Then we leave."

When a week passed and the sheep were all free from their wool, Rosa asked Sergio, "When do we leave?"

"We must wait until after winter," Sergio insisted. "Snow can be treacherous for travels."

Rosa spent an impatient winter feeling like time marched backward. When spring grasses sprung along the lake's shore, she asked, "When do we leave?"

Inés is missing; not until we find her. A traveler warned of a plague in the North; not until we hear news that it's safe. A war, more crops, the ewes are pregnant. The trip was postponed, and every day Rosa climbed to the top of the ridge and stared. Every day Rosa felt more and more withered, like a sheep fenced in a too-small pen.

Sergio made every excuse, except the truth: "I'm too afraid to leave."

Once upon a time, a husband came into his shepherd shack, expecting a hot lunch to be waiting at the table. Instead, his wife held a packed bag in her arms.

"Are you coming?" she asked.

Rosa was jumping first off the branch, Sergio realized, but he was still very much terrified.

And he said, "No."

9

It takes a week to find our rhythm.

A week for my body to stop protesting when the sun spikes past the blinds and wakes me hours earlier than is appropriate for a summer vacation. A week for Mom to stop saying, "Morning's the coolest time of day in the desert," like I should be grateful for six AM.

A week for Dad and Serge to stop glaring at each other when they're in the same room. They're like neighboring cats who are both fiercely territorial, but must live with each other somehow. They circle, they growl in their throats, but the claws stay retracted.

A week for me to get used to the bees. They don't bother anyone but me.

A week of work, of job lists and chore charts. A week of Dad crunching numbers when Serge is coherent and crunching numbers when Serge is incoherent. A week of Alta wandering, drifting from project to project, "helping" with whatever menial task is available. Holding tools. Shooing sheep. Her hands never take anything sharp, and her clothes never get dirty. We are earning our calluses and splinters, and Alta is earning a suntan.

I've been Mom's shadow this week, working with her to empty odd drawers and shelves, filled with clutter so obscure, we don't know how to sort it. An old egg beater, one with a crank you turn by hand. Keep it? Serge won't use it in the Seville. Take it? We certainly don't need it. Store it? Not the best item to take up valuable space in an already-expensive storage shed. But it seems wasteful to just hurl it in the trash. So a strange "to be sorted" pile stacks up outside, next to the driveway. Five drawers, two closets, and ten shelves sorted, and the pile is as tall as Lu.

Open, sort, repeat.

When I'm not busy cleaning out the house, I chase after Lu when he tires of playing with whatever toy—or piece of junk—I gave him. I don't mind, though; Lu and

I have a similar rhythm, embarrassing as that is: my attention span is not much longer than my one-year-old brother's.

Serge has his own rhythm, and we try our best not to disrupt it. Those are Dad's instructions, based on the Seville pamphlet's suggestions to *help decrease the chance of triggering negative behaviors or outbursts by keeping the environment structured and predictable.*

Serge sleeps very little. He's already puttering around the ranch by the time I roll out of my sleeping bag. Mom and Dad put a list of jobs on the fridge, things that have to be done to get the ranch up to snuff, as well as the basics required to move a crotchety, demented, thousand-year-old man to a new home. It's quite a list. Equal parts backbreaking and tedious.

But Serge has his own jobs. He shuffles to the pasture every morning, looking at each sheep's ears, hooves, and tail, meticulously checking for ranch-rot and ticks.

He pulls weeds, taking an eternity to get into a gardening crouch, and even then he seems precarious, like a dead tree branch that's one breeze away from snapping. His spine hunches into a perfect letter *C* and doesn't seem strong enough to hold up his head. It takes him an hour to pull up as many weeds as I could yank in less than ten minutes.

But this is my grandpa's rhythm. Slow, thumping, the ancient heartbeat of the ranch.

Serge and my family work side by side, two separate units, and we rarely overlap. I steal peeks at my grandpa every chance I get.

"How did he eat before we got here?" I ask Dad one day, and he snorts, as if it's obvious.

"He grows his food, silly," he says, and points to the crops.

But I've seen those crops. They're crispy, and so yellowed. Puny potatoes, chalky-red chilies, green beans shriveled like witches' fingers.

I mention this to Dad, and he rolls his eyes. "Then he must order groceries. I don't know." Dad couldn't be less interested in Serge's rhythm.

Serge doesn't have grocery bags. Or groceries. No crinkled bags of Cheetos, or cold cereal, or anything you could buy in a gas station, even. I would know; I've cleaned out so many cupboards and drawers, including the pantry—all he has are jars of his withered crops.

Twelve years of being alone on the ranch, with nothing to eat but the occasional lamb chop and mummified vegetables. No wonder Serge is cranky.

Today's Saturday. Today Mom has to drive back to Albuquerque to work. Part of the reason Mom and Dad were able to drag us to the ranch for two months is because of their jobs. Since Dad's a contractor, he was able to leave town for the summer; he just has to take a phone call every once in a while from a crew member with a question. At least that's how it was originally pitched. He's taken at least five phone calls a day, and trying to coordinate the framers with the electricians with the roofers and the carpet layers, everyone needing confirmation . . . Dad's on edge every second of every day, the heat draining his patience away.

Mom's an ER nurse, and she reduced her hours and switched her schedule around so she can still work every Saturday and be at the ranch the rest of the time. Today she makes her first drive back to the city for a double shift. I'm jealous that she gets the AC blowing on her for the three-hour drive. If it were me, I wouldn't come back.

She emerges from the guest room in a pair of maroon

scrubs, checking everything a thousand times—Lu's snacks, the gas stove, Serge on the porch.

"You're sure you'll be okay?" she asks Dad.

Dad gives her a look. For a second I wonder what would happen if I told him how much he resembles Serge: mouth hanging in an almost-frown, lines creasing his forehead.

"We'll be fine. Make sure you park in the grass when you get back," he tells Mom, just as his phone rings. "I'm repaving the driveway today, and it won't be dry." His glances at the screen. "I've got to take this, it's my electrician."

He walks to the front yard to take his call.

Mom hands Lu to me. "I won't be back until morning," she says, "so good night. Help keep an eye on things, will you?"

"We'll be fine," I echo Dad.

Mom glances at Dad through the window. "I'm not worried about you." She leaves, honking the horn as she pulls away.

Outside, Dad's down on his knees, spreading freshly poured cement onto the gravel. It's weirdly mesmerizing to watch, the teeny rocks erased one by one, like it's a giant canvas and Dad's completing a masterpiece.

Lu isn't as fascinated as I am by Dad's work, so I take the antsy little guy inside. We settle in the living room, me on the futon, playing games on my phone, and Lu, for the moment, entertained by his toy laptop, which asks, *Are you home? Are you home? Are you home?* over and over in an obnoxiously chipper voice.

"Tell it no," I instruct him, but instead he smacks all the buttons at once and giggles like a madman.

"Carol, hey." Dad comes into the room, sipping a Gatorade. "I need you and Alta to keep an eye on Serge and Lu while I run to the hardware store."

"In Albuquerque?" I say.

"No, there's one about thirty minutes from here," Dad says. "Is that okay?"

"Sure," I say. What else am I going to say?

"Serge is on the porch, washing his blanket," Dad informs me. "Alta's in charge."

Inés pushes her wet nose into my hand, so I put my phone in my pocket and pat her head.

"Make sure no one steps on the driveway," Dad adds

on his way out of the house. "Cement is all laid out. It'll be wet for a few days."

I salute him good-bye, and he drives away in the truck.

Lu starts fussing. I try to hand him his talking toy tractor, but he pushes it away and babbles a stream of nonsense.

"What's the matter, huh, Lu-Lu?" I hand him a pouch of baby fruit snacks, which he nibbles at, then drops. When the smell hits me, I realize why he's fussing.

"Oh, Alta!" I call. "Lu needs you."

But it's silent in the back of the ranch house. Alta's either dinking around on her phone or she fell back asleep.

Who am I kidding? Even if I could get her out of her room, there's no way she'd change Lu's diaper.

"Okay, Lu," I say, reaching for his wet wipes. "Let's do this."

I pull my shirt up over my nose and mouth, which blocks most of the smell. Lu's holding perfectly still, his owl-wide brown eyes staring up at me, as if to say, *What are you waiting for?*

"Raúl," Serge calls from the porch. "Raúl, ¿*dónde estás?*"

I sigh. "Hold on," I tell Lu, and leave him lying on the floor, his shorts around his ankles.

Serge is in his wicker chair. "Where is Raúl?" he asks, in English this time. His wool blanket is draped across his lap, dripping wet and covered in suds.

"He had to run an errand," I say slowly, eyeballing the wet blanket on his lap—the same blanket he always washes. "Do you need something?"

"We should not let that boy leave the ranch, Rosa," Serge says, and my heartbeat reverberates in my throat. "One of these days he won't come back." His eyes are dull. Pale. Flat as the desert. Like they were that day in the barn, when he was lost in time.

Your loved one may be unable to remember names, thoughts, or memories. Announce your identity with a slow, calm demeanor.

"It's me, it's your granddaughter, Carolina," I say, but it doesn't work.

"I'll wait here for Raúl to come home, Rosa, and then we can eat dinner together as a family." He pushes the wet blanket back into the tub and stands, staring at the land around us.

"Why don't you come with me," I say, taking Serge's arm in a *firm but gentle manner,* and guide him into the house.

Back in the living room, Lu has torn the room apart. He's opened the cupboard of the bottom half of Serge's TV stand, pulled out the collection of board games, and emptied them. The carpet is completely covered in tokens, coins, cards, dice . . . And he's done all this with his shorts still around his chubby ankles.

"Lu! No-no!" I fly to his side, yanking a stack of slimy Monopoly money from his mouth. He laughs and tosses an entire deck of playing cards, showering us in a storm of hearts and diamonds. How did such a tiny guy cause such a mess? I was only gone for a minute.

"Alta!" I cry, unable to keep from panicking. "I need help!"

I look at Serge, who is still standing where I left him.

"I'm sorry," I tell him. "I'll clean this all up right now, I promise."

But Serge doesn't respond. He eases himself into

the recliner, still blank-faced, no hint that he's noticed the board games scattered everywhere. No hint that he knows his grandkids are in the room with him. His eyes are blurry, rainy-day puddles. . . .

Lu starts to whimper, probably freaked out by my outburst—and upset about his still-dirty diaper. "Sorry, guy," I say, kissing his curly dark hair and clearing a spot on the rug for an emergency diaper change. Alta owes me big-time for this.

Speaking of . . .

"Alta! Come on!" I shout. "You're supposed to be in charge."

I get up to throw away Lu's dirty diaper—and freeze at the sight of the empty recliner. Serge is nowhere to be found.

"You've got to be kidding me," I mutter. *"Alta!"*

I prop Lu on one hip, march to Dad's old bedroom, and throw open the door.

Alta's not there.

"Alta?" I call. "Serge?"

But the house is silent.

"Where is everybody?" I ask Lu, my heartbeat speeding up.

Lu blows a raspberry.

I head outside, my annoyance with Alta trumping my worry about Serge. "One of these days," I tell Lu while stomping down the porch steps, "Alta's going to get what's coming to her."

Scanning the horizon, I don't see anyone—only the sheep, flocking around their trough for a midmorning drink. No Alta—and no Serge.

I'm retreading the fear I felt on our first day at the ranch, when Lu went missing and found a rattlesnake. What if my sister's facing off with a rattler at this very minute?

I recall my words: *Alta's going to get what's coming to her.* "That's not what I meant!" I shout to the cloudless blue sky, dashing toward the barn, Lu bouncing on my hip.

I keep losing everyone I'm supposed to be watching.

Lu and I peer into the shadows, but there's no Alta. And no Serge.

"Don't panic, don't panic, don't panic," I tell myself. Lu parrots the words back at me in toddler singsong.

"That's right, Lu," I say brightly. "Everything is okay!"

Bzzz.

I jump. A bee!

But it's not a bee. It's my phone buzzing with a message. I pull it out of my pocket with a shaking hand, wondering what I'm going to tell Mom or Dad if they ask how things are going. . . .

But the message isn't from Mom or Dad. It's from Alta:

Gone out. Be back by dinner.

A new message arrives while I'm still trying to make sense of the first:

DO NOT tell your dad.

Gone out? Gone out where—and how? Alta hasn't touched her car since she got here; it's still parked out front.

From the barn doors, I peer across the ranch. It's like Alta and Serge have both grown wings and flown away, like Sergio worried Rosa would do in the story. I swallow the last of my fury at Alta—for now—because even though she abandoned me, at least I know she's okay. What matters now is finding Serge.

As Lu and I trudge around the ranch, calling out for Serge, the answer to how Alta sneaked off smacks me in the face: Marco. Alta must have had her boyfriend come pick her up, leaving the ranch without driving her own car. Technically not breaking the rules.

I could almost admire Alta for her cleverness. She's a slicker escape artist than Houdini.

Or Serge.

Should I call Dad? No, I think I'll spare myself a scolding. Serge can't have gone far—I cling to the hope that I'll find him before Dad gets back from the store and realizes Serge was ever missing.

10

I'm covered in sweat, my voice hoarse from shouting for Serge and singing silly songs to Lu to stave off a meltdown—his or mine, I'm not sure—when I hear the slamming of a car door.

Uh-oh.

"Carol!" Dad roars from the front of the house. "Get out here!"

I hike Lu up on my hip and scramble around to the front yard, wondering how Dad knew right away that I'd messed everything up. I don't have to wonder for long: Dad's standing on the porch stairs, quaking with rage, pointing a finger at the driveway.

His finely smoothed work has been destroyed with footprints sunk deep into the soggy cement. One side of his duct tape barrier is ripped apart, the ends trailing uselessly on the ground.

"What happened?" I gasp.

"Didn't I tell you to keep an eye on Serge?" Dad says.

"I tried!" I say. "But he wandered off when I was changing Lu. I've been looking all over for him!"

"He's right over there," Dad snaps, and I follow his pointing finger to the fields, where Serge's head barely pokes above a row of dried-out cornstalks.

I let out a shaky breath and rest my damp forehead against Lu's.

"You have to stay with him, Carol. He could have wandered off and gotten lost, or gone to the ridge, or fallen down the porch stairs . . ." He gestures to the ruined driveway behind him. "And this, this is just—unacceptable."

I open my mouth and close it again, a flabbergasted fish. "I'm sorry, I just took my eyes off him for one second."

"Well, that one second just set us back a week." Dad slaps the porch railing with open palms, cursing.

"I didn't mean to." Every time I speak, my voice is smaller and smaller.

"A week!" he says, looking like he's lost his entire life savings. "One more week to re-prep and re-pour that driveway. Do you want to be here an extra week?"

I shake my head.

Suddenly he looks exhausted, like he ran to the hardware store on foot. "Or maybe I'll try to cram it into our schedule. Stay up a few nights. I don't know." The guilt fills me to the brim.

"I didn't mean to," I say again. I want to tell him about Alta, so he knows I'm not the only one who should be in trouble. But that'll only add to his already rickety load, and Alta will fry me for tattling. Besides, with the mood he's in, Dad just might blame me for her leaving, too.

I open the screen door and step inside.

"Carol," Dad calls. "I'm sorry for barking. I am. It's just . . . We want to get out of here as soon as we can, right?"

"Right," I say, hiding my face in Lu's curls. I don't lift my head as I walk through the dark house.

◆ ◆ ◆

After depositing a sleepy Lu into his port-a-crib, I head to Dad's old bedroom and burrow into my sleeping bag, face-first. *Keep an eye on things, keep an eye on things . . .* Mom's words chant through my head, and a bee finds my rhythm and adds a buzz as a counterbeat: *bzzz, bzzz . . .*

I lie there, drowning in my deadly concoction of remorse and bitterness, and when I look up, the sun is on the other side of the sky. Alta strolls into the room and barely glances at me.

"When did you get home?" I prop myself up on my elbows.

"Now," she says, like I asked the dumbest question in the world. She sets her purse on the bed and kicks off her sandals.

"You were supposed to stay here and help with Lu," I say, my teeth clenched. "Mom said so this morning."

"Well, something came up." Her tone warns me to leave it alone.

In the kitchen I hear Dad putting the dinner Mom made us into the oven. "Does Dad know you were gone all day?" I ask.

"No, and you're not going to tell him." The way she

says it—like it's a statement of fact, like she's already sized me up and figured me out . . . My anger melts, becoming exhaustion in my muscles.

I stare at the sleeping bag and nod.

"Good," Alta says, and pats my head like I'm a Chihuahua. "Let's go eat dinner."

"I'm not hungry," I say to Alta's back, but she's already down the hallway, has already forgotten about me. How can she forget so easily?

On the porch, Serge is soaking his snake-stomping boots in the old-fashioned metal tub, cakey bits of cement breaking away from the soles and floating in the water.

"I tried to walk to the pasture, but the ground wouldn't stay still beneath my feet," Serge says.

"It was wet cement," I tell him. "Dad was trying to fix up your driveway."

"Your father keeps trying to fix things that aren't broken," Serge says.

"Grandpa?" I ask. The name still tastes foreign. Not quite right.

He looks at me with his electric-blue eyes. "You want to hear the rest of the story," he says.

I cross my legs, scrunching myself up against the house.

"Once upon a time," I begin for him, and he continues with me, "there was a tree . . ."

O*nce upon a time, there was a tree. It was taller than the crag where the eagles nested, tall enough to touch the clouds with its tippy-top leaves. It held still in the orange afternoon light, like it was straining to hear the conversation happening beneath its branches.*

Sergio finished saddling the wheat-colored horse and slung a bundle of wool onto its back. "You shouldn't be going alone," he said to his wife, for the thousandth time.

Rosa threw a stone into the lake, skipping it six times across the pale-green water. "The crops need to be brought in," she said. "Sheep need feeding, dosing, shearing."

"Then stay."

She smiled. "And waste a perfectly saddled horse?"

Sergio laced his fingers in hers. "Tell me you'll be fine. Tell me you won't come home in a coffin."

"How do you know about coffins?"

He shook his head. "You think I'm just a silly shepherd? I remember Father Alejandro's stories as well as you."

"I married you for your looks," she joked.

"Stay with me," he whispered, so quiet she couldn't hear. Perhaps he said it more for himself.

Rosa looked at him. His eyes hadn't changed, not in all these years. They were still the color of the sky's first morning breath, blue and serious, the same eyes he had when he was the chubby boy whittling on the tree branch.

Am I going too far? she wondered. To dream of leaving is one thing; to saddle a horse and ride away is quite another.

"Remember how you made that wish?" Sergio said. "One hundred years ago you wished to leave the village, and here you are."

He stared at her like she was a magician, like she had transformed the lake into sand, and her doubts flew away. This was magic. Leaving, actually leaving, was a thing of magic. She never wanted him to stop looking at her this way.

"A hundred lamb slaughters ago," she said.

"Lamb slaughters?"

Rosa nodded. "How else are we supposed to measure time around here? A year might as well be a minute."

And a minute without you will feel like a year, *Sergio thought.*

A breeze rippled the lake and blew warm air through Rosa's hair, carrying the honey-vanilla scent to Sergio. Her signature trail of bees hovered behind her, a constellation of yellow against the black bark of the tree trunk. He wanted to wrap her close to him, pretend that these last few moments together really were an eternity. "Rosa, you must be safe." He kissed her forehead. "If only you could take the tree with you . . ."

Then his eyes lit up. He darted up the tree like a desert fox.

"What are you doing?" Rosa called.

"Chasing an idea." Even with shepherd's soreness making his arms complain with every move, he reached their favorite branch in seconds and pulled out his whittling knife, glancing around. He was reluctant to damage the tree, but the fear of death, of Rosa's death, pulsed through him like his own heartbeat.

Rosa climbed up next to him.

Using the knife, Sergio peeled away a sliver of black bark. Then he waited. Waited for the tree to shudder, or cry. The tree wasn't human, of course, but it was as much a part of their village as any of the villagers themselves.

Moments passed, but nothing happened. He peeked at the tree's bald spot. So the wood under the bark was black, too. A part of him had always wondered.

"What are you doing?" Rosa whispered.

"An experiment," he said, "in the gift of the tree." He slid the piece of bark onto a leather strip and tied it around her wrist. "I don't know if it will work, but promise you won't take it off."

She fondled the bracelet—strange, yet so familiar. "I promise."

The two of them sat side by side, legs dangling as when they were children.

Beneath the tree, their sheepdog Inés lapped up lake water, then curled up beneath the tree for a siesta while the sheep lazed about in the pasture.

But even in the village where years didn't matter, time drained away. Rosa needed the remaining daylight to ride the twenty miles north, to the next mission.

A stack of sheep wools was loaded behind her on the horse. Travelers had marveled for years at this wool—how thick, how soft it was. Wool that never wore out. Rosa had collected it for months, washed it herself, hung it to dry, and planned to sell it to pay to see the world. Her wedding gift from Sergio, finally coming to fruition.

"Stay with me," Sergio said.

"Come with me," Rosa countered, and for the thousandth time since she'd packed her bag, Sergio thought about it. About leaving his flock for the villagers to tend, about finding another horse, about leaving.

"No," he said. Rosa saw the same paleness in his cheeks as when he saw blood or bruises or scrapes.

She would leave. He would stay. But she would come back. Sergio was someone worth coming home to.

He hugged her, metering his breaths with hers, then kissed her. They climbed back down the tree together, and Rosa mounted the horse. She looked like a painting to him, her lips scarlet and full, her braid of black hair escaping her bonnet, her turquoise riding dress smartly buckled at her waist. More beautiful than the lake, more full of life than the tree.

She rode up and over the ridge, a few rogue bees following her, and was gone.

Sergio watched the ridge until the sun faded. He imagined eternity without Rosa and lost his heartbeat for a second. Then he laughed at his wife, her boldness, the way she rewrote the history of the village in one crazy move.

Once upon a time, someone left the lake.

Three months passed. Sergio helped the village bring the crops in, then spent the rest of his days doing manual labor: fixing roofs that had never leaked, straightening door frames that hung perfectly straight, tending to the sheep day and night like a butler. He did anything back-splitting, anything that wore him to the bone, so when night came, he was asleep before his head hit the pillow, lost in a black haze of dreamless slumber.

Three more months passed. Six months total without Rosa, far longer than he'd hoped she'd be gone. Sergio pictured her bouncing around the world like a tumbleweed, rolling in any direction the wind blew. He didn't let a certain phrase form in his mouth. He didn't want to taste the words, but they swirled in his mind: I miss her, I miss her, I miss her.

Inés shirked her sheepdog duties and lay by the door every night, sniffing the air and searching for her mistress.

Sergio climbed the tree one evening and touched the spot where he had peeled the bark away with the knife. The raw, unhealed bark made his throat bubble over with bile. What had he done, cutting into the branch? What had he done, thinking a bracelet of dead tree-skin would keep Rosa alive?

What had he done, letting her leave?

"Have you heard from Rosa?" the villagers asked. "Have you gotten letters?"

They could see it killed him to keep answering "No, not a letter, or a messenger, or a smoke signal, nothing." So they stopped asking. They stopped mentioning her name.

It had been three-quarters of a year since she rode away on that gold horse — a very quiet nine months, since the bees' incessant buzzing was no longer part of Sergio's days. The bees stayed near the tree, flying aimlessly among the blossoms, which seemed withered by the sand and heat and time.

Sergio, too, withered. His worry withered him into a skeleton.

When one year passed and faded into the next, he boarded up his shepherd shack from the inside. There he sat, surrounded by darkness, his hands whittling pieces of wood into unknown objects. Carolina, Rosa's sister, slipped food through the cracks, since he had no will to keep himself fed or even alive. She and the other villagers pleaded for him to come out, to let the village grieve together for the loss of one of their own. For the tragic example of what happens when the gift of the tree is rejected.

But he didn't move. For months. Years.

Until the day he heard her voice.

"Sergio!" A kick on the boarded-up door. "It's me, it's Rosa! Let me in!"

He couldn't yank the boards down fast enough. Sunlight streamed in first and pained him, since he'd spent so many days in the dark. When he finally got to her, and saw that she had all her limbs and wasn't bleeding or broken, he grabbed her. He stroked her face, tugged her hair, sobbed and sobbed as he planted kisses on her skin. Behind her, the bees were already buzzing.

"Are you okay? Are you hurt?" Sergio checked her neck, her fingernails, her ribs, searching for scars or burns.

"Sergio, it worked." She held up her wrist, the bracelet tied tight. "I should be dead, but the tree saved me."

She was down south in the Andes, walking with

the horse along the canyon. A rock slide crushed her flat, but she and the horse jumped up and carried on without a scratch.

"The gift lives on," she said.

Sergio touched the bracelet with trepidation. "How does it work, then? Does it radiate protection like sunshine?"

"I'm not sure," she said, "but it doesn't matter. It works. Sergio, we must have a village meeting tonight."

"But you just got home."

"Gather everyone at the lake." Her eyes glowed wild. "We must discuss what to do with the tree."

"What to do with the tree?" Sergio repeated. "What do you mean?" But Rosa walked past him to greet Inés.

Once upon a time, a village chopped down a tree.

11

One Saturday, as Mom's on her way home from a shift, Dad realizes he forgot to thaw one of the frozen meals she made for nights like this.

"Aw, shoot," he says when he pulls the casserole dish of enchiladas from the freezer and it's a solid brick of pulled pork, tortillas, and red sauce.

My mouth waters. "How long will it take to cook?"

He pokes it with a finger. Hard as a wall. "Hours," he says. His stomach gurgles. He's been doing ranch repairs all afternoon. He's as hungry as I am.

"Don't worry," he says. "I'll find us something else." He opens the cupboards and frowns. There's only

Serge's strange field-grown, dried-out, unrecognizable vegetables and Mom's ingredients for made-from-scratch dinners.

"Hmmm," Dad says, clearly flummoxed by the lack of ramen noodles.

"Sun cakes?" I suggest. Dad can really only cook this one thing. Luckily, they're delicious.

"Good thinking." Dad ties Mom's apron around his middle and turns a burner on the stove to medium.

Sun cakes are really just Mexican pancakes with cinnamon and brown butter, but when I was younger, to get me to eat, Dad told me these round things on my plate covered in syrup had a special ingredient in them: sunshine.

I fell for it every time. They were exactly how I imagined sunlight would taste: soft on my tongue, melting, with a hint of spice and a whole lot of sweet. Plus they were round and golden, like the sun.

It was easy to believe in impossible things as a little kid.

Within fifteen minutes, Dad's whipped up a stack of pancakes taller than the carton of orange juice and is already working on a second batch.

I serve Lu, cutting his pancakes into bits. I get a plate ready for Serge, cutting his pancakes into even smaller bits. I don't even bother asking Alta to help. She's sitting at the table, making a big show of enjoying Dad's sun cakes, probably laying the groundwork in case he finds out what she was up to all day: fiddling with her phone and avoiding chores.

"Sun cakes?" Serge says when he comes in from the porch. "I haven't had sun cakes since you were a boy, Raúl."

Dad shovels an entire pancake into his mouth, but he still purses his lips as he chews. Three weeks here, and Dad still can't stand it when Serge talks.

"You know about sun cakes?" I say.

Serge puffs his chest out. "Where do you think your dad learned how to make them?" I look at Dad, but he's pretending to read the back of the syrup bottle.

So Dad's most famous meal is actually a Serge recipe.

Mom comes through the door with a giant cardboard box in her arms and a stack of envelopes in her hand.

"Mama!" Lu cheers, tossing a confetti of sun-cake crumbs in celebration.

"Oh, man, what a long drive," she says. "I'm beat."

"Hungry?" Dad gestures to the tower of sun cakes.

"I had Chinese on the way. Here's the mail." Mom hands the bundle of envelopes to Dad, who flips through them, frowns once or twice, then tosses them on the table.

"Something for you, Carol." She gives me a letter, which I tear open. It's the registration for junior high. A whole mountain of paperwork, including a map of the school, instructions for accessing the website for checking grades and attendance, a how-to guide for opening my locker, and, most important, my schedule.

Wow, that's a lot of classes. Teachers. Homework. My future school year spreads across an entire grid. I scan it once, and a sentence jumps out at me.

Your locker partner is: SINGLE.

Single?

"What does this mean?" I show Alta.

"It means you don't have to share a locker with anyone," she says. "Cool."

"I don't get a locker partner?" I say.

Alta notices my face. "This means you get it all to yourself," she says. "You should feel lucky."

Mom nods. "No one else's stinky gym socks to deal with."

I try to feel lucky, but I mostly feel left out. I bet Sofie and Gabby both have locker partners. Now I can't even gossip with them about that.

"And look what came, girls." Mom points at the label on the cardboard box. *ForeverTeen.*

School clothes! I temporarily forget my locker-partner woes and tear into the box.

Mom has us buy our school clothes online at the beginning of summer, when stores have sales to make room for new stock. I chose my outfits with a critical eye this year, only picking items that I thought seventh-grade Carol would wear. Finally, I'll get a glimpse of her.

"Can I try them on?" I ask. "Can I? Can I? Can I?"

"If you're done with dinner," Mom says, and I clear my plate as a response.

"I want to see them on you before you take off any tags," Mom warns, and goes to get changed out of her dirty work scrubs.

Alta dumps the box on the bed and makes two piles: Alta clothes and Carol clothes. I pull out my phone and text my friends.

ME: *My school clothes came from ForeverTeen! You guys want to see?*

SOFIE: *Model them for us!*

GABBY: *Yessssss please! Send pictures!*

Hmm, what to try on first . . . There's a sleeveless white eyelet blouse, a lavender chiffon cap-sleeved top, a navy-blue matching skirt-and-shirt combo that screams first day of school . . .

Alta's already slipped into jeans and a black tee, and looks effortlessly, irrevocably chic.

"Put something on," she says, "and we'll walk the catwalk together."

Nice Alta is here.

"Which one?"

Alta selects the sleeveless white blouse and a pair of shorts, and turns her back while I change.

"Well?" I say, smoothing the new clothes with my open palms.

"Cute!" Alta nods her approval, which means it no longer matters what I look like. I'm sold.

"I want to send a picture to my friends," I say. "Will you take one?"

She takes my phone. "Strike a pose," she says.

When I get my phone back and flip through the photos, my breath is knocked out of me.

Who is this girl? There are plenty of mirrors at the ranch, but I must rush past them on my way to help with chores. They've never shown me this girl, staring at me in the photo.

My hair, notoriously frizzy but usually tamed by a straightening iron, is a ball of tangled black yarn.

My skin is leathery with tan, a buzzard's complexion, after only three weeks at the ranch—what will it look like by the end of summer? My eyes, sunken into my face with exhaustion, are dull and black. I have dirt smeared around my mouth, dirt from running after Lu in the pasture today. I'm feral, wild.

The clothes fit okay. But this is not what I pictured seventh-grade Carol looking like.

"Come on, let's show Mom," Alta says.

"No," I say. "You go ahead. I'm going to change."

"Mom wants to see everything, even the stuff you don't like." My sister inspects her rear end in a window's reflection.

"No," I say louder, and heat zooms up my neck and cheeks. "I don't like this shirt. Or these shorts."

"They look fine," Alta says, and I almost laugh. As if Alta would use "fine" as a standard for anything in her life.

"No they don't," I argue.

"Well, try on something else, then," Alta suggests, and so I do. I try on everything I picked out from the *ForeverTeen* website, six weeks ago, when I selected each piece like I was choosing my future.

I hate it all. Every shirt, every bottom, every photo Alta snaps of me.

ME: Nothing fits :(

SOFIE: What??? Oh no!

GABBY: Show us!

But I can't show them. It's not as simple as that— Alta was right, the clothes fit fine. I just don't fit the clothes. I delete the pictures from my phone.

ME: I'll show you when we exchange them for the right sizes.

ME: Hey, did you guys find out who your locker partners are?

SOFIE: *Gabby and I signed up together, remember?*
You were going to ask Bree Anderson, but then
she moved.

I vaguely remember a conversation of this nature happening in the last month of sixth grade, but there were lots of papers I had to fill out.

My own locker. It could be okay.

Mom, to her credit, is sympathetic when I come back in the kitchen in my pajamas. "Not a single thing?" She shakes her head as if *ForeverTeen* personally ruined her daughter's life with their ill-fitting clothes.

"We'll go on a special shopping trip, just you and I," she promises. *When?* I want to ask, but she retreats to her bedroom to recover from her shift, and I'm left alone.

Alta's taken over our bedroom, talking to Marco, so I head to the porch to find quiet.

Instead, I find Serge. He's in his chair, whittling. The porch light casts an overhead shadow, making a thick black line of his oxygen tube.

"Did you use to tell Dad that sun cakes were made of sun?"

"*Sí*," he says. "Sometimes little boys are too busy to eat. I'd tell him it was made of sun, and he'd finally stop running around long enough to sit down and eat five in a row."

I smile, but somewhere in me, there's a sadness. I wish Dad had told me sun cakes were from his childhood. I wish Dad had told me they were from Serge.

Twelve years old and only barely learning about my roots.

"Rosa left," I say. "In the story, she left. Does Sergio ever leave the lake? Or is he too afraid?"

Serge stares into me. "Would you be afraid to leave, Caro-leeen-a?"

I think. "I'd be scared of the newness of it, I guess. Change can be scary."

Serge nods. "Some people are afraid of the future. Your father is terrified of the past," he says, and I can't argue there. That pale fear that was on Dad's face when he wrangled the rattlesnake into the pillowcase . . . that's the same fear that I saw on his face when Serge talked about sun cakes.

Whenever Serge talks at all, actually.

"So does he ever leave the lake?" I ask again.

"I will tell you, *chiquita*. Once upon a time," Serge says, "there was a tree . . ."

O*nce upon a time, there was a tree. A village gath-ered in its shade, shade as big as the moon itself.*

At sunset, on a calm night that belonged to no sea-son in particular, a woman with rose-petal lips waited under the tree. She smelled of foreign wind, snow, and pines, of the sand of other deserts. She smoothed the front of her dress: an expensive-looking, exotic silk number, unlike any clothing ever seen in the village. Her hands trembled with excitement.

Sergio was next to his wife. "Don't do this," he said. "Don't tell them."

But she did tell them. She told the villagers about how she wore the tree's bark around her wrist during her many years of travel. She told them about the rock slide, how she lay crushed under two tons of crumbled canyon wall, breathing and waiting. When people uncovered her, they had planned to bury what was left of her corpse, but instead she picked herself up like a rag doll that had fallen off a girl's bed.

Sergio clenched his teeth as she spoke, whittling a stick to a dagger-sharp point.

"Do you understand what this means?" she cried. She held her bracelet up for them to see, to make it real for them. "We don't have to stay here at the lake. We can go anywhere!"

"Why would we want to leave?" Father Alejandro said. "We have everything we need here."

Sergio nodded. His thoughts exactly.

Rosa laughed, a swan's cluck. She reached into her luggage, still packed from her journey. "Because of this," she said, and held up a leering cougar totem carved into white wood. "From the ruins of Cuzco, in Peru. And this." She held up a hexagonal jewelry box embroidered with golden dragons. "From the Far East. And this, and this. And these." She tipped the trunk over, and the villagers' curiosity couldn't be contained. They lunged forward. They touched the clunking wooden shoes from the land of the windmills, touched the lump of gritty peat from a cranberry bog on the Emerald Isle, touched jars of seashells from three different oceans.

Carolina held a strand of raw, unpolished

freshwater pearls and sighed. Rosa came around behind her and fastened the pearls around her sister's neck.

"Keep them," Rosa said.

"Or I'll get my own," Carolina said, smiling up at her.

"Exactly!" Rosa cried. It was happening, really happening. She had worried about resistance, resistance to adventure, to change. Resistance to new.

But the more they touched the things, the more it seemed something had brushed onto their skin, something contagious, something foreign. Something other. Their desire to stay safely near the tree melted away, replaced by a new desire: to go. Their faces lit up, and they whispered monosyllabic explanations of joy: "Ahhh." "Ohhh." "Yes."

Only one face grew harder and darker. Sergio refused to look at a single souvenir; his eyes stayed on Rosa while she flitted among the crowd like a hummingbird, darting into every conversation. She's doing exactly what Rosa always does, riling everyone up, stoking their flames, he thought. He wished she would sit down and be silent.

"The tree is a gift!" Father Alejandro said. Everyone quieted, and Sergio prepared to call out his agreement. At last, a voice of reason among the madness.

"And Rosa has shown us that the gift has no limits," the Father continued. "Let us take the gift to the four corners of the earth and witness the many wonders of His creation."

"But . . ." Heads turned to Sergio, fumbling his whittling knife awkwardly in his hands. "Father, you always said there is nothing else in the world that compares with the tree."

Father Alejandro stroked his chin, his weathered face crinkling. "When we first came to the oasis, my men and I, after years of fruitless searches for gold, we knew it would be an insult to God to leave this tree, and so we stayed. This is what I have taught—that we must be grateful and always stay here to delight in God's gift. But the Lord has spoken." He pointed at Rosa. "He has spoken through this daughter of God! To have her leave and return in safety is God's way of telling us to go forth and see all of His creation!"

The villagers erupted in passionate, overlapping

conversations. The Father's eyes turned hazy and dreamy. "To sail again," he said softly. "To once again feel the cold sea breeze . . ."

Sergio's heart plummeted into his stomach. "It isn't right," he said. "To harm the tree. To strip its bark."

"But Sergio," Rosa said, "you're the one who cut the bracelet in the first place."

The villagers all looked at him, unable to believe it.

Sergio let out a long breath. Was I the one who started all this madness? *"You're right," he said, and the villagers twittered among themselves like hens. "But I never meant for all this to happen."*

"Our tree survived when you took the bark for me," Rosa said. "Why shouldn't every villager partake of the gift?"

"We could take turns," Sergio said. "One bracelet is enough, isn't it?"

"But we have this whole tree," Rosa countered. "There's more than enough for everyone to have their own."

"God wants us to leave the lake," Father Alejandro said. "We must carry this gift across the whole of

earth's paradise, for to know God's creation is to know God."

Rosa grinned. The approval of the Father meant the approval of the village.

"Let's take a vote," Sergio said, desperate. "Each of us must decide. Do we stay and bask in the full protection of the tree? Never bleed? Never choke, never hurt, never die?"

"Or do we leave, and live?" Rosa said. "See new things, breathe new air?" Bees flew around her head, gleaming in the last gasps of sunset light.

The people cheered. Sergio threw a stone in the lake.

Every villager, the old and the older, cast their votes.

It was almost unanimous. Nearly everyone voted to cut into the tree, take slivers of its wood, and see the world.

Only one person voted to leave the tree alone.

There were odd dreams that night. Dreams of cold square houses with black windows. Giants in multicolored clothing with blank faces. Animals that could only exist in the mind: fishes with coyote heads, *rabbits with eagle wings. The strangest dreams that night were the ones full of nothing—blank spaces that would be filled in with all the things they would see when they left the lake.*

Once upon a time, there was a tree, living on the shores of a green-glass lake, breathing in hot desert air. Its black branches grew green leaves and snowy flowers, and bees lived in the blossoms. The tree was a gift, protecting the people in the village from injury, aging, disease. Death.

Once upon a time, there was a tree, and they were only supposed to use its bark. But they cut it down.

12

It's a Friday morning, more than halfway through my summer-vacation-turned-desert-hostage situation, and I'm alone in the kitchen. Mom and Dad have already stumbled outside to work. I search the cupboards for cold cereal, but all I find is bread and some lumpy gray hash.

Toast it is.

A month and a half has blurred past. Six weeks of packing boxes, detail-cleaning floorboards and heating vents, scrubbing walls.

Six weeks of keeping an eye on Serge and chasing after Lu. Mom and Dad don't even ask me to babysit anymore. They toss my brother into my arms, the two of them already arguing about who forgot to get what at the hardware store or some other silly thing.

I don't know if it's the heat, the exhaustion from a month and a half of physical labor (for a house that isn't even staying in our family), the constant threats of a Moody Alta storm or a Crazy Serge storm looming, or all of these things—but bickering seems to be my parents' only form of communication lately. Not full-on fighting. It's more like they're buzzards pecking at each other in a squabble for some dead thing. And the dead thing is the ranch.

I guess it's better that Lu is safely with me, out of their crossfire.

Two weeks left at the ranch.

We wake, we work, then we collapse one by one, like dominoes. Some nights the TV cooperates and we catch a movie that was actually made in this decade. Those nights almost feel like vacation.

Serge has Good Days, when he only forgets little things, like whether he already watered the sheep or not. He doesn't yell. When he turns on the TV, he remembers which channels are his favorites. He eats Mom's cooking without spilling a drop and says "thank you" in English. He tells us outlandish stories, like the time Inés swallowed Dad's goldfish. On the Good Days, even Dad laughs at my grandpa's stories.

On Good Days, Alta wears a smile to the dinner table, and she stays up late talking with me, like it's a slumber party. Lu is a chubby little angel, going right to sleep without a fuss. Mom and Dad steal kisses when they pass, when they think no one's watching. My friends text me the latest rumors about Manny Rodriguez, about seeing the new boy at the swimming pool, about how much fun it's going to be in homeroom (we all have English together).

We have Bad Days, too.

On the Bad Days, Lu throws tantrums for dumb things, like if we're out of orange juice. Dad sleeps on the futon in the living room, instead of in the bedroom with Mom. Alta slams doors, making the whole house shake. Serge gets so lost in his mind, I worry that he won't make it out.

Luckily, he always reemerges. So far.

Even on Bad Days, I wonder what Dad sees about Serge that's so awful. I do my own detective work, studying their threadbare conversations for a hint. But I'm missing something. I asked Alta; she didn't know and didn't care. I asked Mom again, and she told me to mind my own business. What happened to make Dad, Serge's only child, refuse to speak to Serge for twelve years?

Bees follow me on all days, good and bad. They're as reliable as the sunrise; if it's been twenty-four hours since I've seen one, I know I'm due. But they only find me when I'm alone, which has made it impossible to convince anyone else that they're real.

Dad: "You must be seeing some kind of striped fly; there are definitely no bees around here."

Mom: "I don't know what to say, honey—I don't think Serge has any bug spray. Here, hold Lu while I get dressed, please?"

Alta: "Buzz off, Carol!"

The one person who might actually believe me is the one person I can't tell. Rule number one this summer: don't upset Serge. He made such a ruckus over bees that first day we were here, I don't even dare mention the letter *B* to him.

I shoo a bee away from my toast and see Mom out the window, rebuilding a section of the fence. She smashes her thumb with the hammer, but just sucks on it and keeps working. In no time at all, she's nailed half the fence together. I marvel at her power. Mom's stronger than I ever knew. She's a dragon in disguise.

I wonder if the ranch will bring out the dragon in me. Only two weeks left to find out.

I wash down my toast with milk and head to the porch. The temperature is ninety-seven degrees, according to the thermometer, and it's still morning. We'll be in triple digits by lunchtime. My tank top's already plastered to my back with sweat.

I close my eyes, thinking of that cool green lake from Serge's story. How delicious it would be to jump headfirst into chilly water and wash the sticky sweat away . . .

"Morning, sleepyhead." Mom strolls to the sink and refills her water bottle.

"Want me to hold your nails for you?" I say.

"Actually, I've got something else I need you to do." Mom sets the hammer down and calls down the hallway for Alta.

"Tell me if Grandpa starts walking in," she says. "I don't want him to hear."

Outside, Dad and Serge are fifty feet apart, the pasture between them, but their silhouettes are similar—they both lean to their left sides, using their right wrists to wipe their foreheads. Serge's back hunches over at a sharper angle than Dad's and he's thicker around the middle, but it's like gazing into a crystal ball at Dad's future old-man self.

Serge is cleaning sheep hooves, one leg at a time. Dad's pulling dead, dry plants from the dirt. It's obvious who's working on projects for staying at the ranch and who is working to leave.

"Alta! Shake a leg, we're waiting!" Mom rolls her eyes.

My sister finally comes into the kitchen, sparkling with baby oil, in her pink bikini.

Mom snorts. "Now that's the perfect outfit for a sheep ranch."

Alta shoots laser beams from her eyes. "I just need to lay out for ten minutes, before the rays get too hot."

"Finish your chores first. And the laundry you were supposed to do yesterday," Mom says, "then you can work on your tan. Come on, girls, I'll show you what I need you to do today." She waves for us to follow her down the hallway and barges into Serge's room.

"Um, Dad said I'm not supposed to go in there," I say from the hall. That room is haunted by Serge's memories of Grandma Rosa. Maybe by Grandma Rosa herself. Alta rolls her eyes at my obnoxious display of respect and walks right in.

Mom sighs. "I hereby grant you permission to intrude. Now listen. I'm driving Serge to his doctor's appointment. While we're gone, I want both of you to pack up the closet." She doesn't waste any time with darkness; she rips the cardboard sheets from the windows. Bright white New Mexican sun fills the room, the first time it's seen light in twelve years.

Alta sneers at the grimy room around her. "Ew."

Mom ignores her and opens the dirty windows, and it's like the room lets out a breath it's been holding for more than a decade.

"Dad thinks it'll upset your grandpa to see Grandma Rosa's things," she says. "So I'm going to take these things to the storage unit tomorrow before my shift. Get as much packed as you can while Serge is gone. Boxes are in the living room." She wiggles the closet doors. "Open up," she grunts, and tightens her grip.

A bee—of course a bee—finds me, buzzing in a halo around my head. *Bzzz* . . . I listen—that same collective droning, buzzing, humming I heard coming from the closet on my first night here . . . It's muted, but impossible to miss.

Impossible.

Mom cocks her head. "Do you hear that?"

I freeze. The buzzing gets louder.

"Shoot," she says. "Lu's up early." She bounds into the guest bedroom, and Alta seizes the chance to escape.

I grasp the closet doorknobs and pull, but they won't open, as if a ghost is pulling from the other side.

Ghost bees.

The noise behind the door grows louder, and I have a sudden, irrational fear that maybe it isn't an air force–worthy fleet of bees; maybe it's just one giant bee with a stinger the size of a samurai sword. I blink the ridiculous image away.

I use all my weight to yank on the doors, and when they finally give, I stumble, nearly landing on my back with the force.

The great buzzing is now above me, and louder— much louder. It's a swarm of bees, released from the closet into the bedroom, a gritty gold-and-black-striped cloud. I try to scream, but no sound comes out. Hundreds of them, maybe thousands—they bunch and spread out, bunch and spread out, swimming through the air like a school of fish.

And then they're gone, out the open window and buzzing to freedom. I pant, steadying myself against the bedpost. I wait here, finding my breath, with no way to measure time. Has it been two minutes? Ten minutes? An hour?

Bees, trapped in Serge's closet, after a century of drought . . . It's weird enough to be one of Serge's stories.

"Okay, okay!" comes my sister's exasperated voice from the hallway. "I'm doing it now!"

Mom's carping at her to get to work. Alta reenters the room, robe over her bikini, smelling like success-fully burnt skin. Lu's on her hip, munching a soggy waffle.

"Did you get boxes yet?" she asks, already bored.

"No," I manage to get out, my heartbeat finally under control.

She huffs and trudges back down the hall, reappearing a minute later with some boxes. "Let's get this over with," she says.

I step hesitantly into the closet. There's a strange scent: layers of wet earth and wood, clay baking in sunshine, new rain on green grass. Alta switches on a light, and even she can't hide her amazement.

"Whoa," we both whisper. Lu claps in approval.

The closet is a museum of color, a rainbow in the otherwise drab ranch house. Not only every color imaginable, but different fabrics, textures, feathers, jewels. Shelves and drawers, hangers and coat racks, all filled with clothing, hats, scarves, bags . . .

"What is Serge doing with all this stuff?" Alta says. She sets Lu on the carpet, and he finds an old pair of castanets to clatter together.

"It's not his," I realize. "These are—were—Rosa's things."

I shiver. Like the Rosa in Grandpa Serge's story, Grandma Rosa must have traveled, too.

Alta nearly trips on a pair of red wooden Japanese sandals. "There's something from everywhere in here." She runs her fingers along a peacock-blue silk sari.

"Did she travel a lot? Do you remember?" I ask. Alta was four when Mom and Dad got married.

"I only met Grandma Rosa a few times, and she was sick. Always in bed." My sister's eyes stare far away. "Then . . . she died. I said good-bye before I ever really said hello." I stay quiet. She never talks about this time of her life, when Mom married Dad and the families had to blend. But my sister shrugs back to normal and slips a flamenco dress over her head. The dress jingles; little bells are sewn into its layers of sherbet-colored ruffles.

"What do you think?" she says. "Prom worthy?"

I grin.

"Go on," she says. "Try something on."

For now, Alta isn't a too-cool seventeen-year-old, and I'm not twelve. We're both five, playing dress-up. I drape a shiny crimson matador cape around my shoulders.

Alta shrieks.

"What? What is it?" *More bees?*

I track where she's looking, my heart thumping at double time. An ostrich head peeks at us, stuffed and mounted on the closet wall, tangles of necklaces hanging from its skinny dead neck.

"Creepy!" Alta says.

"So, Grandma Rosa was a bird poacher?" I say.

Alta, miracle of miracles, is about to laugh at my joke, but her mouth opens into a glossy pink triangle. "Oh. Hi," she says, looking over my shoulder.

Someone's behind me. Serge?

It's only Dad.

"What are you girls doing?" His eyes fly over Rosa's things like he's seeing fairies.

I pull off the matador cape and lift up Lu, using him as a shield for my guilt. "Mom told us to pack up the closet while Serge is gone."

Dad gawps. "I haven't seen this stuff in years." He points at the bird's head. "That's an emu," he says. "She got it in Australia. It used to scare me as a kid."

"Australia?" Alta says. "I've always wanted to go there."

"She and Serge sure got around," I say.

Dad raises his eyebrows. "Not *Papá*. He always stayed here. His idea of traveling is walking to the ridge and back."

The four of us stay in the closet for another hour, packing one item at a time. Well, we pack. Lu plays. Dad plays, too—he recounts where everything came from as simply as the alphabet. That mask is from South Africa. Those hats are from Morocco. This painting is from Colorado, when *Mamá* first saw snow. This seashell is from the Pacific Ocean—*Mamá* just loved the ocean.

Dad's face is soft as he speaks, and Alta and I cling

to every word. We set the things in the boxes as if we're packing away vintage china: gingerly, carefully. These are as much Dad's treasures as they were Rosa's.

"You girls should pick something," he says. "This is going into storage until—well, until further notice. So if something calls to you, take it." He leaves the room, carrying boxes.

We glance back at the remaining clothes with new eyes. Permission to bring one of these exotic, exciting treasures home! What should I pick? A creamy robe from Korea with hand-stitched cherry blossoms on the sleeves? A ruby-encrusted lizard brooch? Red patent-leather dancing shoes from Madrid?

Alta's stopped packing and instead has her arms full of things that have called to her: everything, apparently.

Then I find something.

A bracelet. Black bark strung onto a leather strip. It jumps out from all the sparkly, bedazzled jewelry because it's so simple. Like the ranch. I pick it up.

It's like the bracelet from the story.

Alta sets her things down and looks at the bracelet in my open palm. She uses her coral fingernail to prod the bracelet's bark. "Pretty," she coos.

"I know," I say. The bark swirls, grains trickling into formation, a cellular wooden waterfall frozen in time. It feels like staring at eternity, looking at this bracelet.

It calls to me.

"It's really pretty," Alta says again. A flame flickers in my chest. I know what she's doing. She's going to try to con me into giving it to her.

She'll wear it for a month, then toss it out instead of passing it down to me. She hates giving me her old things—she wants to be the only owner of things forever.

"This would go perfectly with a dress I saw at the mall," Alta says.

I'm not backing down. "Dad said I could pick something," I say, "and I'm picking this."

Alta glares. "It doesn't match anything you have."

Exactly, I think. This bracelet matches nothing in my wardrobe, matches nothing in Albuquerque. Nothing in my life. The bracelet isn't anything like who I am; it's a bracelet for who I want to be.

"I saw it first," I say, hating how like a little kid I sound.

"Hey, what'd you find?" Dad comes back from stacking boxes in the minivan. I hold out the bracelet, and he takes in a sharp breath.

"*Mamá's* bracelet. She wore it everywhere." Dad ties it around my wrist. I try hard not to smirk at Alta. "It's kind of perfect that you found it," he says, "since you look so much like her these days."

"I do?" I ask, and I realize that I don't actually know what Grandma Rosa looked like.

"See for yourself." He pulls a sepia-toned photo down from a shelf.

Rosa looks like an old-fashioned movie star. She's tall and curvy as a cello, with pouty lips and black wavy hair hanging past her hips.

At first, nothing in her face is familiar. She's beautiful and glamorous, and I'm, well, I'm like my dad. But then I realize her eyes are just like our eyes, too—squinty, with stubby eyelashes and no color in the irises, just dull black. Looking at Rosa, I see how I can tilt my chin up, glance at the world from beneath my eyelids like they're heavy drapes, and add sparkle to my dark eyes by thinking mischievous thoughts. I practice it while Alta and Dad pack another box. It feels like a grown-up way to see the world.

"Here's *Mamá* in Chile." Dad puts another photo in my hands, patting Lu on the head as he walks by him.

"That's one of her scarves, see?" My grandmother's neck is draped in a knitted scarf that looks softer than clouds. "And here she is at the Olympics." Rosa aims an arrow at the camera, tongue sticking out the side of her mouth in concentration.

"Grandma was in the Olympics?" I say, surprised — no one in our family is athletic.

"No, no," Dad says. "She was at the Olympics selling her scarves and made friends with the Spanish archery team. Everyone loved those scarves. People paid a lot of money for them."

"Was there anything Grandma couldn't do?" I say, entranced by the photos. "She was so . . ."

I pause, overwhelmed by the words that could end this sentence. So adventurous? So talented? So wild and free?

So unlike Serge?

Dad has to clear his throat a few times before he can speak. "She was something, all right." He gives us instructions to finish packing. "I'll haul it out to the minivan later, when the old man isn't looking." Then he leaves, taking Lu with him, and Alta and I are alone.

I flex my wrist, examining the bracelet. Old wood,

young skin. This is how I hoped to feel in my school clothes from ForeverTeen: ready to mount a horse and ride to the other side of the world. Like in Serge's story.

So much of his story is stolen from real life. There's a girl named Rosa who travels the world. There's a sheep ranch in the desert. The world's most persistent bees. A bundle of souvenirs from every country that's ever existed. And now this black-bark bracelet . . . There's even a scabby tree stump beyond the pasture, I realize, that kind of matches up. I wonder if Serge was always such a clever storyteller, weaving reality with fiction as masterfully as Grandma Rosa knit her famous scarves. Or is this another side effect of dementia? Does Grandpa Serge actually believe the stories he's telling me?

Bzzz, bzzz . . . Alta's phone rings in her robe pocket and brings me back to the here and now. "You can just pack all this up." She gestures to the pile of Rosa treasures she plucked up so greedily moments ago.

"You don't want any of it?" I hold up the brocade bag from New Orleans that Alta gushed over. "Not even this?"

Her eyes shift cold: Moody Alta. "It's all just a bunch of junk. She wasn't even my real grandma, anyway."

My chest deflates. Didn't we just talk about Grandma Rosa, how amazing she was, and now Alta won't even claim her? "But you're my sister," I say, "and she was my grandma. So that's basically like saying she was your grandma, too."

"Well, if you want to be technical, you're really only my *half* sister . . ." she says, and I swear, something burns the outside of my wrist. The bracelet presses against my skin, its heat radiating up my body, exploding out of my mouth like I'm breathing fire:

"You're just mad about the bracelet. Well, it's mine. For once, something is mine. Your daddy can't buy it for you, and you can't bat your eyelashes and make me hand it over. It's mine." I love the way that word tastes, so I say it again. "Mine."

Her glare penetrates me—there might be scorch marks on the wall behind me. "You're right," she says. "Your bracelet. Your grandma Rosa, your grandpa Serge, so it's *your* closet to finish packing."

She glides out of the room, a rattlesnake retreating, and my face glows red, like I've just been slapped.

I don't know how long I stand there, waiting to cool down, but when I venture into the back of the closet to finish the packing by myself, it doesn't surprise me to hear a faint buzz. Whenever I'm by myself at the ranch, the bees turn up their volume. This time I'm glad for their company. They make me feel less alone.

I snap my fingers, just to see how fast a second is. Things change that quickly.

Just minutes ago Alta and I were equals, playing dress-up in the closet. If only I could have bottled that moment up and saved it for when I needed it—but moments can't be stored or repeated. They are lived once, then gone.

I measure time with changes.

The bracelet is heavy now, scratching my wrist. It's the prize for winning against Alta, a bittersweet victory. *Not my real grandma*, she had said. *Not real sisters.*

I finish the closet joylessly, folding, draping, and packing in robotic movements. When the closet is empty, I shoo a few rogue bees out the bedroom window, and that's when I spot something on the floor, back in the dark corner. . . . Something small and round. . . .

A seed.

13

A seed, black as a scorpion, the size of a penny. I examine it in my palm. A seed, in Grandma Rosa's closet. A seed that grows into what? I guess we'll never know; it would probably just fizzle and die if buried in the ranch's gritty, sandy dirt.

While I'm puzzling over this, a bee lands on the seed and scurries along its surface. It inspects it, almost sniffing (do bees have noses?), then flies away.

The front door opens and shuts. "Carol?" Mom calls from the kitchen.

"Coming," I say, and gently pocket the seed. The bee disappears out the window.

Mom kisses my cheek when I come into the kitchen. "Thank you," she says. "Did Alta help?" She inspects my face as she asks this.

"Yeah, big help," I say. Mom raises her eyebrows, but I don't feel like going into it, so I change the subject. "What happened at the doctor's?"

She swallows, then swallows again—Mom's procrastinating saying the truth out loud, which is how I know it's not good news. "He's getting worse. His brain is deteriorating faster than they can track it."

My heart lurches. "They don't have a pill that can stop it?" I say. "There's no cure? No machine that can slow it down, or a surgery . . ."

Mom's eyes flood. "Brain deterioration is irreversible. Once the Christmas lights are off, they're off."

I guess I had hoped Serge would stay only comically forgetful, in the shallows of dementia—misplacing his boots, barking at the people on TV like they can hear him, asking if Inés has been fed, over and over. I can live with a Serge like that. But instead Serge is going to drift further out to open sea, lost inside his own broken brain. Mom spots my bottom lip quivering and hugs me.

"Oh, hon," she whispers.

The dam of tears threatens to break, but I hold it in, hold it in, hold it in . . .

"Where is he now?" I ask.

"Where else?" Mom says. "On the porch." I take a deep breath and head out there.

Serge is in his chair, whittling. He doesn't look different than he did this morning, doesn't seem any deeper down the dark, drippy well of dementia.

"Caro-leeen-a," he says, "what is that around your wrist?"

My entire body freezes solid. "A bracelet," I answer truthfully. "A very old bracelet."

"It suits you," he says. "You look so much like her." He breathes in deeply, his oxygen tube sighing. "*Chiquita*, does Inés have food?"

"Yes."

"And water?"

Sigh. "Yes."

He nods. "She's a good dog."

I sit on the top step. "Can you tell me the rest of the story? Do they really chop down the tree?"

He stares at the ridge, eyes in story-land already.

"Yes, they chopped down the tree. Left a scab on

197

the land." Serge's knife moves like a blur. "Once upon a time . . ."

I mouth along with him, blinking back tears, *there was a tree.*

O*nce upon a time, there was a tree.*
And they cut it down.

Not at first.

First, Rosa took Sergio's whittling knife, crawled up to their favorite branch, and removed small pieces of the coal-black bark, the size of ribbons. One for everyone.

The villagers stood around the trunk, whispering prayers of hope. Rosa would free a strip of bark, then toss it below to a giddy soul, who would press it to his heart: his token of freedom. Bees darted around the villagers' heads, annoyed by these confounded humans who blocked the blossoms and skinned the tree alive.

When every villager but one had a piece of the tree, they celebrated with a feast of mutton and grilled cactus flowers. Sergio paced the lake's shore, nibbling his meat. His eyes stayed on the starry sky to avoid watching Rosa, who was the fiesta's lifeblood. Every time she danced, his gut lurched.

The people asked Sergio to use his whittling skills on their bark strips, and at first he resisted. Why should he help them, when they voted to leave the village? To leave him?

But he relented, carving a talisman for every man, woman, and child. He skipped sheep chores to work on them, compelled to touch each piece of bark himself. He carved the wood as penance. Since he couldn't stop the villagers from cutting up the tree, he wanted to make the butchered wood into something beautiful, something to remind them of home while they traveled. He shaped the bark into many things: pendants laced onto string; wooden brooches; barrettes for a girl with wild dark hair; charms shaped like the tree itself.

Carolina asked for such a charm and attached it to her collar as a brooch.

Rosa was the only one who preferred her bark plain—just the raw, untouched bark on the leather strip.

Then it happened. People started leaving. One

family at a time, they tiptoed away from the lake and danced over the ridge. They camped under different stars, then returned.

They trekked into open desert and met up with coyotes. Snakes. Spiders. Cliffs. Rushing rivers with shifting, tricky currents. Purple lightning strikes. But they always returned.

Such a cautious dance for a people who had never needed caution before.

Once upon a time, there was a tree. And they cut it down.

Not yet.

But they did wish to go farther.

They sought reassurance from Rosa. "Will the bark really be enough? Such a tiny piece of the tree will really protect us from death?"

Rosa reassured, but still they fretted. "Take more, if you're worried," she said.

So they sawed off branches—just a few at first—and Sergio whittled fishing poles for the fathers to fish with, toy swords for the boys to fight with, baby dolls for the girls to swaddle. He even made carts for the horses to pull. There seemed no end to the amount of lumber provided by the tree. Gradually the tree was stripped of bark and limbs, a naked black beam pointing to heaven.

Sergio never saw what happened to the tree's white blossoms. Neither did the bees, whose collective angry buzz rang through the village long after sundown every night.

Whole families left. The mission grew emptier night after night, and Sergio walked the halls counting who remained. Once, no one had ever left. Now they were gone, all gone.

This time, when the villagers came home, they fell to their knees at the shores of the green-glass lake and kissed the water. Months away from home made them sentimental. They brought back their own souvenirs this time, evidence of their own bold travels: their own totems, their own treasure boxes from the East, their own seashells.

They returned greedy. Hungry for more of the world—for more of the tree.

They hacked wood from the bald tree, clawed it from the trunk, tore it, ripped it away at odd angles, splintered and raw. Instead of prayers under their breaths, they spoke loudly and grandly of their travels, sharing stories around the bonfire at their annual summer festival. Sergio tended to his sheep and watched his people take, take, take, like buzzards plucking flesh from a man still pumping blood.

"She's gone too far," he murmured to Carolina, while Rosa exchanged upcoming travel plans with neighbors.

Carolina widened her eyes at Sergio. "She's only just started," she said, and walked to her sister.

The white blossoms never grew back. That sweet honey-vanilla scent faded from the village, replaced with the smell of sweat. Bee clouds swirled above the remnants of the tree, their buzzing louder than the new harsh wind that howled across the lake. The bees were desperate for pollen. But the blossoms were now a thing of the past.

The past. The village was supposed to be a place immune to pasts, presents, and futures, but now there would forever be a division—a before and after. Before, when the tree was living. After, when the villagers were living and the tree was not.

A new way of measuring time.

Father Alejandro asked Sergio to carve him a canoe, so Sergio, his heart heavy, shaped a chunk of tree into a sleek one-man boat, which the Father took on his trip to a northern sea. A deadly hurricane struck, but the Father survived and brought the boat back. "The gift lives on," he said, and smiled in a wild way that reminded Sergio of Rosa.

A village family with three daughters had Sergio make a frame for a portable longhouse. The girls painted symbols and pictures on the wood, then they carted it up a treacherous mountain range in the West. When an avalanche of snow buried them alive, they climbed out and walked away, unharmed. "The gift lives on," they said.

"The gift lives on," Rosa repeated to her husband, the rare times she was home.

"So it seems." Sergio scanned the once-bustling village in the oasis, now a row of dusty abandoned shacks.

On a morning Sergio had planned to spend caring for his pregnant ewes, Rosa rode into the pasture. Inés abandoned the sheep to greet her, and Sergio helped her off her horse.

"Welcome home, mi cielo," he said. "Back so soon? You only left three weeks ago."

"I wanted to be home."

Sergio raised his eyebrows—all the glorious world to travel to, and Rosa chose the village? "How long will you be staying this time?"

"Until the spring," she said.

Sergio stared. "You're staying for eight months?" Could it be she was finally cured of her wanderlust?

Rosa smiled, her eyes soft. "I'm staying until our baby comes."

Sergio's legs shook. He felt a thousand things at once: fear and nerves and complete, childlike elation. "A baby," he whispered, and his heart nearly burst.

Once upon a time, there was a tree, and Rosa sat on the grass, leaning into the trunk, her husband at her side with his hand on her swollen belly.

"What shall we carve for the little one?" she asked.

"Carve?" Sergio repeated.

"For when the baby travels," Rosa said. "A carriage, of course, and a crib made of the wood. But you *could carve the baby some toys—a rattle, a doll, a set of blocks . . ."*

With a pang, Sergio realized his child would only ever know the tree as lumber.

Once upon a time, there was a tree. And they cut it down.

14

It's always hot at the ranch, but tonight, our last night, the heat's suffocating.

Lu's been fussing for twenty minutes straight. I've tried everything: peekaboo, a puppet show, tossing "dog treats" (Cheerios) into his mouth like he's a puppy. But Lu fusses in a steady stream until it's background noise. I check one of the ancient fans we have propped in the windows around the ranch house. Yes, it's cranked up to full blast, but the fans don't cool anything off. They just push this hot air around in circles.

It's driving me crazy.

"Mom." I fuss a little myself. "Make him stop."

"He's got the big three going on," Mom says. "Hot, hungry, and tired."

"Aren't we all," I mutter, and drag him to Mom. She's zombie-tired, too, her hair a black nest at her collarbone, but she cuddles Lu to her shoulder while hunting through the pantry for dinner inspiration. Most of the kitchen is packed at this point, which makes our meal options slight.

"Shh," she tells Lu. "I know, I know, it's the witching hour."

That's what Mom calls this time of day, right before dinner: the witching hour. It's the perfect description. The border between real life and the impossible feels thin, hazy.

Also, we all turn into grouchy, pouting witches. If I knew a spell that could snap dinner onto the table and smiles on our faces, I'd do it.

Alta's at the kitchen table, her huge fuchsia headphones covering half her head (sister code for "do not disturb under pain of death").

Mom's now opened the fridge for the third time, groaning when no new food magically appears. She forgot to hit the grocery store on her last drive back from Albuquerque.

"Can't we just call in a pizza?" I say.

Mom shakes her head. "It's too far to deliver."

"It's too hot!" I moan, and lie flat on the kitchen linoleum.

Mom steps over me to get to the sink. "Move, please? You're in the road."

I roll until I'm barely out of the way. "I can't breathe," I say.

"Carol," Mom says, and I stop the whining. I hate when my own name is used as a weapon.

I roll one more time and reach in my pocket to rub the seed. I've carried it with me since that day I found it in the closet. In a house where death hides around every corner, it's reassuring to touch something so alive. At least, I hope it's alive.

The witching hour . . .

Even the sky is witchy tonight, halfway between light and dark, sun and sunless, blue and amber, starry and blank. My own fuse feels shorter than usual. I want Lu to be quiet, Mom to cook dinner, and me to be zoning out, watching the Disney Channel until bed.

Impossible. The TV is packed, anyway.

Tomorrow we'll put the big-ticket items into the moving van Mom brought down instead of the mini-van: tables, couches, beds. We'll fit the rest of the boxes in, too, filling the gaps and holes in a 3-D version of Tetris. We'll sweep the floors, turn out the lights, and head back to Albuquerque on that long, lonely highway.

I've been counting down the days all summer. I thought I'd be more excited to go home.

There's a crash outside. The whole house rattles.

Alta rips off her headphones and points out the window. "Fire!"

"What?" Mom nearly drops Lu in her rush to the window.

I smudge my face against the glass. The evening has an orange glow. Yes, a fire—but where?

There's yelling, too. One of the voices is definitely Serge, hollering from the porch in curse-laced Spanish. Dad responds with a few choice phrases of his own. He sounds underwater.

Serge practically bounces out of his chair with fury, sucking oxygen in gulps. "Put it out, put it out!" he cries.

Mom, Alta, and I beeline it to the porch. Across the

pasture, the barn is ablaze, burping balls of fire into the evening air. Wooden beams snap, walls crumble. The whole thing will be gone in minutes.

"Should I call the fire department?" Alta holds up her phone.

"What fire department?" Mom says, bouncing Lu on her hip. "The closest one is fifty miles away." I guess in the desert, when something's on fire, you just let it burn.

"Barn's on fire!" Serge yelps. Mom touches his shoulder, and he jerks away, looking pained. "Make it stop, make Raúl stop!"

"Raúl!" Mom grips the porch rail with white knuckles.

I'm paralyzed, staring at the fire. Flames look so different on TV, almost cartoonish; in real life, the fire's as big as the sun.

"Burning, burning, too hot!" Serge cries.

"Alta, go get Serge some water," Mom says. Alta, to her credit, doesn't put up a fight—she rushes right away.

"Is dinner ready?" Dad calls from the pasture.

"The barn, Raúl!" Mom shrieks.

"I know. So do we have dinner ready or what?" Dad

says. "I'm starving." He's burning the barn on purpose; why else would he so casually stroll into the front yard while the rest of us gawk at the fireball shining behind him like the world is ending? Even with the flames amplifying the desert heat to core-of-the-earth temperatures, I shiver; the image of my dad silhouetted against a fire is eerie.

"You started a fire in a drought? Are you nuts?" Mom shoves Lu into my arms, heavy as a sack of flour, and charges down the steps.

"It's fine," Dad snaps. "It's contained." He finds his beer on the porch railing and swigs it.

I gasp when the firelight illuminates his face—Dad's eyes are bloodshot and watery, swollen from a summer's worth of work on just slivers of sleep. Sweat glistens on his forehead and neck. He doesn't look like he'll even last until tomorrow.

Serge is mad enough to melt into a puddle of flabby skin. His sentences start in English, then run off a cliff and fall into angry, broken Spanish. "You burned my barn. You're coming for me next. You'll roast me alive with the sheep!"

"Calm down, *Papá*," Dad says. "The barn had termites. Wood with termites has to be burned, you know that. No one's coming for you."

"You are." Tears leak down Serge's cheeks, bending like rivers around the bumps. "You put my things in boxes. You're going to put me in a box. Then you'll burn it all down."

"*Papá*, none of that is happening."

"Uh, Mom?" Alta comes outside with Serge's water, forehead wrinkled in what appears to be genuine concern—a rare sight. She angles her whisper out of Serge's earshot: "Something's wrong with the dog."

My throat tightens. Not Inés.

Mom passes Serge his water. "Raúl!" she calls. "Come quick!"

When Dad walks past his father's chair, Serge cries once more, "You're going to burn everything down!"

I don't want to leave Serge alone, babbling and blubbering in his wicker chair, but Mom calls for me to join the family in the kitchen.

We gather near the counter, and my heart is shipwrecked at the sight: sweet, strong Inés lies cold on the linoleum, legs stiff.

"Is she breathing?" Mom asks.

Dad kneels beside the old dog, stroking her head, her neck, her face. "Barely," he says, a tremor in his voice. Yes, if I watch around her collar, Inés's neck rises and falls, but slowly, like each exhale hurts.

"Oh, Inés," Dad says, and I can't tell if he believes this is really Inés, pet of his childhood, or if he's still just playing along. Maybe it doesn't matter anymore.

"How old would she be, again?" I ask.

Dad looks at us, his exhausted eyes brimming with a lifetime of memories. "Old Inés has always been around." He rubs her floppy ears.

Lu fusses, then turns to Jell-O and slides out of Mom's arms. He coos, patting Inés on the head, then looks mystified when she doesn't respond.

"Say bye to the dog, Lu." Dad can barely choke this out.

Then it happens. Inés takes her last breath, and when her chest falls, it doesn't rise again. She's gone.

No more early morning scratches at the front door. No more tail whacking against my knee at the dinner table. No more dog sighs punctuating the sweltering afternoons. I could have measured my summer with that dog.

How will Serge take this? He asks if Inés has been fed as often as I hear bees buzzing. My heart hurts so much, I ache down to my toes. I've never seen anything die. I put my hand in my pocket and hold on to the seed.

We wait, silent, until Dad dries his eyes and lifts Inés's body, cradling her like a newborn.

"She lived a long, happy life," Mom says.

"What does that matter now?" Alta says. "She's dead."

"It matters," I say. "It's all that matters in the end." My sister puts her headphones back on and wanders off, but I stay.

"Don't tell Serge," Mom says to Dad.

He shifts the dog's weight in his arms. "I have to. She's been with him for years. He'll notice she's gone."

"He goes to the Seville tomorrow, Raúl. Can't you fib a little?" Mom says. "Tell him we took Inés to the vet? Buy him some time to process?"

"Rule number one," I pipe in. Serge came unglued when Dad burned his barn down. What will it do to him to lose Inés?

"You're right," Dad says. "We won't tell him." He lifts the dog. "Carol, peek out at him, will you? I don't want him to see me." I look out the front door.

Serge stares at the flames as if he's watching a movie. His back is to us.

"Go," I tell Dad, and he carries Inés down the porch steps and around the opposite side of the house, off to find a proper place to bury her.

I wait until my tears dry up, then walk to Serge.

"First the barn, then the house," he whispers. "Then they'll pack me in a box and send me away."

I touch his shoulder the way Mom did, and he doesn't shove me away.

"I've never been anywhere else, *chiquita*," Serge says. "Will my new home have a ridge? Mesas? Will it smell like the ranch smells? There won't be sheep, but will there at least be stars?" His voice is laced with all his love for this place, this ranch that I try so hard to understand, but I always fall short.

I've never felt that way about anywhere. Not even home.

"You're right," I say. "It'll be different. But think of

the new things you'll see, the new air you'll breathe." I use words from his own story, the same words Rosa told the villagers.

Dad climbs up the porch steps, dirt coating his jeans. Arms empty.

Serge growls through yellowed teeth. "You're packing all my things in boxes, taking whatever you want, stealing my treasures . . ."

"No," Dad says weakly.

"You want to put me away in a box! You're burning me down!" Serge propels himself up and out of the chair, hands flying in slow motion, aiming to attack his son.

"I was just trying to kill the termites, you crazy old man!" Dad shouts, his cheeks chili red. He pushes Serge away, hard, and my grandpa lands back in his chair with a sickening crunch. His oxygen tube has fallen from one ear, making half his face look strangely bare.

I swallow away a bitter taste. Dad hovers over Serge with hands tensed in fists, a cobra coiled to strike.

"Raúl," Mom gently calls from the doorway, and breaks Dad's spell.

There's a buzzing. *Not now, bees,* I think, and search the air. But it's not bees, it's Dad, sobbing. His fists fall open, then he falls to his knees, howling like a coyote pup.

"I'm sorry." He grabs Serge's snake-stomping boots and holds himself there. "*Papá,* please, I'm so sorry."

Serge stands and extricates himself from Dad's touch, pulling his loosened oxygen tube taut. "You won't burn me down," he says, his face blank of emotion, and disappears into the house, his metal oxygen tank clinking behind him.

"Guys," Mom says to Dad and me, "I'm beat. Fend for yourselves for dinner, okay?" She goes in.

I'm not hungry. I don't think I'll ever be hungry again.

Dad sips his beer, and when he locks his puffy eyes on mine, it's not even debatable: he needs me more than Serge does right now. I sit next to him on the porch steps. Smoke billows above the pasture—the closest thing to fat gray clouds this ranch has seen in a century.

He wipes away sweat and tries to speak, but all his sentences start, stop, then start again, the way his truck freezes up in winter. "I'm sorry you had to see . . . Dementia does funny things . . . Sometimes Serge's brain just . . ." He shakes his head, over and over and over. "I shouldn't have yelled at him."

"Dad," I say, "why'd you do it?"

"Do what?"

"Why'd you burn down the barn?"

"You heard me," he says. "Termites."

"Termites," I repeat. "You couldn't have just used some bug spray?"

"We can't afford commercial-grade pest repellent. Termites travel. It was either fire, or else they'd catch a ride on a sheep running downhill and munch all the wood in the house."

I think about that morning, at the beginning of summer, when Serge and I dosed sheep in the barn, when he told me about measuring time, keeping track of his years by counting the sheep he sheared. When the sheep are gone, Serge will lose that time. Lose those years. In the Seville he'll have to use a clock to measure time, just like everybody else.

The image infuriates me. I can't let Dad off the hook that easily. "You really hurt him, Dad." I'll never forget the way Serge screeched while he watched the flames take his barn—like he was the one on fire.

"Termites!" Dad's voice is in shreds. He sounds like Alta when she's been caught sneaking in after curfew—insisting on the same half-baked excuse, over and over, even though everyone knows she's lying. "It was the right thing to do, okay?" He gives one of the porch railings a good shake. It's extra wobbly, even for how old it is. "*Papá* thinks he's the only one who wants to keep this house standing."

"I thought you hated the ranch," I say.

"This was *Mamá*'s home," he says. "Everything here—every room, every wall, even the sheep. It's all hers, too."

I sit with Dad until he's out of tears (and out of beer), then fix us both a peanut butter sandwich for dinner—chalky peanut butter, bland bread, but it fills the pit in my stomach.

In the living room, Serge stares at the wall where the TV used to be. Dad approaches him slowly, no sudden movements, a hunter approaching a wild animal.

"Did you feed Inés?" Serge says.

I hold my breath. But Dad just says wearily, "Yes."

"She's a good dog," Serge says, and the two of them get lost in the silent emptiness of this last night at the ranch.

I retreat to my room and nestle into my sleeping bag, clutching the seed in my hand.

My phone buzzes.

SOFIE: When do you come back???

ME: Tomorrow.

SOFIE: Yayyyy! Will you be able to come to Manny's
         barbecue? We're doing boys vs. girls for
         volleyball.

ME: I don't know yet.

SOFIE: Are you so excited to come home?

ME:

I plug my phone in and wait in the darkness—for sleep. For bees. Neither finds me.

15

Around midnight, when Alta's in teenage dreamland, I walk out to the porch.

Serge whittles, the wool blanket draped over his lap. "My eyes are old, *chiquita*," he says. "My nose is old, too. But both are telling me rain is coming."

"Tell me the story," I say. I'm out of words tonight. What I want is to listen. "Does Rosa stay now that the baby is coming?"

"The bees will bring the rain." He barely says these words, but they've spilled out of his mouth so many times this summer, they're predictable as the cloudless sky.

"Once upon a time," I prompt. *The ending*, I think. If I can hear the ending, then I'll be able to sleep.

I'll be able to go home.

"Once upon a time," Serge says, "there was a tree . . ."

*O*nce upon a time, there was a tree. It was no longer the most beautiful thing in the desert. Emerald leaves, gone. Milky-white blossoms, gone. The boughs that braided themselves into a network of places to climb, places to sit, places to swing and leap from, gone. All that remained was the black trunk, stripped of bark and branches.

Sergio's only comfort when he saw the desecrated tree was that it was still a tree, technically. It still towered above the earth, its roots still clinging to the dirt like a burr clings to wool.

Once upon a time, Sergio's only comfort when he saw his sweating, screeching wife in the pains of childbirth was that it was still Rosa: still her rose-petal lips, though sometimes pursed in pain; still her mischievous eyes, shining with courage when not clouded by agony. It was still his hand she grabbed when a surge hit and shook the scream out of her.

"It's time," she had said so calmly hours ago, patting her giant belly. Sergio had nearly jumped out of his skin. Time, at last, to meet his . . . daughter? Son? So far, he'd only thought of the little baby as a lamb, a bumblebee, a teensy new offshoot of Rosa blooming in her womb.

But was it time already?

Eight months had rushed past since Rosa had returned. Eight months of the marriage Sergio had dreamed of: a wife who was there when he woke before the sun, who made him coffee with cinnamon. A wife who sheared the sheep while he held them, because this almost violent task was the worst part of running a band. A wife who brought in bouquets of wildflowers for their home. A wife who relaxed with him by the fire in the evenings, a wife who was there when he fell asleep.

Sergio had tried hard not to begrudge Rosa her travels. He was well aware that the woman he loved had a wanderlust that could never be contained, and to order her to stay home would be like putting a brightly feathered bird in a cold iron cage.

But the joy of these last eight months, watching

her belly swell with life while the rest of the village flirted with death, with their lamb-slaughter festivals and dangerous trips . . . This happiness was unmatched.

Rosa let out one last, long, great moan, and then her head flopped back in relief. Her wailing was replaced by a much smaller, sharper wailing.

Carolina was the first to hold the baby, and she swaddled the little one in a clean blanket. "A son," she said, and Sergio's next inhale was different, the most important breath of his life. Breathing as a father.

Rosa reached for the baby, and Sergio reluctantly handed him to her, then tapped his foot until his son was in his arms again. "I see you have my mouth," he said, "but I hope you only use it for smiles, not for frowns. And you have your mother's eyes. Do you see the world like she does?"

And the thought filled him with fear.

Once upon a time, Sergio, his wife, Rosa, and their infant son, Raúl, watched Inés chase a bird along the shore of the green-glass lake.

"Such a spring we've had," Sergio said. "The best I've seen in all my years."

Rosa snorted. "Certainly we've had better springs," she said. "No more flowers, no more shade. Just all this brown." She gestured to the dying land around them. As if to illustrate her point, a hot, gritty wind blew past them.

"There's so much more to this spring than flowers," Sergio said. He beamed at his wife and his son. The life he had always dreamed of—so what if the springtime was a little on the dry side?

"You'll have to tell me if the summer is as lovely," Rosa said.

She looked at him, and he saw the answer to his unasked question right in her eyes, dead center.

"A child should be with his mother," argued Sergio.

"Then come with me," Rosa said.

"Not when Raúl is so young," Sergio said.

Rosa sighed. "There's still so much world to see," she whispered, and for a second, Sergio didn't disagree. How many nights had he spent alone in his marriage bed, imagining the far-off places his wife was? What was the view like, where she was?

They had a new world in their son to explore. But for Rosa, this would never be enough.

Raúl grew strong, but slowly, like babies in the village always did. Sergio and Rosa relished every second they had with him.

Rosa sang the baby to sleep, introduced him to all the lambs, let him feel the grass with his fat little feet.

She rested her head on Sergio's shoulder, and once Raúl was asleep, they watched the stars come out of their daytime hiding. Same stars for hundreds of years, trickling across the sky.

But once upon a time, on an unremarkable day, Rosa packed a bag and saddled her horse. Sergio put Raúl on his hip, and the baby bobbed a chubby wrist up and down in farewell to his mother.

"Three days," she promised. "I'll be back in three days."

And she was. Sergio tended sheep and tended Raúl, and watched over the village while everyone was gone, as was his usual post. Rosa returned home, and she stayed for weeks, or months, or even years. Time didn't exist when she was home. Then she left and returned and left again.

When Rosa was home, the village was paradise on earth to Sergio. When Rosa traveled, the village was Sergio and Raúl's father-son playground.

"This is our lake, Raúl," Sergio said. "And our village. And this is our tree, and we will never cut it down."

The remaining lumber from the amputated branches was piled on the lake's shore. The villagers had taken more than they needed—now Sergio saw the remnants of their greed every time he passed by the lake.

"You haven't made anything for yourself yet," Rosa said to Sergio during one of her sojourns home.

You haven't left yet, *she meant.*

"I'm not interested in jewelry or trinkets," he said.

I'm not going, *he meant.*

But when Rosa pointed out that it was silly to let the wood go to waste, he dragged the lumber to the pasture, and with this supply of midnight-black wood he made himself, Rosa, and Raúl a sprawling, stunning ranch house. Not a talisman, or a bracelet, or a cart, or a boat. Not something for traveling.

Something for staying.

They used the old shepherd shack as a barn.

Time whipped past him, and much of that time, he was alone with Raúl. Rosa bounced home, then bounced away days later.

"Stay with us," he'd beg her, but she'd smile that sly Rosa smile and slip out of his hands like a gecko. He lost track of where she was heading: the Alps, the Arctic, one of the oceans—it was all the same to him. She always brought things back for Raúl, whose toddlerhood stretched to fill many years, as though his body refused to grow on days his mother was gone.

Sergio sheared the sheep dutifully, providing the wool for Rosa's scarves. These scarves, she informed him, had quite a reputation by now. They fetched enough money to fund not only her own adventures, but those of the other villagers as well.

Sergio replanted the crops and kept up with the communal gardens. Despite the parched land and the coarse winds that now howled across the oasis, the harvest was still enough to feed the whole village. Sergio saved what he could—stocking his pantry with can after can—but most of it rotted now before it was eaten.

A ghost town doesn't need food.

Every year, when seeds went in, the dirt got drier. Hot wind blew sand into his eyes and lungs. The bright green of the oasis faded to a sickly gold, and all plants disintegrated to grit. Without the shade of the tree, the sun beat down in violent punches. For the first time, Sergio felt like he lived in a desert.

Once upon a time, Sergio walked through the pasture, Raúl in a sling on his back, and heard the hiss of a rattler. Before he could spot it, the snake struck his ankle.

The bite folded in on itself and healed before a drop of blood was spilled. "The gift lives on," he said, relieved. But that evening his heart still thumped. Snakes had never been so bold before.

He made a request: the next time Rosa traveled, she bring him and Raúl each a pair of boots.

She laughed. *No one in the village ever wore shoes.*

"Snake-stomping boots," he said. "My bones feel old for the first time, and they tell me that things are changing around here."

"Change is good," she said, folding her arms. But she did bring the two of them each a pair of black leather cowboy boots, beautifully embroidered with fleurs-de-lis. Sergio never let Raúl leave the house without them. When Raúl's feet grew, Rosa brought a bigger pair.

Things changed in the village, yes, slowly. Rosa reported to Sergio that things were changing outside the village, too—but rapidly. It was a world of industry, she said, of horseless carriages that ran on steam, and women who wore trousers, and machines that let you stand in one corner of the world and talk to someone on the other side. "It's the turn of the century," she explained.

"What's a century?" he said.

"Outside the village, no one measures time with sheep." She spoke to him like he was the child, not Raúl.

She brought home a new language. "English," she said, "is the language of the future." Rosa taught it to Raúl, and it was all Raúl wanted to speak.

"What is this?" Sergio would point to a sheep when he and Raúl were cleaning the barn.

"Sheep!" came the tiny reply.

"No, Raúl," Serge would correct. "La oveja. Oveja."

"Sheep!" Raúl would say, and clap at his own cleverness. "Sheep, sheep, sheep!"

And every time he said it, a cactus rolled over Sergio's heart. Sheep, he tried saying, but it sounded too prickly a word for these white fluffy things he tended.

But he learned enough English to keep up with his son, who was turning out to be as stubborn as his mother. Raúl asked about the world outside the village constantly, asked where the sky stretched to beyond the ridge, asked why he couldn't go with Mami, asked why the bees' buzz sounded like an angry song, asked and asked and asked.

"Another Rosa," Sergio sometimes thought when

he looked at Raúl, and his gut lurched with a mixture of pride and dread.

Once upon a time, there was a tree. And they cut it down.

They cut it down.

Sergio never learned who did the chopping, but one day the hollowed tree was on its side. The stump was left, an ugly black wound on the land, a scab that would never heal. The sight of it made Sergio sick, like when he saw blood: stomach clenching, nausea spreading.

"Too far," he said to Rosa. "You've gone too far!"

"The tree lives on in our talismans," she told him. "In the home you made from its lumber. In the canoe you built for the Father. In this bracelet you made for me."

Once again, Sergio remembered that fateful day when he made the first cut into the bark of the tree. How had that one small act led to all of this?

Years after the tree was gone, the stump had shriveled and hardened, a pockmark on the lake's shore. Sergio sat on the porch of this house he had built from the tree, in a cream wicker chair Rosa had brought back from one of her travels. One of those horseless carriages Rosa had told him about drove up the long, winding dirt road toward the house, rattling like thunder, snorting out peppery smoke. What an ugly thing, he thought, a rusty black beast with a humpback and a stench like sheep manure on fire.

The beast pulled right up to the house, its rubber tires flattening the grass, and the driver said to Sergio, "I'm looking for the family of a Carolina de Vaca."

Sergio stood, surveying the man suspiciously. "I am her brother-in-law, sí."

The driver asked Sergio to come to the back of the beast and opened a door.

Lying inside was a corpse, marble-eyed, staring at nothing: Carolina, Rosa's beloved sister, dead.

Sergio took the body from the hearse and laid her on Father Alejandro's bed in the mission, flat on her back with her hands folded in prayer.

Raúl asked, "What do we do now, Papá?" but Sergio had no answers. He didn't know how to mourn.

"We stay silent," he said.

They didn't speak until other villagers returned, lighthearted, from their travels, chattering like magpies. They fell, gasping, when they saw the body. Death wasn't supposed to happen, not to them.

Rosa was the last to come home, and when she saw her cold, dead sister, she couldn't speak for three days.

"But how?" Rosa's whisper was hoarse, shredded after three days of crying. "We know the gift lives on."

"No, it doesn't," Sergio said bitterly. "Not anymore." When the tree was chopped, the gift must have flickered, sputtered out its last sparks.

Died.

No, not a gift, he decided. The Father had been wrong. Gifts are not taken away. And he let himself use that word, "magic." The magic had died.

More bodies came back to the lake. More death, but now there was no lumber to build coffins.

Once upon a time, there was a tree. But they chopped it down.

16

Moving day.

When I wake, it's early enough to watch the sunrise. The house is dark. No bees buzzing, no truck engine revving in the yard, no sheep bleating. Just Alta's breathing, heavy as a scuba diver, from the bed above me. I wait on the floor for Serge's usual hacking cough from the porch, but the world is silent.

Are you so excited to come home? Sofie's message is still unanswered on my phone.

No, I'm not. I'm not ready to leave yet.

I pad through the chilly house with the seed in my hand. Inés, dead. Carolina, in the story, dead. More and more villagers, dead, dead, dead.

I want the seed to live.

Drought dries everything to dust, as Serge says, so the seed has as much chance of survival as Serge's mind. But I have to try.

Dad's zonked out on the futon. I scoot past him and through the front door. Serge's asleep in his wicker chair, the oxygen *shoosh*ing through the tubes and into his nose. He doesn't stir when I sneak by.

The sky is the color of an apricot, and a few weak stars are visible along the horizon. It's neither hot nor cold. My throat clinches when I see a spot of recently dug-up dirt behind the house: the place where Dad buried Inés.

I'm no gardener, but I take the little seed to the only logical spot on the ranch, the only place with evidence that a seed once grew there and thrived, once upon a time . . .

The scabby old tree stump.

Three feet away from the dead trunk, I dig. The dirt is rough as a cat's tongue, impossible to gather into a fistful. With every scoop of dirt, planting a seed feels more and more ridiculous. The land is dying. This is no place for a seed to grow.

But I have to try.

The stars fade into morning light by the time I place the little seed in the hole. It looks so helpless in there. "I'm sure you're thirsty," I tell it, "but there's a drought." *Get used to it.*

A bee buzzes to the hole, crawls along the seed, then flies away. Another bee lands on the seed, then takes off; a third bee replaces it.

What are they doing? The seed is probably dead; drought dries everything to dust, to bones. But even if it's not, it's still just a seed. There's nothing there to attract a bee, let alone a steady stream of them.

I lean forward to get a closer look, and I can't believe what I see.

Each bee carries . . . *water.*

A single drop of water.

They place the water on the seed, then buzz away. I barely breathe.

The bees are bringing back the rain. I stay and watch. The bees water the seed, a drop at a time, until the sun brings up a nice peach snow-cone morning. Then, as quickly as they appeared, the bees are gone.

They watered the seed, I think as I push dirt back

over the hole. No rain for a hundred years. No bees in a drought.

Impossible.

I brush desert dust from my pajama pants and walk to the house with tingly legs, determined not to think about it.

"Buenos días." It doesn't surprise me to hear Serge ahead of me, awake on the porch. I set my demeanor to normal—rule number one, don't upset Serge.

"It is a good morning," I say.

"A morning for leaving," he says, and I hurry inside before my face falls.

In the bathroom I get ready, every movement robotic. When I tuck my toothbrush in my duffel bag, I'm officially packed.

Everything at the ranch, except for the few things that Serge is taking to the Seville, is going right to a storage shed in Albuquerque, saved for another day when we'll have to pull it all out and re-sort it into more piles: keep, toss, or back into storage.

Mom hands me a wet rag and asks me to wipe down the light switches in the house. I had no idea that moving required so many nitpicky chores.

The slap of my sandals echoes in the house as I walk into the empty guest room. Wipe light switches, turn off lights. I walk into Dad's old bedroom. It's empty—Nintendo consoles and hairy-rock-star posters long gone in the trash bin. Wipe light switches, turn off lights.

I take a breath and walk into Serge and Rosa's old bedroom. Empty, even of dust. It could be anyone's bedroom, anywhere in the world. Wipe light switches, including the one in the empty, hollow closet, turn off lights.

I leave the door open when I'm done.

Grandma Rosa's things—her silk clothes, the emu head, all that jewelry that would make a pirate salivate— are in boxes, packed in the moving van. I picture these treasures in a pitch-black storage shed, alone and neglected for another twelve years.

In the kitchen Mom's front end is in the fridge, smell-checking what food is salvageable: a mom job, indeed, since the cheese she just chucked had a patch of fuzzy blue-white mold on it.

"When do we leave?" Alta's wiping down the kitchen windows, with sunglasses on so no one can see her glaring. She and Mom must be in the intermission of an argument.

"Soon." Mom delivers a typical parent response—one syllable, frustratingly vague.

The kitchen feels cold without the spicy aromas of her Mexican meals. I doubt she'll keep cooking like that at home. Back to Hamburger Helper, I'm sure.

"When's soon?" Alta says, phone in her hand.

Mom shuts the fridge, a Tupperware container of noodles and a wrinkly orange in her hands. "If you're in such a hurry, go take Carol's things out to the truck."

Even through the sunglasses, Alta's eyes shoot laser beams at me. "I've got it," I say quickly, and carry my duffel bag outside.

I hear Mom tell Alta to take the stinky fridge rejects to the trash bin, and my sister grumbles down the porch steps behind me.

"What are you going to do first when we get home? Take a thirty-minute shower, or hit the pool?" I say.

"Nap first." Moody Alta. She bangs the trash-bin lid shut, then tromps back up the porch steps, slamming the door behind her.

I'm trying to remember the parts of home that I've

missed all summer, but instead my mind flashes a slide show of the ranch: the way Serge gently held the sheep for dosing, the purple stripe on the ridge, the grainy wood paneling in the living room. Midnight black, just like in Serge's story.

I let myself think it: *I'm going to miss the ranch.*

The moving van and the pickup truck are parked in the pasture, sheep grazing between the tires. Dad's talking on his phone. I don't mean to eavesdrop, but two sentences in, I know what's going on.

It's Mr. González, the real estate agent. The ranch sold.

"Wow," Dad says. "That soon? No, it's no problem. I'll stop by and grab the contract on my way into the city."

I'm punched inside out. I realize I was holding on to a secret hope that the ranch wouldn't sell, and Serge would make a miraculous recovery at the Seville and move back home, and the land would heal. I was hoping this summer wouldn't end this way.

When Dad hangs up, he squeezes me to his side. "Good news, *niña.* That was Mr. González."

"The ranch sold." My voice is flat and dry as the desert.

"Well, not the ranch. Just the land." He shrugs. "I guess they're not interested in buying an ugly old Spanish-style ranch house—"

"You said you liked the house," I say.

"Me?" Dad guffaws. "I mean, I'm sad to let it go . . ."

Papá's not the only one who wants to keep this house standing. That's what Dad said last night when the barn was burning.

"What about the sheep?" I demand. "Where are they going?"

Dad tosses my duffel bag into the back of the truck. He's going to drive it straight to the Seville, with Serge in the passenger seat. "Are you old enough for the truth, or should I lie?"

I raise my eyebrows.

"They're probably going to be dog food."

"Dog food!" I cry. "Why?"

"They're just too bony," he says. "Drought's been awful to them."

"We can't do that!" I say, tears stinging.

"There's nothing else to do," he says. "*Papá* wanted to stay at the ranch forever, but—"

"But things change, don't they?" I finish. Dad looks

at me like he just realized I'm twelve years old, not three. I let him take my hand and we hold still, until my heart feels like it's being squeezed in a waffle iron. Dad leaves to finish loading the truck, and I look out at the pasture.

My phone buzzes with a message.

GABBY: *Guess what??? Manny's locker partner moved
and she's looking for a new one! I gave her
your number. Hope that's ok.*

ME: *Sure, thanks.*

GABBY: *You could be Manny's locker partner! I'm so
jealous!*

ME: *Yep, haha, lol*

But I'm not really laughing. By the time I put my phone in my pocket, I've forgotten what the message even said.

I stand as tall as I can, like I'm the tallest thing for miles — taller than the house, taller than Alta. Taller than the red mesas — tall enough, almost, to peek into the sky and see if bees are bringing rain.

Things are only impossible if you stop to think about them.

But I can't stop thinking about them. The little seed will probably die. The barn has already been burned.

The sheep will be ground up into dog food. The ranch house will be bulldozed to the ground . . . Rosa in Serge's story was wrong. There's nothing good about change.

"Carol!" Mom calls. "Come eat, then let's hit the road!"

Mom has peeled a bunch of oranges and set them on the counter. "Sorry." She apologizes for the sparse food offering. "Gotta clean out the fridge."

"It's fine," Dad says, practically swallowing his orange whole.

"Where's Serge?" Mom says. "Isn't he hungry?"

But Serge has disappeared.

And in a flash, our easy moving day transforms into a search-and-rescue party.

"I knew this would happen," Dad says, after checking the porch for the umpteenth time.

"He can't have gone far," Mom says.

"Do you think he took off? Called a cab?" Dad runs his hands through his hair.

Just like it did the day Serge destroyed Dad's newly poured driveway, my mind runs through all the dangerous places Serge could be.

What if he's having a dementia slip right now? He

could think he's petting Inés when he's really petting a coyote. He could get tired while wandering and decide the ridge looks like a nice place to sit and relax, between the rattlesnake nests.

Worst of all: what if he walks straight into the desert wilderness and just never comes back? The vultures would get to him before any human did.

We look everywhere. For the first ten minutes, Mom and Dad are annoyed. After twenty minutes of searching, Mom's worry lines crease her forehead. When it's been forty-five minutes and Serge seems to have evaporated into dust, my parents are frantic.

I am frantic.

"Any other place you can think of?" Mom asks. "Even places you can't think of?"

"That doesn't make any sense." Alta's stayed in a "just annoyed" phase — she must have a date with Marco planned for when we get home, and Serge's vanishing act is costing her precious primping minutes.

A whole summer at the ranch, and for Alta, nothing's changed.

"Hush," Mom snaps. "And put your phone away."

"I'm going to drive around one more time." Dad

stalks out to the truck, muttering, "Unbelievable, this is just unbelievable . . ."

I check and recheck Serge's usual haunts: the porch, the tree stump, the pasture. I check the chicken coop for the hundredth time, even though he's too big to squeeze in there. I squint at the ridge, again and again.

Bzzz . . .

I whip around in a circle, searching for a bee.

It's a phone call.

Manny.

Manuela Rodriguez, most popular girl in our grade, calling to offer me the equivalent of an Olympic gold medal: the privilege and honor of being her locker partner.

I hold the phone in my hand.

"Did you find him, Carol?" Mom's voice snaps me back to the present, and I decline Manny's call. My phone goes back in my pocket, and I continue my search for my grandfather.

"No, not yet," I call as I race to the porch.

Mom's got one hand on the wicker chair, and she's deep breathing. "What if we find him somewhere and he's . . ." My insides coil.

"Should we call the police?" I ask.

"What police?" Mom whispers. "There are no police out here." But she pulls out her phone anyway.

I hear a creak in the back of the house.

I run into Serge's old bedroom, a place I've checked six times in the last hour.

But here he is, in the empty closet, tucked back in the shadows, wilted like a sunflower on a stormy day.

"It's gone, all gone," he says. "It's like she never traveled at all." His eyes grow distant. "Like she never lived at all."

"We've been looking everywhere for you!" I say. "What are you doing in here?" He fiddles with something, and I reach out, like he's a child, and make him show me.

He's holding his rusty whittling knife in his right hand, and the flesh of his left hand is split into a grisly canyon.

I shake when the blood pools in his palm. "H-hand me the knife." He passes it to me, and I try to ignore the blood shining on the blade.

Bzzz, bzzz . . . A bee flies above me. I barely notice as I scramble for something to stop the bleeding. But there's literally nothing left in the house. Everything is packed, even the toilet paper. I yank the fabric belt out of my shorts and wrap it around his wound, my knees turning to jelly.

"Summer's turned up its heat, *chiquita*. Time to slaughter the lamb and make a feast of the blood." His oxygen tube murmurs with air.

Stop saying "blood," I silently command. "That's only a story," I remind him. All of it, just a story he cooked up.

"It is my best story," he says.

"We're supposed to get in the truck. We're moving, remember?"

"Moving," he repeats, staring at the blood seeping through the fabric of my belt.

I grasp the closet doorknob, suddenly light-headed.

"I don't like blood, either, Caro-leeen-a," Serge says, his voice far away. He's pale, his bee-sting lumps extra purple. "My knife slipped. Old hands, very old hands." The red stain blossoms, bigger and bigger. I can see the layers of his skin, like a cake . . .

"Grandpa, I can't . . ." My world is spinning to a pinhole, the bee buzzing around and around, a shooting star.

"Mom!" I cry. "He's here . . ." But I'm going, going, gone.

17

When I open my eyes, Mom's waving her hands an inch from my nose and I'm flat on my back, Dad elevating my legs.

"What happened?" I say.

"You fainted," Mom says.

Serge putters into the room and pushes a cool glass of water to me. "Here," he says. "Drought dries you out. Dries you to the bones."

I sip.

"Must be the heat," Mom says.

But that's not why I passed out. I remember. "Is Serge's hand okay?" *Don't think of the blood, don't think of the blood.*

Mom raises her eyebrows. "Did something happen to it?"

"He cut it."

Serge holds out his hand. The palm is whole, not a scratch in sight.

"But . . ." I try to speak but my head spins, and I trail off into silence. Did I just imagine the cut? I must have. How else did Serge's hand go from torn and bleeding to the clean, weathered hands of an old sheep farmer?

Mom links her arm in mine and walks me to the moving van. "I want you to wait in here with the AC on. We'll finish loading up."

I don't protest, and moments later I bask in my first air-conditioning of the summer. Alta glares at me while she lugs things to the van.

Did I really pass out from the heat? I swear I saw a slice in Serge's hand, deep as a gully. I used my fabric belt to stop the blood, didn't I? I glance down; the belt is missing from my shorts.

But the AC cools my head, and as my world stops spiraling, I think about it logically. I must have dreamed up the cut. This isn't one of Serge's stories. Wounds don't just heal themselves.

I rest my legs against the dashboard, AC fanning my hair, and look at the ranch house—probably for the last time. If I squint, the windows turn into flat glassy eyes and the front door is a sad, square mouth, sighing. If the house could speak, what would it say? Would it sneeze out red desert dust, then talk about the bees, the bees, the bees? The ranch saw Rosa come and go. It saw her die. It saw Serge's mind slowly darken, lightbulbs dimming year after year. It saw my family arrive and turn our noses up at its ancient beams, its funny smells, its old-fashioned ways.

I was wrong about you, I want to say to the house. *We were all wrong about you.*

My family comes out of the ranch house for the last time. Serge follows them, slumping, a defeated soldier. He stops on the porch and turns back for a final look, but no one else does.

The air-conditioning is supposed to be cooling me off, but something inside of me is snapped open, burning, festering.

We can't sell it. As the thought pops into my head, I say it out loud. "We can't sell it." Dad was right when he said Serge isn't the only one who cares about this house.

I care, too. I care so much.

I get out of the van and nearly trip; my legs still feel like warmed-up Jell-O.

"Carol, slow down! You're supposed to be resting," Mom says.

I ignore her, ignore my knees, which threaten to buckle. "Dad, please, don't sell the ranch!" I sob, and choke on a scratchy gust of desert dirt. "Don't let it go, Dad, please!"

"Carol, honey," Dad starts. "The land belongs to someone else now. It's a done deal."

Anger boils up and out of me. "But the bees!" *I sound exactly like Serge.* It's a fleeting thought, and I brush it away. "The bees have been flying around the ranch all summer. You guys don't believe me, but it's true! I found a seed in Grandma Rosa's closet"—Dad winces and peeks at Serge—"and I planted it, and the bees came and . . . and . . ."

I can't say it. I can't say, *The bees brought back the rain.* Of all the things that have come out of Serge's mouth, that sentence sounds the craziest. But it's not. Now I know it's not.

Alta heaves a sigh that could be heard from the ridge. "Can we go already?"

"Yes," Dad says. "Carol, it's time. Say good-bye."

"Nooo!" I cling to the porch railing. "We can't sell the ranch!"

"Stop!" Mom stomps over to me and wraps her arms around my middle. I hold on tighter as she pulls, clawing the wood, making a tug-of-war game out of this: Mom versus the porch, me as the rope. "Carol, this is ridiculous!"

"Please, nooo!" I howl.

"Come on, Carol! Stop acting like such a baby," Alta says.

Her words sting the parts of me that are trying so hard to leave childhood behind. But I grip the porch railing tighter, digging my nails in.

"Caro-leeen-a." Serge walks, calmly as a cat, into the eye of our storm. "Come get in the van, and I'll tell you the next part of the story."

He freezes me. I stare, Mom's hands still around my middle.

"I'll tell you what happened to the village and the tree," he says. "To Sergio and Rosa."

And just like I have been all summer, I'm drawn to Serge like a magnet. I let him help me in the van, where he buckles my seat belt. His wizened hands are steady, his breathing lulling my own inhales and exhales to half time.

Mom and Dad murmur behind him, and I know what they're saying: *What's going on? He's supposed to be the wreck, not Carol.*

"Grandpa," I say, and my eyes flood. For the first time, that name clicks—a summer shifting into autumn, a minute hand ticking a new hour into place. Not Serge, but Grandpa. It finally feels right to say it.

I say it again: "Grandpa. We have to say good-bye today."

"Shh," he says, patting my hand with his hand, just like a real grandfather, one whose brain isn't being eaten away by dementia. My grandfather.

"Do you remember where you're going today?" I whisper, before he launches me into a world of bees and lakes and cuts that always heal.

"Caro-leeen-a," he says. "Just make sure Inés gets fed."

My heart disintegrates to dust, and I lean into the seat, eyes closed. I'll keep them closed the whole way home. I don't want to see the ranch shrink in the distance. I don't want to see telephone poles start to pop up or artificial, man-made colors trickle into the landscape. I don't want the desert to end.

"Once upon a time," Grandpa says, and I, on the border of sleep, listen.

Once upon a time, there was no tree. Strangers hadn't passed through the village in years. There wasn't even an off-ramp from the highway. Cars zipped past and didn't know that beyond the mountain lay a ghost town of time-eaten, abandoned shacks and swampy green water, which was now more pond than lake. The tree-stump scab baked on the shore; the whole village was a scab, parched and brown and dead in the desert.

If a stranger was to pass through, he would hear thunder rolling above the village. Always thunder, never rain. But it wasn't really thunder—it was bees. Bees scurrying in the cracks of the boarded-up windows, bees crawling over every beached lake rock, searching for the white blossoms and the gnarled black tree that had been their world.

Sergio sat in his wicker chair on the porch of the

ranch house. This is where he was every evening, frowning at the drying-up lake while sunlight faded into darkness. He stared right at the spot where the tree would have been, as if he could see it. As if trees had ghosts.

Raúl had shot up these last years, ripening faster than any child had ever grown in the village. He was now big enough to be Sergio's right hand, to learn the business of sheepherding.

Only Rosa kept returning to the sleepy village. Everyone else had taken their slivers of the trees, their "gifts," to the four corners of the world, and gradually, over the years, they died.

The tree's magic was gone.

Some died on the front lines of the wars in Europe. One minute they were storming the enemy lines, unafraid of gunfire because of the protection of the tree. Then they lay broken in the mud, their first tastes of pain, of blood, of mortality also their last, still clutching their pieces of the tree against their chests.

They all died.

Some died of old age, their bodies centuries past their expiration dates. Most of the old ones died tucked into quilted beds, closing their eyes for sleep, not realizing they would never open them again.

One girl died in a train crash. A corn farmer died when he fell from a silo. Whole families died within minutes of each other, even when separated by thousands of miles of world.

Beloved Father Alejandro died of influenza. Sergio didn't speak for a full month after he went into the ground.

Rosa walked the halls of the mission while Sergio glared at the treeless horizon. Raúl played with Inés on the crunchy grass. Inés — a miracle, the magic dog — was one of the last villagers still alive.

With no one living in it, the mission was an echo chamber, a new home for baby jackrabbits. A tomb.

Clack, clack, clack . . . Rosa had invested in a pair of her own snake-stomping boots, because now a rattler's bite would kill. No more bare feet.

One day Sergio took Raúl out in Father Alejandro's old boat, rowing across the lake-pond. Such a good boat, still seaworthy. The slimy green water sloshed the boat's sides, the only sound penetrating Sergio's cobwebbed mind.

"The lake is still here," he said to his son. "The tree is gone; the blossoms are gone. But at least we still have our lake."

When they came to shore, Rosa came up behind them. "There you are."

Sergio jumped. "You startled me." She was much quieter, now that a cloud of buzzing bees no longer followed her.

"Come on," she said. Raúl quickly left Sergio's side and ran to Rosa. "I have a surprise for both of you."

Sergio noticed a strand of gray in her hair and networks of wrinkles lining her mouth and eyes. When did she start to look so old? Did he look as old as she did?

"What is it this time, huh?" he said. "A riverboat? A unicorn with wings? A train that travels upside down in the clouds?"

She held out three paper tickets. "An airplane."

"Airplane?" he repeated.

"Airplane!" Raúl jumped up and down.

"A silver machine that flies in the air like a bird. I bought us tickets to Spain. We'll see Madrid, Barcelona, Seville—"

Raúl shouted, "You mean we get to go with you? Hooray!"

But Sergio shook his head. "We cannot leave," he said. "Look around us. The tree is dead."

"It isn't dead," Rosa argued. "It lives in the wood. In the house, in my bracelet. It lives in the hundreds of years we had. It lives in us."

"But its magic is gone," he said. "How many more years could we have had, if you hadn't cut down the tree?"

"How many more years would you have wanted, stuck in this village?" she said.

A congregation of vultures squawked and danced around their rabbit-carcass feast. "You see?" Sergio pointed at the birds as his evidence. "We never had a buzzard here before, not in a thousand years. We cut down that tree and let death into our camp!"

"We cut down the tree so we could live," she said. "See things. Feel things, feel pine needles, and dolphin's skin, and cold winds, and—"

"Pain," Sergio said.

Raúl shuddered. He knew that word, from Papí's stories. Pain was a fire in the flesh.

"Yes, pain," Rosa said. "Pain is how you know you're alive."

"Your sister, dead," he said, shaking his head. "Father Alejandro, dead. The old ones, dead. All our friends, dead. Dead, dead, dead! Such an ugly word." He hurled a stone into the water. "This village was never supposed to taste death."

"You're scared." Rosa waded into the lake in her boots. "Scared little boy in the tree."

"Scared of death? Of course," Sergio spat. "Everyone is."

"I'm not," she said.

"I'm not, either," Raúl said.

"The tree was a gift, Father Alejandro told us." Sergio tried again. "A gift. And we chopped it up, for lumber, and toys, and jewelry."

"For life," Rosa corrected him. "We did it all for life."

"But now we will die," he said.

"But at least we will have lived."

Once upon a time, an old man and an old woman stood where a tree once stood, a tree that would have shaded them and their young son. Instead, the sun glared on their backs like a spotlight, boiling their tempers and pushing harsh words to the surface.

Harsh words that were interrupted by a buzz.

Raúl heard it first. "What is that?" he said.

Rosa shielded her eyes with her hands, searching the skies. "It sounds like a helicopter."

"What the devil is a helly-copter?" Sergio said.

The buzzing grew louder.

"One of those newfangled flying machines. Just like an airplane. You'd hate it," Rosa said, folding her arms.

"Sí, I would!" Sergio yelled.

It wasn't a helicopter.

It was a storm. A storm of bees, yellow-and-black stripes, an angry buzz.

Rosa accepted Sergio's arm around her, protective and strong. Even though they argued, she was his wife and he was her husband, and their love was deeper than the old tree's black roots. Raúl nestled between them.

"What's happening?" Rosa asked, but Sergio had no answers. There were no answers, no words. Only bees. They tipped their heads back and watched.

A million bees, maybe more. An uncountable storm of bees, flying in a cyclone, stirring up dust, blocking the sun, making it midnight dark on the lake's shore. The bees plummeted down to the water, then back up, down and back up.

"Is this it?" Rosa cried.

"Is this what?"

She drew back to meet his sky-blue eyes. "Is this how we die?"

Sergio swallowed. He was panicking, but she was reveling, head thrown back, mouth dropped in awe at this glorious, terrifying sight. Raúl, too, wasn't afraid—he reached out to touch one of the bees, but Sergio yanked his arm back.

Then the bees moved.

Each bee dipped into the lake and took a single water droplet, clutching it between needle-thin black legs. Bee after bee, in militarized lines, rocketed down, took water, and flew away. The lake's shore began to recede. Somewhere behind them, the dog barked.

"They're taking the water!" Sergio rushed to the

shrinking lake, now only fifty feet in diameter. He swatted at the bees, arms flailing. The lake shrank to twenty feet. Then ten.

Then the lake was gone.

Once upon a time, a storm of bees lifted up a lake and carried it away.

No more clear green water, only a dried lake bottom, the sand already crackling in the vicious heat. The desert was quiet as a cemetery.

"We took their tree," Sergio whispered, "so they took our lake."

"You got stung." Rosa touched her husband's swollen face, covered in red bee stings. His skin burned with the new maze of bumpy stings. So this was pain.

This was what Rosa cut down the tree for.

"No more water," he murmured. "No more bees."

"Now where do we go?" Rosa said.

"What do you mean?"

"It's time for us to leave, like everyone else," Rosa said.

"We're not leaving."

"We have no water." She absentmindedly stroked

her black wood bracelet. Was it Serge's imagination, or did she seem unsure of herself for the first time in her life?

He cleared his throat, taking advantage of her silence. "We do have water," he reminded her. "The village wells."

Raúl ran with Inés across the crusty lake bottom, now just a bowl of land, hollow and haunting.

Sergio and Rosa looked at the new landscape of the village: no tree, no people, no lake. She looked at the new landscape of his face, the bee stings that would never heal.

Once upon a time, there was no tree. There was no lake. There was no rain.

And a drought began.

18

Home.

I snooze through most of the drive home, and when I wake, we're snaking off the freeway. It stops smelling like wide-open spaces and starts smelling like a city: exhaust, hot asphalt, flower delivery trucks, steam from metropolis buses.

The smell is everything I love about home. So many people feel tiny in such a huge city, just one of millions. I've always felt the opposite in it—huge by association.

Today I don't feel larger than life. These buildings used to be the tallest, shiniest things in my life. But every time we drive past one, I think of the mesas at the ranch, how they're so much taller.

I roll down the window to get some air; instead I inhale a blast of car exhaust and cough for three straight minutes. How could I ever have thought I could breathe here?

We get stuck at a red light for ages, only to drive forward and hit another red light.

It's loud. Not just the traffic, but the city itself. A million people talking at the same time, no one listening. A million televisions on full blast, no one watching. The humming and buzzing of the bees has been replaced with the sound of electricity . . . It's deafening.

Noise clutter.

Dad's on the other side of the city, getting Grandpa settled in the Seville. The Seville: a place without a porch, without the ridge, or sheep, or air.

There's no air in this city. Not anymore.

I dig the last slivers of the porch railing out of my hand as we pull into our neighborhood. I thought I'd left my tantrum back in the desert, but it's right here, bubbling in my throat. The ranch, gone. Grandpa, gone. And I didn't even get to hear the end of the story. Does Sergio ever leave? Does Raúl have to stay forever?

Alta drives in the lane next to us, pouting her lips like a supermodel, pretending she's alone in the world. Once upon a time, I would have tried to copy her, but now I just laugh. Oh, Alta, always wanting to be the black sheep, romanticizing what it's like to be the outsider. The truth is she fits in perfectly with the rest of my family. I'm the one who doesn't fit. I'm the one who would rather be back on the ranch, listening to Serge's bewitching stories. I'm the one who feels like she will never be the same.

Being the black sheep is lonely. I don't think my sister knows that.

Our house is still here: cheerful yellow siding, white shutters, surrounded by a manicured yard lined with chrysanthemums. I step out of the moving van and into the green grass, so spongy my feet sink into it. Nothing wild grows—no weeds, no cactus. This air . . . I fill my lungs, but it's not real air, not like out in the desert.

If the air of the wide-open desert is Mom's delicious homemade Mexican meals, this city air is from a box. It's Hamburger Helper.

Has our yard always been this teeny? Our street is a row of birdhouses, all of us boxed into our own yards by identical picket fences.

"Everything looks smaller," I tell Mom.

She smiles. "Maybe you're just bigger."

Alta parks her new car and carries her things into the house with one hand, her other hand scrolling on her phone's touch screen.

"Your purse is falling," I say. She tucks it under her arm without a word to me, then disappears into her bedroom.

My own room is a palace compared to Dad's old bedroom at the ranch. I crash-land on my bed, my clean, sweetly scented bed. A luxury after the sleeping bag on the floor. I lie on my stomach, face squished into the mattress, shoes still on . . . My phone vibrates.

GABBY: *Are you home yet?*

ME: *Yes, just barely.*

GABBY: *Coming to the pool party tonight?*

ME: *Maybe. I'm really tired.*

GABBY: *I miss you!*

ME: *I miss you, too.*

I don't tell her the truth, that I have no intention of going to the pool party. I do miss my friends, but I'm wrecked. All I want is to spend the evening lying in front of the air conditioner.

Mom orders pizza right away, clearly grateful to be back within delivery range.

Dad comes home from the Seville just after the pizza gets here, massaging his neck, and I roll my eyes, Alta style, at his dramatics. Did he drop off Grandpa, or slay a dragon?

"How'd that go?" Mom asks.

He sits on the couch, a slice of pizza in his hand. "As good as these things can go, I guess."

I picture Grandpa, alone in the Seville, so far from the endless desert, his beloved stars . . .

"Can Grandpa have visitors?" I say.

My family turns their heads.

"Sure," Dad answers. "We'll go see him soon. Great idea."

"Tomorrow?" I say.

Alta rips into her pizza like a wolf tearing a carcass, eyes boring craters into me. She wants me to shut up;

she doesn't want to be forced to visit her silly old stepgrandfather with her pesky, meddling little sister. Oh, wait, pesky, meddling little *half* sister.

I say it again. "We could go tomorrow, right? Shouldn't we make sure he's okay?"

"Not tomorrow," Dad says. "Give Grandpa some time to adjust. We'll try for Sunday."

I nibble my pizza, disappointed. Grandpa will have to spend a whole day by himself. "Fine. Sunday," I say.

"That's the day before school starts," Alta complains.

"It'll be good to do something as a family," Mom says.

"We just did a whole summer as a family," Alta mumbles.

"Hey," Mom warns, and we stop talking and eat.

The next day is Saturday. Lu sleeps in, which means Mom is able to sleep in, so she lets everyone sleep in. Only my body is still on ranch time; it rises with the sun, even though my curtains block the light.

When I make plans to go shopping with my friends, I'm genuinely excited.

Mom slips something into my hands on my way out the door. "This is for watching Lu all summer."

It's a twenty-dollar bill.

"And this is for your help watching Grandpa."

Another twenty-dollar bill.

I try to hand the money back, but Mom won't take it. So I leave, swimming up to my neck in guilt.

"Backpacks are out," Manny says at the mall. Alta was saying this very thing a few weeks ago at the ranch. Is there some sort of club where popular girls meet and vote on what's trendy and what's not?

My friends each buy a messenger bag, so I fork over my forty bucks so I can coordinate with them. When we pose in the mirror, our bags all slung over our left shoulders, I think of the sheep at the ranch, how they would stand so close together they blurred into a single pulsating puffball. If one of them stood just a little taller, his head would poke out of the collective wool. Then anyone could see him. A coyote. A hawk.

Dare to poke your head up, dare to stand out from the crowd, and you risk being gobbled up.

Sunday: Seville day. We pile into the minivan, Alta huffing because Mom and Dad won't let her drive her own car there. My parents act nervous, clenching hands, just like that first day at the ranch. "Don't let it break your heart," they tell me, "if he's not ready to see us yet."

The Seville's complex spreads over half a block of prime New Mexican property. There're tennis courts and a swimming pool, and the main house is a mansion, with white Ionic columns and gilded trim.

"This is way nicer than a hotel!" Alta says when we pull in. "Why was Serge complaining so much?"

Some people prefer ranches, I think.

We head to the sliding doors. Dad looks at something on his phone and punches a code in the number pad: 1412.

"This place needs codes for the doors?" I ask as we march into the maroon-and-gold lobby. "Who would want to break in here? Do the old people really need that much security?"

"It's not to keep people out," Mom explains, adjusting Lu in her arms. "It's to keep residents in." She explains that you have to punch the code to exit, too. I ponder this with mild horror. What if Grandpa wants to take a walk? Get some air? See the blue sky? He can't even walk through the front door without permission?

Even if he had the code, he has dementia—he'd never remember it, anyway.

"That's why we chose the Seville," Mom says. "It'll keep Grandpa safe."

Right, because what's safer than a prison, I think.

"This place must cost a fortune," Alta whispers to Mom. "I thought Serge was supposed to be a poor sheep farmer."

"Alta." Mom *tsks* at my sister's bluntness, then answers, "Why do you think Grandpa sold the ranch?"

My stomach coils. Grandpa sold his ranch to pay for his own birdcage.

"This way." Dad leads us down a corridor that, though carpeted, still stinks like a hospital: bubble-gum soap and mop water.

In the Seville pamphlet, photos show these same halls filled with old people so happy, they look one denture-y smile away from flying up to heaven. There are pictures of old people playing cards, soaking in hot tubs, having a movie night with vintage red-and-white popcorn buckets. But I don't see anything like that here. It's as empty as the desert.

"Where is everyone?" I say to Mom.

"Everyone who?" she says.

"All the old people."

"How many grandparents are you visiting today?" Mom asks, trying to be funny.

I don't laugh. This place is too eerily quiet, like they're getting the residents used to the endless quiet of cemeteries.

Dad knocks on door 104. *"Hola,"* he says, and walks into the room. We tiptoe in behind him.

Like my first day at the ranch, I'm not prepared for how different Grandpa looks.

No one else has eyes that blue, but it's all I recognize of my grandpa. The person lying in the bed is bloated like a fish with infected gills, chalk-faced, drooling.

"Buenas tardes, Papá," Dad says.

"Mmmm," Grandpa says.

Dad brings a cup of water to his lips, and Grandpa sips through a straw, then collapses on the pillow, as if exhausted by that simple chore.

"What's wrong with him?" I don't even bother to keep my voice down. I'm so shocked, I'm beyond being polite or proper.

Mom shoots me a look. "Shh. Not now."

But I'm thirsty for an answer now, right now. "Dad, what's wrong with Grandpa?"

Dad doesn't seem fazed. "Grandpa is still adjusting to his new medicine."

"There is no medicine for dementia," I say. "Mom told me there was no cure."

"There is no cure," Dad says. "He's on a mild sedative while he gets used to things here. The doctor just wants him to be comfortable."

This is the opposite of comfortable. The TV flickers, barely audible. Grandpa's eyelids flutter—not asleep, but not awake. "Mmmm," he moans again.

"He can't even talk!" I say.

Why am I the only one who's horrified? The Seville is supposed to be a vacation for his rusty, broken-down mind—instead, this place has turned my grandpa into a zombie.

"So they just . . . leave him in here, like this?" I say. "What if something happens to him?" I picture him having a stroke, or a heart attack, or simply dying, with no one here to help.

"Nurses do checks every two hours, like clockwork,"

Dad says, as if that explanation justifies why my grand-father should be parked in a bed, barely distinguishable from the pillows that surround him.

"Hey, Grandpa," I say, walking up to the bed. "How about you tell me the end of the story?"

Grandpa blinks, his eyelashes mostly crusted together.

"Carol," my dad warns.

"I just want to hear the end. Can you do that for me? Come on, once upon a time . . ."

"Mmmm." Grandpa closes his eyes, asleep or close to it.

"No," I say, touching his shoulder. "No, wake up! I've got to hear the end of the story!"

"Carol!" Dad barks. "Enough!"

Lu whimpers, disturbed by our tense words. Dad drags me into the hall. "What is wrong with you?"

I slump against the wall. "It's just . . . I never got to hear the end of the story." *And Serge looks an inch from death,* I add silently, *and I can't bear it if the ending dies with him.*

Dad pinches the bridge of his nose. "The one about the village that chopped the tree down?"

"How did you know?" I say, amazed.

He laughs. "What, you think you're the first one to hear it? *Papá* told it to me every night when I was a kid. The tree, and the bees, and the lake . . ."

I'm dumbfounded. "I thought . . . Maybe his dementia . . ."

"Dementia has done a lot of damage," Dad says, "but he's always spun a good yarn."

"I just wanted Grandpa to tell me the ending," I say.

"I'll tell you how it ends," he says.

But I don't want to hear the ending from Dad. I want to hear the ending from Grandpa. I straighten. "Would you tell me a different story?"

Dad raises his eyebrows.

"What happened between you and Grandpa?"

"Carol . . ." He takes a deep, cleansing breath, watching me the whole time. "Okay. It's probably time you knew. When *Mamá* was—"

"No," I say. "Once upon a time . . ."

He nods. "All right, all right. Once upon a time . . ."

"There was a tree," I finish.

"A tree stump," he corrects.

19

Once upon a time, there was a tree stump. An old man sat on the stump with more wrinkles in his face than there were cracks in the dirt. He looked at the bleak land around him and sipped his water. It tasted like the metal barrels that now held the water. He was always dry in the drought. Even his bones were dried out like jerky.

He whittled a block of wood, eyes following the headlights that pulled in the driveway. A white car, with blue and red lights on the top: the police. Again.

A sheriff stepped out of the car, and the old man took his time crossing the pasture to reach him.

"Buenas noches, Sergio," the sheriff said. "How's the night out here in no-man's-land?"

"Hot." Sergio waited. The sheriff always asked about the weather, and Sergio always answered with the bare truth. Weather was hotter than hell. Always.

"Found something of yours trespassing in Sumpter's Gulch." The sheriff opened the back door of the car. "Come on out, Raúl. Time to face the music."

A teenager in a flannel shirt climbed out and smoothed his black hair. "Thanks for the ride home, Sparky. Same time next week?"

The sheriff chomped his gum. "You pull this kind of stunt after next week, and I'll be dropping your butt off at the jail, not home with Daddy. I know you have a birthday coming up. The big eighteen."

The old man waited some more. This part was always the same, too. The sheriff coerced Raúl to confess the details of his misbehavior, then Raúl made some smart comment that stayed just on this side of appropriate. Finally, the sheriff peeled away, kicking dust all over the pasture.

It didn't matter what Raúl had been doing. For the old man, these nights blended together in one word: disappointment.

"Help me with the sheep," he said to his son, and tucked his whittling knife in his pocket.

"Sparky's got a real power trip going." Raúl ran to keep up with the old man, who headed toward the barn. "We weren't doing anything illegal."

"Trespassing is illegal." The old man felt like he had said these lines a hundred times; he wearied of them before they even escaped his mouth.

"But we weren't trespassing."

"Who's 'we'?" his father asked, barely interested.

"Me. Jacob. Neil."

The usual suspects, the old man thought. They were the last sort of boys he wanted his son hanging around.

"To trespass," Raúl said, "you have to set foot on private property. Technically, we didn't set foot in the gulch."

Sergio coughed.

"Honest," Raúl said. "We were in the tree the whole time. Above the gulch." He smiled at his own cleverness. *"Sparky's trying to get us back for last week, when he thought we got into the school trash. We told him it was probably coyotes, but he doesn't believe us."*

Sergio opened the barn doors, and sheep trudged out.

"You're not saying anything," Raúl said.

"What is there to say, Raúl?" Sergio sighed. *"Every week you sneak away from the ranch. Every week a sheriff brings you home. You're as predictable as the stars. Predictable as death."*

Raúl stared at the old man, at the mouth that always curved down, at the skin that was lumpy from bee stings that never healed properly, at the electric-blue eyes that looked straight through him. He hated this place, his dry, boring home. He hated his father, who looked so much older than his friends' fathers. Or even their grandfathers.

Sergio was right. Raúl ran off every chance he got. Papá never let him leave. Not for public school, not for a minimum-wage teenager job, not for a date. Raúl's friends could only scrape up enough gas money to pick him up once or twice a week.

He'd never been desperate enough to run all the way to civilization on foot, but tonight might be the night. He'd only been home five minutes, and he already couldn't breathe.

"The officer is right," the old man said. "If you try these shenanigans after your birthday, you go right to jail. The world treats you like a man when you're eighteen, even if you still act like a boy."

"When does Mamá get home?" Raúl muttered.

"Who's to say?" the old man said.

Raúl scoffed. "Then I'm going to Neil's. Call me when she's back."

"You're not going anywhere." The old man's face was a blank sheet of paper. "You're grounded."

"Grounded?" Raúl clenched and unclenched his jaw.

"You insist on acting like a child, so I'll treat you like a child." The old man could barely look at his son—too much of his wife peered out through Raúl's eyes.

"You can't ground me," Raúl said. "I'll be eighteen in a week."

"Then you're grounded for a week."

Raúl kicked the barn wall. "You can't trap me here forever."

"Don't talk to me about forever!" Sergio boomed. "You don't know what forever means."

"Oh, don't even start with your weird tree stories."

"Those stories are your heritage," Sergio said. "Your roots, Raúl. You don't remember. You've run away so many times, your memory's lost in the desert."

"They're just stupid bedtime stories!" Raúl said. "I'm not a little kid anymore, Papá!"

He ran into the ranch house and threw his belongings into the suitcases Mamá had given him. If people's yells had distinct flavors, Papá's voice would taste like onions plucked before they were ripe, boiled in bitterness, and left in the refrigerator.

Mamá only yelled in excitement, never anger. Her yells would taste like stars and jelly beans, ones that wouldn't stop jumping in your mouth. He adored his mom, even though she was always traveling. Mamá was warm like sunshine—no, she was the sun, and Raúl was happiest when he was orbiting around her.

But he couldn't stay. Not a day longer. He'd miss Mamá, but no one would understand his need to leave better than her.

When the old man came in, he found his son latching his luggage, his drawers and closet empty. "Where are you going?"

"Anywhere," Raúl spat, "that isn't here."

Silence, and an angry stare-down between father and son.

"What do you think is out there?" the old man asked. "You think life's perfect everywhere else? You think it's safe?"

Raúl knew what was out there. Books. Paintings. Girls. Fast cars. Birds other than eagles and vultures, animals other than sheep and rattlers. His shelves were lined with souvenirs from Mamá's travels: Santiago, Madagascar, shiny New York City, snowy Alaska . . .

If he opened his mouth right now, horrible things would spill out, things he'd wanted to say to the old man for seventeen years. If he said those things, there would be a hole the size of the Grand Canyon between them.

"Everything," he said. "Everything is out there."

"You're grounded," the old man reminded his son.

"No! You can't keep me here!" Raúl's own yell tasted like rotten bell peppers and bleach. He pounded his fists into his suitcases, and he spoke the magic words: "You can't even keep Mamá here for a full week! She's too desperate to get away from here. To get away from you!" Those words had rolled around in his mind for years. He had been saving them up like coins, and they came out as bullets. Raúl didn't care; he wanted them to hurt.

Sergio quivered. He could see the rolling, raging lake inside Raúl. All that passion and fire should have reminded Sergio of Rosa, but instead, Sergio looked at his son, and it was like staring into a mirror.

"You can't keep Mom here, and you can't keep me here, either." Raúl grabbed all his bags at once, a bouquet of luggage.

Sergio tried to stand in the way, but Raúl laughed and dodged him easily; the old man moved like he was a thousand years old.

A door slammed, and Raúl ran into open, lonely desert, never looking back.

Once upon a time, Sergio let the quiet wash around him—how still the house was and, without Raúl here, how much bigger.

How much time passed? An hour, maybe? He refused to wear a watch, to measure time in that newfangled way.

Then he heard the engine of a car. She was home.

The old man walked outside, trying to set his face back to neutral. Rosa had no patience for his fights with Raúl. She thought her son should be free to come and go as he pleased. She had a selective memory, too. Had she forgotten about Carolina and the Father? Had she forgotten about death?

She grinned brighter than the white desert sun during solstice. "Hola, Sergio!" she cried, running to him. Her hugs still smelled like honey and vanilla. They held their faces close together.

"Where are you coming from this time? Somewhere new, or somewhere old?" Sergio whispered.

"Very old," she said. "The oldest. The Cradle of Life in Ethiopia."

This, too, was a routine conversation. Sergio didn't care where she traveled to, not really, and Rosa had given up long ago trying to convince him that the world was fascinating. But it was routine, and such routines were difficult to break after marriages as long as theirs.

"Are you wearing your bracelet?" he asked.

She held out her wrist, the bracelet smartly tied. "You're a worrywart," she said. "Always fretting."

Suddenly her smile turned into a gasp, and she bent over, arms holding her waist, as if something had snapped in her spine.

"What is it?" Sergio grabbed her.

Rosa closed her mouth, then rolled her eyes to the sky. She collapsed in the dirt, limbs buckling like a dropped marionette.

"Rosa!" Sergio made her a pillow of his elbow and held her there.

She stared at the sky as if she were on another planet. "Something's . . . happening. Something's *wrong." With obvious effort, she turned her head toward the house. "Where's my Raúl?"*

"Raúl is . . . gone." Sergio hated that word. "I'll get the truck right now and find him."

"No." Rosa coughed, and blood splattered the earth. She looked at her husband. "Stay with me."

Fear. He never thought he'd see fear in those brave black eyes. He muttered prayers in Spanish under his breath while she coughed and coughed, the sounds of drowning echoing off the ridge.

"So this is how it all ends," Rosa whispered.

"So you want the ending, the real ending?" Dad's eyes lock on to mine. "The real ending is death."

"I thought Grandma Rosa got cancer," I say.

"She did," Dad says, and his sentences are tethered inside him; he has to force them out.

But I push. "I don't get it. What did Grandpa do?"

"She got cancer, but *Papá* wouldn't take her in. A doctor came every once in a while and checked on her, but *Papá* always refused further care. He wouldn't let her leave the house."

So that's it, then. The feud is because Dad thinks

Grandpa's responsible for Grandma Rosa's death. He thinks Grandpa let her die.

"*Mamá* took another ten years to die, and *Papá* grew more and more scared, and more and more protective. She was finally stuck at the ranch, and she hated it. I came back to see her as much as I could, even though *Papá* and I wanted to strangle each other." He shakes his head slowly, over and over. "He trapped her there, to keep her safe, but she still died. She died because he wouldn't let her leave."

"What about the tree?" I whisper.

"What about it?"

"Does it ever grow back?"

"That tree only belongs in a story, Carol, a made-up story about a world that never existed, a past that never happened," Dad says.

"I know," I mumble.

"Grandpa's stories were ones he made up to make losing her easier." His bottom lip trembles, and he holds my hands like they're anchors. "What story am I going to tell, huh? To make losing *him* easier?"

Before I can answer, he straightens, wipes his nose, and says, "Oh, kid. Let's go home."

20

I measure time in school supplies. A binder, six pencils, four billion sheets of college-ruled paper, and an eraser shaped like a watermelon.

I measure time in glances from Alta. She looks at Grandma Rosa's bracelet on my wrist and throws stones with her eyes.

On my first day of seventh grade, I walk with my friends to school, the four of us wearing our messenger bags.

Mine digs into my shoulder. "This thing's giving me welts." I rub my red skin.

"But they're so cute," Manny says.

Why did I agree to this silly bag? I spent forty bucks on it, and now I'm wishing I had my ratty old backpack. At least those straps are comfortable.

The morning sky is pale blue, so watered down it's mostly white. The lack of color makes me ache for the ranch. At the ranch the sunrise would be striped like a bowl of rainbow sherbet, and when the light hit the ridge, the sand would sparkle.

I half limp, lugging my bag, to catch up with my friends. "We're kind of ridiculous," I say.

The three others stare at me, as if I shouted swear words.

"Admit it. These don't really work so well as school-bags."

Gabby clutches hers defensively, even as pencils spill out the front pocket.

"What do you suggest?" Manny says. She lifts her nose in the air, and I almost laugh. She thinks I'm challenging her, but I'm not; I just really hate carrying this bag.

"I should have bought snake-stomping boots," I say.

"Snake-stomping boots?" Manny repeats. "Carol, what are you even talking about?"

"My grandpa—" I'm about to explain Grandpa's

boots to my confused friends when there's a sound, one I haven't heard in days, not since we left the ranch.

A bee, buzzing around my head. I search for it in the air, and even though I can't spot it, I hear it.

I'm sure I look insane—demented—as I spin in a slow circle on a stranger's lawn, searching for the bee. "Are you okay?" Manny asks.

The buzzing fades, lost among the noise of city birds chirping and cars driving. I breathe out and let it go—let it all go. The bee. The ranch, lost forever to some buyer. Grandpa, lost to the Seville and sedatives—and to dementia. This is junior high, the moment I've been waiting for all summer. I've got Manny as my locker partner. New school clothes. New schedule. New Carol.

"I'm okay," I say. "And I love our bags. I do. I just have to get used to the strap."

We reach the school and find our homeroom, and my friends chat with our classmates, but I have nothing to contribute to the conversations. No gossip to share, since I was gone all summer. I'm as still as the desk I'm sitting at.

There's a letdown when our teacher's just a normal teacher. We're in junior high now; we're supposed to get young, good-looking teachers who wear silly ties and read us books for teenagers but still let us into the candy stash. This guy's hair is snowy white, and his tie is plain blue. MR. ADAIR is written on the whiteboard behind him.

"When I call your name," he says, "stand up and tell us how you spent your summer. If there's a nickname you prefer to go by, let me know."

A report on our summer — how original.

"I'm Gabriela, but I go by Gabby," Gabby says. Mr. Adair makes a note. "This summer, I stayed home, and hung out with friends. We had lots of sleepovers."

Gabby also spent the summer getting taller. I can't stop gawking at her legs — when did they get so long?

"I'm Sofía, but I go by Sofie." Mr. Adair makes a note. "This summer . . ."

My ears shut off, muffle all sound. Sofie's always been pretty, but the new eyeliner she wears makes her look like a real junior high girl. No — she looks like Alta. I'm like a little girl in her mom's lipstick.

My friends are blooming into trees, and I'm still just a seed.

It's my turn, and suddenly I'm aware of a still-healing

scrape on my knee that makes me look like a clumsy little kid.

"I'm Carolina," I say, and stare at my messenger bag dangling off my chair, "but I go by Carol." Mr. Adair makes a note.

Caro-leeen-a. Caro-leeen-a.

"I spent my summer at my grandpa's ranch."

My bottom half thuds into my seat, relieved to have the spotlight off me, but the teacher doesn't let me get away so easily.

"What does your grandfather keep?"

"Sheep," I say, "but he can't take care of them anymore."

"Takes hard work to raise sheep," Mr. Adair says. "I'll bet you learned a lot from him."

I nod, and Mr. Adair prompts, "Such as?"

How can I answer this? I'm just now unraveling the hundreds of things I learned from Grandpa.

I look out the big square window while I think.

It's raining.

Navy and gray clouds stain the sky, and the rain falls like someone turned on a faucet. "Rain," I say, and point. The class looks, unimpressed.

"Sorry," I murmur, trying to cleanse my cluttered mind.

"I haven't seen rain in two months. There's a drought at my grandpa's ranch. It hasn't rained in a hundred years."

"The southwestern desert?" Mr. Adair asks, and I nod. "I'll bet your grandpa's happy the drought's finally over."

"What do you mean?"

"It's been raining there all morning. Drought's over just like that." He snaps his fingers.

I forget I'm in school, forget that the other kids are staring at me like a cactus grew out of my ear.

No rain for a hundred years.

Caro-leeen-a.

The teacher calls the next kid on his roll. I pretend to sharpen a pencil while Eduardo, call me Eddie, shares about his summer at camp, and I watch the rain drizzle down the windowpane.

No one else gapes at it like me. I trace the dark clouds as far as I can see them. Rain's common in Albuquerque. But it's raining at the ranch? After a hundred years? The drought is over, just like that?

I think of the bees landing on the seed, the water they carried, one by one.

When the teacher's back is turned, I pull out my

phone and Google it. He's right—the drought is over. Flash-flood warnings in southern New Mexico.

Did the bees really bring back the rain?

Something flies past the window.

A bee. It feels like an answer: yes.

My heart flutters the rest of the day.

Manny sits with Sofie, Gabby, and me at lunch. The entire cafeteria is whirring with whispers at this new social development, but I'm still rain-shocked.

"I just can't believe it's raining," I say.

My friends don't even try to mask their boredom with this topic. "So what?" Gabby says. "It rains all the time."

"You heard the teacher," Manny says to me. "The drought's over. You should be happy."

"I am happy." Then why is my heart pounding so hard, it feels like it'll burst from my chest? Like something strange or wonderful or terrible—or all of these—is about to happen?

When they ask if I want to come to Manny's after school, I make an excuse. "Uh, Mom wants us to have family time," I fib.

"You were with your family all summer," Manny says.

"Yeah, come on, we didn't see you for two months!" Gabby says, and I almost give in. I *did* miss my friends. But Grandpa's rumpled face flashes through my mind.

"I really can't, sorry." I push my lunch tray to the center of the table. "Who wants my cookie?"

When school is done, my friends walk me home, but before they can invite me over again, I run across our slick grass. When a bee buzzes in my ear, I don't flick it away.

Alta's powder-blue car is parked sideways in our driveway, like she was in too much of a hurry to straighten it out. I guess Alta won the battle of the convertible.

"Mom!" I cry before the front door is even open all the way. "You won't believe it! It's raining!"

No one's in the living room.

I take the stairs two at a time and find Mom in her bathroom, putting makeup on. Lu's reading a stack of board books. Mom and Dad's TV is on, but no one watches.

"Hi, hon," Mom says, widening her eyes for the mascara wand. "How was your first day?"

First day?

Oh. School. "Good. Fine," I say. "But Mom—"

"No, come on," she says, more energy in her voice than there ever was at the ranch. "I need more than 'fine.' Your first day of junior high! Was it as bad as you thought it would be?"

I think for a minute.

But it's not my first day of junior high that I think of; it's my first day at the ranch. When Lu went missing and all the dangerous things at the ranch rolled through my head like a horror movie: *What if he drowns in a trough, swallows a rusty nail, gets attacked by a sheep or a coyote or a hawk?*

For months I've had every dangerous junior high school scenario on a loop in my mind, too: *What if I get lost? What if my teachers are mean, or I don't understand the homework assignment, or my locker gets stuck and I'm late to class?*

But today I didn't worry about any of that. I didn't even think of those things once. My mind was in other places. It was twenty minutes away, in an assisted-living facility, wondering if they served lunch the same time my school did. It was three hours south, wondering if that little seed was drinking rain. I don't think I've gotten braver; I think I've just found other things to be scared of than tripping in the lunchroom or walking down the wrong hallway.

Things like a lonely grandfather who still has a story to finish.

"School," I say, "is going to be just fine."

Mom smiles her famously melting smile. "Well, Alta's on a date with Marco, and I'm running some errands with Lu. You'll have the house to yourself for a while. I'm sure you have some homework."

"Where's Dad?" I ask.

"Work," she says. "He'll be home late."

"Mom," I try again. "Look, it's raining. Isn't that amazing?"

She glances out the window, the rain still coming down in buckets. "So?"

"And it's raining at the ranch," I tell her. "It's been raining all morning. The drought's over!" I wait for this announcement to rock her core, for her to gasp, sigh, maybe drop her makeup bag.

"Oh, yeah, I saw that on the news," she says, pulling on a blouse. "Now that's some cruel timing, isn't it? Right after Grandpa moved?"

"Can we go see him?" I ask.

She nods. "Of course."

"Now?" I hold my breath.

She scrunches up her eyebrows. "What's the rush?"

"It's raining," I say, but Mom still looks confused. I'll

299

have to connect the dots for her. "I want to make sure Serge sees the rain."

"I'm sure he can; he has windows," Mom says.

"He was a zombie last time we were there!" I say. "What if he can't get to the window by himself?"

"He's got nurses."

This conversation is treading water, about to go under. "I just need to make sure."

Mom sighs. "Not tonight, hon."

"But the rain!" I say. "What if it's not raining tomorrow?"

"Saturday," she promises.

"But that's too far away!"

"Carol! It's a school night, plus I have errands to run." She picks up Lu, and I follow them downstairs. "Look," she says, by way of consolation. "Get some homework done. Relax. You've got a nice quiet house to yourself. We'll be back before dinner."

I must be frowning still, because she gives me a little hug and says, "Why don't you try calling the Seville? You can talk with Serge as long as you like. Tell him it's raining. The number's on the fridge." She and Lu leave.

I turn off the TV. The house feels even emptier than

it is. Every room is an echo chamber for my unspoken thoughts. Mom couldn't have been more off—I don't want to be alone. I want to be with Grandpa. After about an hour of homework, I try calling Dad to see if he'll take me to see Grandpa. But he doesn't answer.

Maybe I am being dramatic. Maybe I should just call. I dial the Seville's number. A nurse with a sickly-sugary voice connects me to room 104, but the phone just rings and rings, buzzing and buzzing, until the nurse picks back up and says, "Sorry, dear, he's not picking up."

Of course he isn't, I think. *He's probably still zonked out, asleep with his eyes open, sedated past the point of even knowing what a phone is.*

I wish I could be there right now. He needs to know it's raining at the ranch. After a lifetime of drought, Grandpa needs to know the bees brought back the rain.

I call again and again and again, until the nurse asks me to stop calling, please, and I hang up, defeated. I try to get lost in my pile of classroom outlines and first homework assignments, but my mind won't concentrate on anything but rain.

I close my eyes and wish, with the force of a thousand bees, that I could find a way to get to Grandpa.

But it doesn't happen.

Slowly, the house fills back up. Dad comes home first. He takes a shower and turns on a baseball game. Then Mom and Lu, bearing Chinese food. Alta trudges in an hour past her curfew, eyes slitted, snapping at anyone who talks to her but pouting when no one asks her what's wrong.

I fall asleep disappointed, hoping I'll dream of bees.

But my dreams are empty.

The rain wakes me.

It's one in the morning, and it still hasn't let up. I watch out the window. The rain *plink-plink*s onto the windshields of the cars below—Dad's pickup truck, the minivan, and finally Alta's little speck of a car, parked crooked at the end of the driveway.

The night is black, but the raindrops glisten silver as they fall. I wonder if Grandpa can see the same thing.

I go downstairs for a drink of water and wish I had stayed in bed, because I'm about to do something crazy.

Alta's car keys are on the counter.

21

An ideal time to practice driving is about one in the morning, on the highway leading to the south part of Albuquerque. There's almost no one else on the road, so you can just glide along at your own pace, alone. Which is a good thing, since I've never driven with any other cars around.

Today—or yesterday, I guess, technically—Mr. Adair made me stand in front of the class and say my name. If I could stand in front of my class now, I would say different things. I am different. On the inside.

I'm now the kind of person who sneaks out in the middle of the night and steals her sister's car to tell her sick grandfather about a rainstorm, shattering probably a hundred laws: underage driving, running away, car theft.

I can't think about it—it makes my hands shaky, and I need full concentration to drive.

Rain slaps the car, and after a few failed attempts, I crank up the windshield wipers.

Driving Alta's car is way different from the truck. The truck is a beast, and you have to force it to succumb to your will. Alta's car is smoother, touchier. The slightest tap on the gas, and it takes off. It's a car that does what it wants. Not that I would expect anything different of a car owned by Alta.

A jackrabbit dodges the driver's-side tire, and I jerk the wheel in surprise. It takes me ten whole seconds to steer back into my own lane. Sweat collects on my forehead.

A car whizzes past, headlights blinding me. "Oh, please, oh, please," I whisper, clutching the wheel. I keep the car straight, muscles like steel, and try not to think about how crazy this is.

Finally, after what seems like hours later, I pull into the Seville.

I stop the car behind one of the boxy vans in the

parking lot. Parking takes a minute to figure out, but when I'm sure that the car won't roll away, I get out and pocket the keys—this will all be for nothing if I get murdered by Alta for trashing her car. Going through the front lobby is out of the question; visiting hours ended over four hours ago, at nine PM.

I run around the building until I find the back door, amazed that I actually made it here, that I'll actually get to see Grandpa—until I see the number keypad, the same number keypad that locks the front entrance.

Of *course* they lock the back door, too! Otherwise, the old people would split in no time.

What was the number I watched Dad enter just two days ago? I try combo after combo, but nothing makes the light on the number pad flash green and the doors slide open. I rack my brain, but all that comes to mind is a mosaic of numbers from my first day of school: mine and Manny's locker combination, the numbers of my different classrooms . . .

Rain pelts my back and soaks my hair. This was a stupid idea. I should head home now, before anyone wakes up and realizes I'm gone.

Just when I'm about to trudge back to the car,

defeated, a flash comes to me: Dad, staring at his phone, punching in the code with the rough fingers of someone who's been working all summer on a sheep ranch.

I put in the numbers: 1412.

The sliding doors open, and I slip into the hallway. I can't believe it's this easy. No blaring alarms. No flashing lights. No armed security guards escorting me off the premises. But even though I'm grateful, I can't help feeling annoyed on behalf of the residents. Is this what their life savings are paying for? A measly four-digit code is all that stands between them and middle-of-the-night burst-ins from anxious granddaughters?

The storm rumbles, and I jump and give a tiny squeal. One more number to remember: my grandpa's room number. I tiptoe until an intersection of hallways looks familiar and see his door, room 104.

A clipboard next to the door has his name on it and a printout of his schedule for the next day. Wow, they schedule everything for him now, I realize. When he watches TV, when he showers, when he eats, when he pees. Everything's scheduled . . . except me.

Footsteps.

Someone's walking down the hall. I tuck myself

around a corner and watch a nurse emerge from the lobby. Could she possibly have heard the noise I made? I imagine having to explain myself to the nurse, and for a second, I'm scared stiff. What was I thinking, coming here like I did? I could have died on the drive here. And when Mom and Dad and Alta find out what happened, I'll be as good as dead. I should call Mom, confess to stealing the car, and tell her where to pick me up.

But then a familiar buzz sounds near my ear.

"I wondered when you'd show up," I whisper. A bee flies around my head twice, then buzzes down the hall. As though I told it what to do, it heads straight for the nurse and buzzes in her face. She tries to flick it away, but the bee corrals her back toward the lobby.

Seizing my chance, I turn the corner and creak open Grandpa's door.

I'm surprised to find him out of his bed, and awake. He's staring at the TV, which isn't even on. His wicker chair's been replaced by a maroon recliner, its cushions nearly swallowing his frail body. The curtains at his window are shut. Have they been like that all day?

"Grandpa?" I whisper.

But he doesn't move.

"Grandpa, it's me, Carol," I say, a little louder. "I'm sorry to come so late, I just . . . I couldn't sleep."

He's still a wide-eyed corpse, as flat as the desert horizon. I have to double-check that he's breathing, but yes, his chest rises and falls in slow motion.

I walk right past him and throw open his curtains. "Look, Grandpa. It's raining. And guess what else? It's raining at the ranch! Drought's over." My words flow out smoothly, though I'm a knot of nerves.

That burgundy wool blanket is tucked over his legs. His wedding blanket, I realize. The gift from Rosa to her groom on the night they got married.

I shake my head. That was from the story. I'm no better than Grandpa, losing sight of what's real and what's make-believe.

Right as I think this, I see his hands, splayed open, palms facing up. I remember when he slashed his hand in the closet—I *know* he cut it; the memory of his blood makes me queasy even now. His hand, sliced like a potato, and seconds later, clean. Healed.

The gift of the tree . . . What other explanation could there be?

No. No. It was only a story.

But the story is the reason I'm here.

I close my eyes and tilt my head. "It sounds like bees," I whisper, and I'm not exaggerating. The pitter-patter of rain against the window could be an army of bees, droning as they fly. "One hundred years of drought, and Dad made you leave right before it ended," I say, eyes misting over.

Why is Grandpa so quiet? Why isn't he looking up at me with those magnetic eyes, echoing me: *Caro-leeen-a, did you say it's raining at the ranch?* The sedatives have worn off—he's not pale anymore, not stuck in his bed, like he was two days ago—so why is he just sitting there, barely even blinking?

Suddenly, fear trickles down my back like an ice cube. Maybe I'm too late, and he's already forgotten everything—the ranch and the drought and the story about the tree.

Maybe he's already forgotten me.

Another savior bee flies to the rescue. It hovers between us, buzzing loudly against the backdrop of rainfall. I point triumphantly to the bee. "Grandpa, they follow me! Just like they followed Rosa. In the story."

I don't know whether it was my words or the bee,

but Grandpa finally smiles, his eyes lighting up, blue ringed with gold. His voice is crackly, the first words spoken to me—or maybe to anyone—since the ranch: "Take me home, Caro-leeen-a."

"Take you . . . home?" I shake my head. "Grandpa, this is your home now."

"I want to see it," he says.

"Maybe in the morning." I hear myself say this and cringe; I sound exactly like my parents, my wonderful parents who just don't understand.

"Take me home, Caro-leeen-a," Grandpa says again, and sits up with strength I didn't know he had.

Home.

An idea is flooding my mind, a big one, taller than the mesas.

Things are only impossible if you stop to think about them.

And so, I don't think. "Grandpa, listen," I say. "I can take you home, home to the ranch, but we have to go right now." I look around. "Can the window open?"

He shakes his head, and his sedation shakes off him like water. "This place is a box. Sealed like a coffin. Codes to get in and codes to get out."

"The code to the doors?" I say. "I know it! It's one-four-one-two."

He looks at me like I've just solved a calculus problem.

"How else do you think I got in here?" I say.

Grandpa smiles, then gives me instructions. "Go out the back door and pull the car up as close as you can, *chiquita*. And make sure no one sees you."

"What, are you going to make a run for it?" I say, incredulous.

"Just be waiting, Caro-leeen-a," he says, and pulls on his boots. He's so frail, but his snake-stomping boots make him seem stronger, taller.

I sneak down the hallway and out the back door, into the rain, palms sweating. With less difficulty than before, I bring Alta's car to the curb and wait.

But waiting means thinking—and thinking means doubting. How exactly is Grandpa getting out? And did I really let a dementia-ridden old man convince me to drive my sister's stolen car three hours south in the pouring rain? I must be crazy myself.

The car clock says 1:45. If we get right on the road, we can be at the ranch by sunrise. I wince; it'll be a miracle if I can get Alta's car back before anyone notices it's gone.

Don't think. Just do.

Grandpa suddenly looms from the darkness of the doorway, like a ship out of fog. He hobbles on his stiff, ancient legs, and I'm reminded of Inés, the ancient, magic dog, hobbling down the porch steps on that first day at the ranch.

An alarm rings inside the Seville, red emergency lights blinking along the windows. My heartbeat picks up the pace.

"What happened?" I cry as Grandpa climbs into the passenger seat and slams the door. "Why are there alarms?"

"Everyone has to stay in their boxes," he says. "Now go."

I squeal Alta's car through the rainy parking lot— the alarms are still audible from the main road. "What happened?" I repeat. "Did you forget the code?"

Grandpa says nothing, his face turned toward the window, staring at the rain.

Even though I know it's not his fault, even though I know that his mind is slippery enough to forget even the most important of details, I slap my hand against the steering wheel in frustration. "How could you forget it? It was only four little numbers! Now they're going to know you're gone."

What on earth have I done? Now there's no chance our middle-of-the-night escapade will remain a secret.

As if on cue, my phone buzzes in my pocket. And even without looking, I know it's Mom calling.

I pull over, fumbling to turn the hazard lights on before answering.

"H-hello?" I answer.

"Carol! Oh, thank God—she's okay, she's alive." In the background, Dad sighs with relief. My guts twist with guilt.

"Where are you?" Mom shouts. "Is Serge with you? We got a call from the Seville. Oh, Carol, please tell me you didn't take Alta's car!"

"Mom, we're fine, we're safe."

"Carolina, tell us where you are, right now. I'm coming to get you."

I consider. I'm already busted. Grounded, at least, but possibly—and justifiably—in enough trouble to become the stuff of legend in junior high schools around New Mexico. How much worse trouble could I be in, really?

"Carol?" Mom says. "What's happening? Where are you?"

I feel awful as I do this, but I mutter, "I'm fine. Be home soon," and shut my phone off completely.

I steer back onto the highway and drive. When we pass out of the city limits, the radio crackles into static, and we're left with silence brewing, fears bubbling. I speak only once we are through the purple, rain-stained mountains, once alarms and civilization and buildings fade away.

"How does it end?" I say. "The story."

Grandpa's hands fly to cover his eyes. "Death," he says, just like Dad said when he told me his version of the ending. "It ends with death. Rosa knew it, and now I do, too. There's no other way."

"No," I say, tears prickling. "It can't end like that. You said it yourself. Stories don't end—they have new beginnings. We've got to find the new beginning, Grandpa."

"All things end," he says. "I am afraid of endings. Stories, lives . . . It all ends."

My knuckles bulge, I'm gripping the steering wheel so hard. "Of course you're afraid," I say. "What's scarier than death?"

"Rosa was . . . was not afraid of the ending. She was not afraid to go. To die," he says, with some difficulty. "Me, I feel like I've been dying for a thousand years."

I force my concentration back to the road, but Grandpa's words stay with me the rest of the drive.

The rain gets worse as we near the ranch, heavy splotches thudding Alta's windshield.

"It's really coming down," I whisper. I try to slow down through the puddles, but we slide no matter what I do.

"A hundred years." My grandfather is reverent as he surveys the familiar land.

In the muted light of the rainstorm, the ranch is gray and faded, like a photograph still developing, a filter of dust and water.

I'm about to pull off the dirt road and head for the driveway when it happens.

We hit a slick patch, and the car gets a mind of its

own. It spins like a bumper car, rain pelting the vehicle in loud thumps. I can't tell if I'm screaming, or if it's just noise in my head.

Grandpa claws at the dashboard, but his fingers are too weak, and still we're spinning, spinning. Two rotations we've made, and my head is permanently cranked to the right with the force of the curve.

I clench the wheel, wanting control. But grasping the wheel forces the car out of its graceful spin, which was coming to a slow end. Instead, we tip over.

We tumble over, so we're upside down, then we're right side up. Now we're going over again, and my hair's in my face so I can't see my grandpa. I reach for his arm. It's mostly dangling flesh, but I grasp it. We're upside down, hanging by our seat belts.

We rotate once more, thud, and land. I look out the window.

"Oh," I murmur.

The car is in a lake.

A green-glass lake.

22

"Are you okay?" I gasp.

"Did you bring . . . my oxygen?" Grandpa says.

I crumple. That's why he looks so vulnerable to me: his face is missing its oxygen tubes. "No."

Alta's car is half driven into the water, the lake's surface washing over the hood. I put it in reverse and try to back out onto the dirt road, but the car growls at me and doesn't budge.

"Okay, let's stay calm," I say, more for myself than for Grandpa.

I turn the car off, and the clunking sound in the engine dies. Alta's going to hang me, if we ever get out of here. I'll be babysitting and lifeguarding the rest of my life to pay her back.

I wish she were here, and the thought takes me by surprise.

I undo both our seat belts, Grandpa wheezing beside me. The doors won't open, no matter how hard I try—the lake's water pushes against them.

"Hold on," I say. "I'm going to open the top, then we'll climb out." I flip the switch to unleash the convertible top. Instantly, we're soaked by the rain, which falls in drops as fat as pebbles. I scramble onto the back end of the car. "Come on, Grandpa!" I cry over the noise of the downpour. "Grab my hand!"

He reaches out a shaky hand, and, slick as it is, I grip it and yank with everything I've got. Slowly, clumsily, he wriggles out of the car and collapses next to me on top of the trunk. We turn and stare at the impossible.

A lake. A pale-green lake, clear as glass, where the ridge dips down, filling the pasture and kissing the driveway, the water rolling in the windy storm. Across the water, a few sheep are bunched on the porch, terrified. I wonder where the rest of them got to and hope they're okay.

"Grandpa, what's going on?" I say as we slide off the back of the car. "How'd this lake get here? It's only been raining for a day." Goose pimples the size of speed bumps break out all over my skin as I pull him to the shore.

He points to the bracelet tight on my wrist. "Aren't you glad I made you put it on this morning, Rosa?"

"I'm not Rosa—I'm Carol," I say, my gut twisting. *Don't zone out on me now, Grandpa!*

"You should never be without it, Rosa."

"I'm Carol—Carol, your granddaughter," I say, but my voice melts in the noise of the storm.

This is too much, too much, too much. Grandpa needs help, and I can't do it. I shouldn't have brought him here.

I reach in my pocket for my phone, but it's gone. "Crap!" I cry, patting myself down head to toe. It must have fallen out when we waded to the shore.

"Grandpa, stay right here!" I say, grabbing his hands and making him look right at me. "I'll be right back. Just don't go anywhere, okay?" He nods, seeming to understand, so I run through the rain and mud into the ranch house and find Grandpa's old phone, the one with the curlicue wire, on the base attached to the wall. I cross my fingers that it hasn't been shut off yet and lift the phone to my ear.

A weird buzz comes out of the speaker — is that normal for old phones? I dial 911 and hold my breath, staring at the place on the linoleum where Inés died . . .

"Nine-one-one, what's your emergency?" The response is tinny and far away, but I do a happy dance at the sound of another human.

"I'm in the rainstorm, and we need help! The car crashed . . . and the lake, and —" I realize, as I'm speaking, how much word salad is pouring from my mouth.

"I'm losing you, sweetie." I can't tell if it's a man or a woman speaking to me; the connection is too weak. "Are — there — tell — name —" The person's words flutter in and out, and then there is a click and the phone goes silent.

"Hello? Hello?" I dial 911 a few more times, but nothing happens. Finally, I run back outside. I've got to get Grandpa to safety somehow. He's got to come out of his dementia slip; I need his help. I have no idea what to do.

Grandpa stands on the shoreline, his bare feet sunk

in the mud. What happened to his snake-stomping boots?

"Stay out of the water," I direct him, rushing closer. I squint—what's he pushing into the water?

A boat. A hand-carved wooden boat.

"Grandpa, what is this? Where did this come from?"

He pats the boat's side. "It's Father Alejandro's boat. Remember? It's still seaworthy. Come, Rosa. Hop in."

Now I'm the one who needs oxygen. I'm woozy, raindrops spiraling. "I'm Carol!" I say, my voice cracking. "Carol, your granddaughter! Grandpa, we need to get inside, out of the rain."

But he clambers into the boat and shoves off with a paddle.

"No, no, no!" I shout, splashing into the lake after him. I grab the side of the boat and haul myself in.

"Where are you taking us?" I ask.

"To the tree!"

The tree. Grandpa thinks the story is real, that it's really happening.

But it can't be real, can it? It's too impossible.

But what about the lake? my brain asks. *What about the boat?*

Grandpa rows us out into the phantom lake. I'm going to call it that, because it doesn't actually exist. I'm hallucinating—I must be. I hit my head when I crashed Alta's car, and now I'm imagining this huge green lake. My hand isn't really in cool water; it's dipping into the sand in the basin. This isn't a boat; it's a rock.

"The bees, Rosa! See?" he cries, pointing up at the rain clouds. "They came back! They brought our lake back to us!"

I was in bed just a few hours ago, wasn't I? Maybe I still am. Maybe this is all just some crazy dream.

The lake's choppy in the storm, and we're halfway across it. Lightning flashes.

In the burst of light, I see a tree. A tall, fat, black tree that's big enough to block out the sun, its outstretched branches crisscrossing like a spider's web.

The lake churns, and I grip the edges of the boat, my stomach carving itself out. "A tree," I whisper. "How . . . ?" I remember the little seed I planted. But it couldn't be that.

Could it?

Is dementia contagious? Maybe Grandpa coughed

out a spore of his dementia and I breathed it in. His story of the lake, the bees, the magic tree that isn't magic . . . it sprouted and grew in my own brain.

Grandpa laughs. "That tree's been there for thousands of years. Since this world was patched and sewn together. And we will never let the tree die again, will we, Rosa? We've come home, and the bees have come home with us!"

"Grandpa, it's Carol! And I think we should head back to—"

To where? To the cold, dark house? To the highway?

I was wrong. So wrong. I should have kept Grandpa at the Seville, where he'd be safe.

I want to laugh at the bitter irony. Grandpa's always been afraid to leave the ranch, but now it's the most dangerous place on earth for him.

As though proving my point, a wave hits.

The boat capsizes, and we plunge into the water—so cold, I ache. All I see is green, and my arms and legs flail until they're senseless. Somehow my head breaks the surface, and I find the boat, clinging to it like a drowning rat. I gulp water, choke, sputter.

"Grandpa?" I scream, but then I spot him. He's on the other side of the boat, trying to hold on to it with slipping hands.

"Hang on!" I swim around and shove him as hard as I can up and into the boat. He flops inside like a fish. I'm still overboard, one arm draped over the boat, trying to catch my breath.

"Rosa," he sputters.

"I'm not Rosa!" I cry. Suddenly I miss my name, my stupid, Spanish name. I want to hear my grandpa call me *Caro-leeen-a,* just like that. I want to wear that name every day. "Grandma Rosa's gone," I say desperately. "She died twelve years ago. Remember?"

His expression doesn't change. "The bees," he says. "The bees."

My frustration rages, despite the icy water. "Caro-leeen-a, Caro-leeen-a!" I say until my throat is raw. Then I say it some more. I'll keep saying it until I break through, until he looks up and sees Carolina, not Rosa.

"We're going to die, Rosa," Grandpa says, and I feel like I've slipped underwater. "But I'm not afraid, because I'm not afraid to live. Not anymore."

"Don't say that!" I choke, my throat slimy with

lake water and snot. "I don't want to die, not here, not like this!"

Another wave scrambles the water, tossing me against the boat. My legs struggle to find the bottom of the lake, but it's too deep.

"I shouldn't have brought us here." I grip the side of the boat and feel a splinter in my palm, one I missed last week when I held on to the porch railing and refused to leave.

The lightning flashes again, and a silhouette of the tree burns into my sight. When I squeeze my eyes shut, I see it still, white tree on black sky.

A wave picks up the boat, and this time it slams against my head. I'm knocked to stars, my brain prickling. I float back in the water, Grandpa and the boat slipping out of my reach.

I drift on waves, lightning flashing, rain still pouring. I could swear I hear buzzing . . .

My back hits something underwater, something hard and scratchy. A tree branch, jutting into the lake. I let it hold me, lie on it like an open palm, and I pray for sleep. I'm so exhausted, so cold.

Beneath me the branch moves. The tree drinks in

the lake water and grows, lifting me, like a hand raising me to the skies. I stay flat on my back, the branch my bed. The only place to look is the sky, and it swirls black and gray.

And gold.

"Bees," I whisper. "Bees."

As the lightning flashes, I see them in the millions. Each bee holds a drop of water, and as they fly, they toss the water into the lake. Drop by drop. *Bzzz, bzzz,* I hear, as I float in the tree.

The bees brought back the rain, just like Grandpa said they would.

They watered the seed, and the tree grew, and then they brought back the rain.

Impossible.

Then it's black.

23

I wake with a mouth full of water.

My eyes won't open. It's too bright. I slept with my blinds open by accident.

"Caro-leeen-a," someone says. Time for school. *One more minute, Mom.*

It's too hot. My bed's lumpy. This mattress is awful; I don't remember it being this bad.

I grab my pillow, but grainy wood meets my fingers.

I pry my eyelids open, one at a time. The sun is heavy and round and white on the horizon, the sky a watery blue, and I smell my own dried sweat. It's dawn in the desert, and I'm in a tree, flat on my back.

The tree.

Like a flood, it crashes back: Alta's car, the jail-break at the Seville, the lake. Sometime in the night, the bees stopped dropping water, then faded to stars. Stars became sunrise.

My hair is crispy when I sit up, dried out like beached seaweed. I can feel my pulse in my head.

With my eyes still half closed, I turn and peek behind me, down beyond the pasture. If I'd been imagining the events of last night—our boat ride in an imaginary lake—then I should see the golden desert stretching into the horizon. No bees, no rain, no lake.

But I'm in a tree, above a green-glass lake.

I stand on shaky legs and look down. Beneath me, the trunk stretches thirty feet down, black and twisted. Next to the trunk is the scabby stump of the old tree. I gawk at the green leaves springing from the branches of the tree I'm standing in, white blossoms surrounding me like a snowstorm. Bees dart about, buzzing in and out of the blossoms. . . .

I spot the boat on the ridge, tippy-top, meatball on spaghetti. That must have been one crazy storm, to toss the boat up so high.

But where is Grandpa?

The fastest way down is to leap into the lake. I tighten my bracelet. It's time for courage, just like Rosa. I hang my toes over the edge of the branch and put my hands up. I don't wait to feel afraid. I just close my eyes and jump.

The nose of the boat juts into the sand, like it's been buried there since the dinosaurs. The top of the ridge is dry earth, so hot it's crackling beneath me. I follow the pattern of shingled ground around the boat.

"Caro-leeen-a." I hear him before I see him, his voice nails on a chalkboard, a dust-choked muffler.

"Grandpa?" I whisper as I creep around the prow, afraid of what I'll see.

My grandfather is on his stomach, pitched from the boat with arms and legs at odd angles like a busted toy.

"Grandpa!" I screech and throw myself at his side.

"Caro-leeen-a," he says. "Water."

I blink tears away. This is all my fault. "I'll get you some lake water. Hold on."

"No, *chiquita*." Grandpa rolls onto his side. "The water. The bees."

"I . . . I know," I say. "They brought it back."

For a minute I kneel here, baking in the sun. What do we do now? Grandpa can't even walk. How will we make it back to the highway? Or even back to the house?

Maybe I can find my cell phone in Alta's car. Maybe I can call 911 again and give them directions before it's too late.

But that would mean leaving Grandpa here on the ridge, alone. Without his oxygen tank. Without his snake-stomping boots.

Tears choke me. *What do I do?*

"We need to get out of here," I say, my words slurring with exhaustion. "Come on, Grandpa. I'll help you up, then we'll go to the house." And once he's inside, out of the hot sun, I'll figure out what to do next.

One more minute, then I'll move. I'm so tired.

I hear buzzing.

No, not buzzing—*rattling.*

A fat rattlesnake coils near Grandpa's feet, its noisy tail paralyzing me. "Don't move," I whisper.

But he's trying to stand. "Bees, Caro-leeen-a," he says. "I hear bees."

"It's not bees—it's a rattler!" I work to keep my voice from edging into shrillness. But Grandpa is on another planet. Slowly, laboriously, he folds his legs beneath him, so he can stand.

"Please!" I tell him. "Hold still!" His bare feet are so white, they're lilac.

Grandpa stands, and the snake hikes up on its muscled body, scales glinting like rusty corn in the sunlight.

"Grandpa!" I stretch out and push my grandfather out of biting distance.

The rattler strikes. It happens faster than thought, a blur. I shriek and wait to feel fangs sink into my skin.

But the bracelet—Rosa's bracelet, made of bark as black as midnight—takes the rattler's fangs.

The bracelet is a shield.

I laugh and tears fall like bombs in the dirt.

"Caro-leeen-a!" Grandpa's voice breaks with concern. He crawls toward me.

This time the rattler gets him, right on the ankle.

Grandpa crumples with the pain.

The snake slides away, damage done, and camouflages itself on the ridge.

"No. Oh, no." I lean over my grandfather. His breathing is raspy, like he's getting all his oxygen through a

Capri Sun straw. He's lily-faced with dehydration, his eyes blue holes in his face, wide and scared.

"Aren't you glad . . ." he says faintly, "you were wearing . . . that bracelet, Caro-leeen-a?"

Caro-leeen-a. My name has never sounded so sweet.

"What do I do, Grandpa?" I'm only twelve, just a little seed. I'm not smart enough or strong enough to fix this. My grandpa's going to die, and it's all my fault.

He's muttering to himself, a blend of Spanish and English, sense and nonsense, just as he did all summer. But it isn't word salad. I know that now. It's the truth. The twisted, demented truth.

"Tell me what to do," I say. "Please, Grandpa."

"Bees," he whispers.

"No. We need to get you out of here, right now," I say. I'd hoped saying these words would invoke some kind of spell, that an actual plan would spill into my mind. "You stay here. I'll run to the highway and—"

"No," Grandpa says. "Stay with me."

I swallow a sob and curl up against my grandpa, head on his chest, feel him rummaging for air.

"Caro-leeen-a," he says. "I'm not afraid. Not anymore."

For a terrifying moment, he stops breathing and stops moving. His eyelids relax, and the rattlesnake bite stops bleeding, festering raisin brown in the sunshine.

Grandpa takes another breath, but they're too far apart for comfort. Too far apart to measure time. *Don't play on the ridge,* Dad told me. *It's dangerous.*

None of that matters now.

We bake in the sun. I fight the urge to sleep, seeing terrible snakes when I close my eyes. I don't know how long we lie here, intertwined, as the sun climbs the sky. I don't hear the cars pull into the driveway, don't hear the squishy footsteps through the wet pasture.

A hand with neon-orange fingernails touches my shoulder.

"Carol." Her voice is like it was when I was five and she was ten, and we'd play dress-up and I'd fall in the high heels and scrape my knee, and she'd lean over me and whisper my name, calling me back from the brink of pain.

Alta.

I'm pulled up into my big sister's arms, almost forcibly, and she hugs me until all her muscles quake.

"Grandpa . . . he's . . . Alta, look, he's . . ." I'm a snot-drenched, sunburned catastrophe.

She strokes my head, shushing me. "The paramedics are here," she says. "They'll take care of him."

"I'm sorry," I sob. "I'm sorry." The words are too insignificant to explain how I feel; maybe if I say them over and over . . .

"Don't you ever scare me like that again." She pinches me, and it hurts so much, my eyes sting. But then she pulls me to her, tight enough to crush my ribs.

"How did you find me?" My teeth grind into her skin when I talk.

She leans back and peels a soggy leaf from my cheek. "When we got a call saying Serge was missing and then found your bed empty, we figured it out. But when you stopped answering your phone, we all thought—" She sniffles, tightening her arm around me. "I'm so glad you're okay." Her voice is soft as lamb's wool, and she rests her chin on top of my head. I'm suddenly introduced to another Alta, one I've never met: Soft Alta.

"Your car!" I remember. "I ruined your car."

"I don't want to talk about the car." A storm of anger

flashes in her words, not that I can blame her. "You're lucky that I love you, little sister."

I gulp. "I thought . . . I thought we weren't real sisters."

Alta looks like I smacked her, color draining from her cheeks. "Is that what you think?"

"No." I shrink. "It's what you think."

Alta frowns. "I don't think that."

"But that's what you said. Remember?" I hear myself, echoing in my brain, sounding more like a needy, squeaky mouse with each word. "When we were cleaning Grandma Rosa's closet?"

"Oh, that." She laughs, high and pretty like bells. "You can't always trust what teenagers say We blab any crummy thing that pops into our minds."

Yesterday, I would have accepted this lame excuse, and left it alone forever. But today I want more from my sister.

"Alta . . . It really hurt my feelings." I hold so still, I can hear her pulse.

She thinks for a moment. "I'm sorry. I am. But I was miserable out here at the ranch, okay? Stuck here for a whole summer, with Mom on my case about every little thing. Plus you and Raúl and Mom and Lu—you're, like, the perfect little family. My dad would never cook me sun cakes for dinner or sit next to me and laugh at some crappy movie on TV. He barely talks to me."

"I didn't know," I say.

"And Serge didn't want to talk to anyone but you," my sister continues.

"Wait, you *wanted* to talk to Grandpa?" I'm stunned.

"Of course," Alta says. She's almost embarrassed. "He's the closest thing to a grandfather I'm ever going to have."

"I . . . I had no idea," I say.

She shrugs. "I'm sorry if it hurt you. But Carol, you're my sister—half or step- or whatever you want to call it."

My waterworks begin again. Alta smooths my crunchy hair away from my face and holds me.

Mom, Dad, and Lu reach us, and I'm wrapped into a family hug. While the paramedics carry Grandpa down the ridge on a stretcher, Mom and Dad alternate between yelling at me and squeezing me tight.

Finally, my parents look around, taking in the ranch's changed landscape. Dad gapes at the tree and the lake. "How . . . Where . . . I don't . . ."

"From the story," I say, barely believing it myself. "Grandpa wasn't making it up. It all really happened."

"Carol . . ." Dad says, the start of a warning. But he stares out at the transformed landscape and shakes his head.

My family and I make our shaky way down the ridge. I'm convinced a snake is hiding in every crevice, but Alta is the very essence of brave, her face neutral, swollen cry-eyes already back to normal. She never once lets go of my hand.

The paramedics insist on taking me to the emergency room too. I lie in the ambulance on a stretcher next to Grandpa, who clings to life, in the worst condition possible.

I let them check my bones, my blood pressure, my temperature. But I don't take my eyes off the tree, not until we drive around the mountain and it disappears. Then I turn my head to the side, and sleep, and sleep, and sleep.

24

I have second-degree sunburns on my arms, neck, shoulders, and chest. Also minor heatstroke and dehydration. Doctors insist that I stay overnight and tell me I'll have to cover up with long sleeves for the next six months.

I have to grow new skin.

Other than that, my night of reckless lawbreaking hasn't done any major damage.

Besides, of course, to Alta's car. It gets a ride back to Albuquerque on a tow truck. Dad thinks Alta's insurance will pay for most of the repairs. The rest I'll have to pay for with lifeguarding money and extra chores for the rest of my life. I'm back to being Alta's slave—just the way she likes it. And, if I'm being honest, the way I like it, too; it's nice and safe being under her thumb.

I'd take a harder diagnosis than sunburn, if it meant Grandpa would live.

He's not going to survive the day.

The doctors try to soften the blow. *He was already on his way out,* they tell us. *His heart wouldn't have made it another month, another week,* they tell us. *We'll try to make him as comfortable as possible; you take all the time you want to say good-bye.*

It's remarkable he's held on this long, they tell Dad, when they think I'm sleeping. *His organs look like they've seen five lifetimes, not just one.* And through my grief, I smile.

Mom sets Lu on my bed. He tests it for bounciness and claps for himself. I laugh and cry at the same time, thinking of the day he found the rattler under the porch, how close we came to losing him, too.

Death is around every corner at the ranch. But now, so is life. Isn't one always part of the other? An old tree dies; a new one is born.

A doctor pokes her head in the doorway. "How are we doing in here?"

I give her a thumbs-up, and she comes to check the clipboard at the foot of my bed.

"Drinking lots of water?" she asks.

I hold up my drained cup and nod.

"Good. Keep it up." She smiles as she surveys my sunburn. "Your swelling's gone down. Good. You must have been sitting in the lucky chair."

I raise my eyebrows. "Lucky chair?"

She gestures to the antique-looking rocking chair where Alta sits. My sister jumps up. "Did someone die in this chair or something?"

"No, nothing like that," the doctor says. "It's made of special wood. Very old." She touches the smooth black chair. "We call it the lucky chair because everyone who sits in it winds up feeling a little bit better."

Black bark, wood grains swirling.

Dad shuffles in and is so choked up, he can only speak one word at a time. "He's . . . almost . . . there . . ."

Alta pushes my wheelchair into Grandpa's room. She's cracking her knuckles, over and over, nervously wrenching them from their sockets, her eyes wide and fearful. My cool, composed older sister, an over-cried, overwhelmed mess.

"It's like when Grandma Rosa died all over again," she says.

I remember what she said in Grandma Rosa's closet that day. *Saying good-bye before you're finished saying hello.* I pull her hand into mine, not caring if it's lame or babyish. "I'm scared."

"Me, too," she admits, and squeezes my fingers.

Sisters.

We crowd around Grandpa's bed, all except Dad, who paces near the window, his hair standing straight up from him running his hands through it over and over.

My grandpa's covered in tubes and lines that dig into his skin and round white electrodes that look like the tentacles of a monster. Brave, strong, dragonlike Mom goes first. She leans over Grandpa and kisses his leathery cheek.

"*Te queremos,* Serge," she says.

Grandpa's eyes flutter open. "Beautiful . . . Patricia . . ." His words come out in tiny bunches. "If your daughters . . . grow up to have . . . even half your strength . . ."

Mom quietly says good-bye, lets Lu babble to his grandfather, and then leaves the room to cry in private.

Dad is staring out the window, looking lost.

I guess it's our turn.

I climb out of my wheelchair, still holding hands with Alta. Together, we walk over to the bed.

"Ah," my grandpa says, and somehow rustles up enough life to beam at us. "The two brightest blossoms . . . on the tree." He lifts his fingers to stroke Alta's face. "I wish . . . your grandmother . . . could see you . . . Her beautiful granddaughters. She would be so proud."

"My . . . *my* grandmother?" Alta repeats.

"Your grandma Rosa," Grandpa says. "Surely you know . . . you're our granddaughter . . . whether our blood courses through your veins or not." Each phrase uses a whole lungful of his breath. He reaches into the nightstand beside him and pulls out his whittling knife and a scrap of wood.

"Grandpa, I don't think now's a good time—" I say.

But he lays his whittling knife on the bed and puts something in Alta's hands. "For you, Alta," he says. "Caro-leeen-a has one. Now you'll have one, too."

Alta's already crying. I strain my neck to peek at what he gave her. It's a bracelet, made with sandy-colored wood. It looks just like mine—a long piece of bark, strung onto a leather strap. Only Alta's bracelet is intricately decorated with flowers, leaves, curlicues, and bees.

"This is what you were working on, all those months," I whisper.

"You made this for me?" my sister says. I lift up her hand to tie the leather straps for her, then admire our wrists together with the matching bracelets. One light, one dark. One new wood, one old wood.

"*Chicas,* you must never spit on your roots," Grandpa replies.

Alta kisses Grandpa's forehead, her tears dripping onto his pillow like rain. "Thank you," she says, and leaves to find Mom.

My turn.

I'm not ready. Not yet.

I look at Grandpa, at his papery-thin eyelids, his yellowness. His body is too weak to even sit up. But for the first time, he's teeming with life. Life in his blue eyes, serious, electric. Rings of a tree trunk.

I bend down, until our faces are near. "Are you scared?" I whisper.

"What's scarier than death?" he asks, and once again I feel he's testing me. But this time I know the answer.

"Not living," I say. "Not living, being frightened of life, is much worse than dying."

"Squeeze the juice out of every day, Caro-leeen-a," Grandpa says. "Do not be afraid to live . . . and you will not be afraid to die."

Then he reaches for my dad. "Raúl," he croaks.

"No," Dad says, and backs into the wall, nearly knocking down a shelf. "You can't go. Not yet. I have . . . I have too many things I have to say . . ."

Grandpa blinks. "First . . . I want you to listen to me. I want you to hear . . . the ending."

"The ending?" Dad says. "I know how it ended."

"No," Grandpa says. "I want you to hear . . . the real ending."

"Save your breath, *Papá*," Dad pleads.

"Even if it takes all day," Serge says. One word at a time. "Once upon a time . . ."

O*nce upon a time, there was a tree stump. A scabby stump where a beautiful tree once stood. There was a splintered porch railing, a house made of old beams, a wood barn on a sheep ranch rotten with mildew.*

Once upon a time, an ancient woman sat on the scabby tree stump. When the coral sunset light cut across her face, she smiled with rose-petal lips. She inhaled, long and low, like she was trying to breathe in the light.

She held a bracelet in her age-gnarled hands and turned it over, thumbs rubbing the bark.

Sergio stood on the porch. He counted to one hundred, then counted again. Why was he so nervous? Why wouldn't his feet move? Walk to the tree stump?

They both knew a good-bye was coming. Measuring time had never felt so wrong. That day she collapsed in the driveway had been ten years ago, but Sergio still felt the fear like it was yesterday. And a decade of cancer divided by three hundred and sixty-five days a year . . . All those mornings, wondering if she'd wake up, even after all the tests and treatments — they weren't a guarantee, doctors said. All those meals, spoon-fed, choking, sputtering. Nights with no rest, sleep with no dreams. When a loved one is sick, the days are long, but the years are short.

He could measure time with their almost-daily conversation:

"Rosa, let me take you."

"I don't want to leave."

"But if you don't get to a hospital, you'll . . ."

He could measure time with how many unspoken dies should have ended this sentence. The word stacked up on his tongue like firewood.

"If we don't get you to a hospital, you'll . . ."

"Stay with me," she'd say, and pull him closer, as close as two people can hold each other before they melt and mold and become one being.

Tomorrow, he'd think to himself. I'll take her tomorrow. But no one had ever been able to tell Rosa what to do.

Perhaps it was selfish of him, but he wished he had one more year, even though they'd had more than their fair share together. Yes, he would give anything for even one more sunrise.

Rosa watched her husband cross the pasture, felt him nestle next to her on the stump. She clutched his shaking hands, flesh she knew as well as her own.

"Raúl called," she said. "They had the baby—a healthy baby girl. They named her Carolina. For my sister." She smiled, her lips still red and full despite her lined face. "Life goes on."

Sergio's face was stormy. "We never should have cut down the tree."

Rosa raised her eyebrows. "That is your great regret?"

He looked at her. "You're dying. Do you still think we were right to cut down the tree? Are you still glad you left the village?"

Rosa laughed. "I can't believe I didn't leave earlier. There're so many places I never got to see."

Sergio stared. "You went to two hundred countries," he said. "You saw countless rivers. A thousand forests."

"But not every forest. There's always more to see."

The time Sergio had had with this woman, if it could be stretched out like string, would have wrapped around the earth over and over. And yet, she still surprised him.

"There are places I wish I had seen," he admitted. "I wish I'd seen the ocean."

"You speak as though you're the one dying," Rosa said. "Go now, and see it all. There's still time."

But what was the point of time, if there was no Rosa to share it with? "There are things I never knew about you," he said. "Things I never understood."

Rosa squeezed his hand. "Maybe in the next lifetime."

"I wish for a hundred more lifetimes with you."

"But we only get one, don't we?" She closed her eyes. "We did pretty well with the one we had."

Sergio leaned his head into her lap, and she held him there while death chewed away the last of her lungs and guts. When her breathing lagged, he sat up, horrified.

"Rosa," he said, panic rising up in his throat, tasting of bile. "Get in the car."

She shook her head.

"Then I'm calling the ambulance."

She smiled. "All these years, I begged you to come with me, and now that I want to stay, you're finally ready to leave."

Sergio's hands trembled in her hands. "I pushed him away." He shook the words out. "I pushed him away like I pushed you away."

"You didn't push, you held on tight," Rosa said.

"How do I get him to come back?" he asked.

"You don't," she said. "You wait. He'll come back. I always came back."

She used her final breaths to creak to a standing position on the tree stump, toes over the edge, her hands pressed together, as though in prayer. "I'm on the tree branch," she whispered, "and I'll jump first." She smiled a wild Rosa smile. "As usual."

"Rosa," Sergio whispered back. "Stay with me."

"Only you, Sergio. Only you could have made me a life worth staying for."

And then she exhaled, and her hands became white blossoms, and her body became white blossoms, and finally her face became white blossoms, milky-white petals, honey-vanilla scent reaching Sergio while she burst into bloom.

Full of life, even as she died.

A hot wind blew over the roof of the ranch house, blew across the pasture, tickling the fleecy backs of the sheep, and picked up the blossoms, carrying them over the ridge.

Amid the white blossoms, almost too small to notice, was a tiny black seed. Sergio mistook it for a bug at first but clapped his hands around the seed and saved it from flying away.

The gift lives on, *he thought, and put the seed in his pocket.*

Sergio stayed at the tree stump, watching the blossoms fly like white butterflies until the flat desert swallowed them up. The last of the blossoms. The last of life, gone.

Except for the seed. The seed was life.

Once upon a time, there was a tree, and they chopped it down, so they could live—and die.

Once upon a time, there was a seed.

The room is quiet, still, a sanitized, all-white tomb. My heart is my whole body, taking up space so my lungs can't expand, my limbs can't move, my brain can't think.

"I wanted . . . to take her in, *mijo*," Grandpa says. "I wanted . . . her to live. I wanted . . . her to live . . . forever."

Dad takes a minute before leaving the window. His entire world, shattered. Twelve years of a feud with his father, unzipped in one story. "*Papá*," he says, "I'm so sorry—"

"No," Grandpa says.

"Please, let me say it," Dad insists, his fists balled. "Let me say it now—"

Grandpa won't let it fly. "No, Raúl," he says. "You want to apologize . . . now that I'm dying. But death . . . is not a reason . . . to do anything. Life, *mi cielo*. Life . . . is the reason . . . to do everything."

"The seed," I say, nearly as out of breath as my grandpa.

His lips twist into a parched smile. "It fell . . . out of my pocket . . . I thought it was lost . . . forever . . . But you found it . . . Caro-leeen-a, didn't you?"

"The ranch, *Papá*," Dad blubbers. "I can't—I called it off, okay? I'm not selling it."

My jaw drops. "You saved it?"

"You're keeping . . . the ranch?" Grandpa's eyes are the bluest I've ever seen them.

"That's our ranch," Dad says, knotting his hands together. "It belongs to us. I don't know what I was thinking. It's our land. It always has been, and we shouldn't ever let it go."

The three of us fall silent for a moment, the only sound in the room the faltering *beep . . . beep* of the monitors.

"All these years," Grandpa says at last, "and now . . . I'm the one . . . leaving."

Dad sobs, climbing into the bed next to his father, and puts his head on Grandpa's shoulder. "*Papí,* stay with me. Don't go—stay with me."

One corner of Grandpa's mouth turns up in a weak smile. "How many times . . . did I say that . . . to Rosa? And to you?"

"I should have stayed," Dad says. "I should have come back."

"You were . . . my tree," Grandpa says. "My source of life."

"Stay, please." Dad's shuddering speech is an arrow, straight through my middle. If I walk outside, people will see through the hole.

"Through you," Grandpa says, "the gift lives on . . . Through you, Raúl, and your children . . . and the tree . . . Caro-leeen-a planted."

"And we will never cut it down," my dad whispers.

"Raúl?" Grandpa whispers, his eyes going cloudy, the blue washed away. "Would you make sure . . . Inés gets fed?"

Dad's crying is long and loud, a coyote's howl. He clings to Grandpa until I peel him off.

And then we wait, my father and I.

When Grandpa's breathing slows, he closes his eyes. A machine kicks in—the sound of the end. It whirs and hums, a drone.

"The bees," Grandpa whispers, so quiet it's like a sigh. "The bees . . . are coming."

I should look away, so my last image of him isn't this struggle. But I can no more take my eyes off him than Sergio could take his eyes off Rosa. Grandpa and I, drawn to our loved ones like magnets, even in death.

Grandpa's chest stops rising, and I know the exact moment when he releases his last breath. His eyes open wide, and he smiles at some invisible thing out the window. Then he freezes.

And then he's gone.

I don't know how long I'll be alive. It could be another year, or another thousand years. But I do know this: It doesn't matter how long I live. It matters what I do with the time I'm given.

Do not be afraid to die, and you will not be afraid to live, my grandpa told me.

I am not afraid to live.

THE BEGINNING

O nce upon a time, there was a tree.

It was a young tree, recently bloomed from a seed that had been lost in a closet for many years. The tree had sleek black bark, the color of night, and leaves that were spring green and contrasted with the dry brown desert. Its branches didn't block out the sun, not yet. Its white blossoms were just tiny. But the tree would keep growing, forever, and the blossoms would get as fat and fluffy as the sheep munching the grass at its trunk.

The tree had strong roots.

A not-so-little girl, her baby brother, and her father drove to the tree in a pickup truck. When the girl ran to the trunk, she hugged it first, then picked up a rock and tried to skip it across the green-glass lake.

"Carol!" The dad set the baby, Luis, down on his chubby legs and swung onto a low-hanging branch. "Beat you to the top!"

The girl scurried up the tree, wincing when the bark scraped her almost-healed shoulder. The dad won, and it figured, since he had told her once that he spent his teenage years climbing every tree, fence, and telephone pole in the greater New Mexico area.

"No fair," the girl panted. "You're part monkey."

"Then you're a quarter monkey," he shot back, grinning.

They sat on the highest branch, legs dangling above the water. Luis gathered rocks on the lake's shore and piled them into castles.

"Pool table," the dad said.

"My own fridge in my room," the girl said.

"U2 posters, all over," he said.

The girl scrunched up her nose. "Dad, that guy's hair is so tacky!"

"No way! Bono is timeless."

"Timeless means old."

He mock-pushed her off the branch, and she giggled and shrieked, "Okay, U2 posters! U2 is officially cool!"

"What else should go in the new house?"

The two of them thought and looked at the land around them. The ranch house was gone. Termites had munched through most of the wood. Reluctantly, like he was giving orders to take a loved one off life support, the dad had demolished it, but he was going to build a new house.

A house for staying.

This was land for staying now. Next year, the girl would have to bus to school, a new school full of other farm kids who lived down south, but it was worth it. And she would hold on to her old friendships for as long as she could. She had already invited her friends down for a weeklong visit next summer. Manny practically burned up with jealousy when the girl showed her pictures of the ranch on her phone. "You're so lucky you get to live there!" And the girl was lucky.

Green grass shot out in an almost-perfect circle around the tree and the lake. An oasis.

"A garden," the dad said. "Now that the drought's

over, I want to plant a big garden, and we'll all help keep it up."

"Good luck getting Alta to pull weeds," the girl said.

The dad laughed. *"What else?"*

She picked one of the white blossoms and tossed it down onto the water. *"Beehives,"* she said.

"Beehives?" the dad said.

"Yes, rows and rows of beehives. We can sell the honey."

"So we'll switch from being sheep farmers to being bee farmers," the dad said.

"Exactly."

She knew the dad didn't believe, not really. He didn't believe the bees brought back the rain, or that the seed grew the tree. He was still trying to make sense of it, pulling up weather reports to explain the flooding and obscure horticultural articles to explain the tree.

But the girl knew better. She didn't think; she accepted. Things are only impossible if you stop to think about them.

A shiny red truck pulled into the driveway. The

dad and the girl climbed down to meet a man in pristine leather cowboy boots.

"Mr. González," the dad said, and shook his hand.

"Wow, you've really turned this place around," Mr. González said. "I don't blame you for wanting to keep it."

"I don't know what I was thinking," the dad said. "It should stay in the family. Always. It's our roots—where we came from."

The girl walked around the tree trunk to find a stone for the top of Luis's rock castle while the two men talked about zoning and measurements. There had been a few things from Grandma Rosa's closet that were worth a lot of money, and the dad had sold them to build a new ranch house.

They kept the emu head, though.

The girl heard bees buzzing behind her, following her, just like they had followed her grandmother.

Bzzz, bzzz. Her new phone vibrated in her pocket. One new message.

ALTA: You want to go to the mall with me and
       Mom tomorrow?

THE GIRL: Yes, please! :)

*Her wooden bracelet slid up and down her wrist
as she tapped her screen.*

Bzzz, bzzz.

A bee, just one bee, flying near her ear. "Hola,
Grandpa," *she whispered.*

*She ran to find her dad. He smiled when he saw
her, the same smile she had. The smile her grandpa
had given them.*

Mr. González said, "Is this Carol or Alta?"

"Actually," *the girl said,* "it's not Carol. It's
Carolina."

Caro-leeen-a.

"There is no ending," I explain to Luis, "because stories
never end. They just turn into new beginnings, forever
and ever. Like the rings of a tree trunk."

"Tree," Luis says.

"Say *árbol*," I say.

"*Árbol*," he repeats, and claps his hands. I nod, a
proud teacher. He's learning Spanish, slowly, a word
a day.

Measuring time with words.

Story time is Luis's favorite part of the day, when I get home from school and grab an apple for us to share, and take him out into the backyard.

We'll have a new beginning soon: next summer we'll drive down to the ranch again, but this time, we'll stay.

Luis wanders across the yard, determined to catch a bee that has landed on a petunia.

T*he girl climbed back in the tree and listened to the bees buzz in the flowers until the stars came out, and all she heard was the great loud silence of the open desert.*

Once upon a time, there was a tree.

ACKNOWLEDGMENTS

To my dear peach of an agent, Sarah Davies—your patience and wisdom deepen and strengthen my writing and my life. Thank you for all you do.

To my stellar editor, Kaylan Adair, who is everything a writer could want in an editor—you get me. You make me better. Thank you for making my debut experience a positive and beautiful thing. Here's to many more inbox exchanges.

To everyone at Candlewick Press, for championing this book and working tirelessly to get it into people's hands—thank you. I am honored to be part of the Candlewick bookshelf.

To coffee. Thank you.

To Clint Mansell, whose hauntingly gorgeous soundtrack to *The Fountain* was my soundtrack and sonic map while writing *Hour of the Bees*—thank you.

To everyone who read *Hour of the Bees* before it was book-shaped—thank you, for the brainstorming sessions, the gripes, the cheerleading, all of it.

To my family—my parents and siblings, for listening to all my stories, and to Kenneth and Finley, for making new ones with me. Thank you.